AN ARTFUL ASSASSIN IN AMSTERDAM

AN ARTFUL ASSASSIN IN AMSTERDAM

Michael Grant

This first world edition published 2019
in Great Britain and the USA by
SEVERN HOUSE PUBLISHERS LTD of
Eardley House, 4 Uxbridge Street, London W8 7SY.
Trade paperback edition first published
in Great Britain and the USA 2020 by
SEVERN HOUSE PUBLISHERS LTD.

British Library Cataloguing in Publication Data
A CIP catalogue record for this title is available from the British Library.

ISBN-13: 978-0-7278-8904-1 (cased)
ISBN-13: 978-1-78029-637-1 (trade paper)
ISBN-13: 978-1-4483-0336-6 (e-book)

Typeset by Palimpsest Book Production Ltd.,
Falkirk, Stirlingshire, Scotland.

To Katherine.

ONE

I t was quite an original murder attempt. I approved of the ambition if not of the practicality. I'd probably have approved even more had I not been the intended victim.

It was not some panic move, some spur of the moment thing, a sudden outburst. No, this was deliberate; calculated not improvised, unique, interesting, unusual. You could say it had a local vibe to it as it used the geography of the urban terrain to effect. This was not a method of murder you could use anywhere else, aside from Venice.

Bespoke murder, locally sourced and no doubt carbon-neutral.

I was in Amsterdam, where I'd been lured aboard a thirty-foot open boat by a woman I was seeing – an Englishwoman named Tess who was beautiful, in her late thirties with red hair, quick wit and talent. We had struck up a conversation in a coffee shop of the Amsterdam variety, where I had been mildly high and had stared a bit too long at her diamond earrings.

I no longer steal jewelry – or anything, really – but in the same way that a long-retired carpenter will still gaze fondly at a nice piece of hardwood, seeing the rocking chair within, I had automatically calculated the likely street value of Tess's diamonds. The earrings were yellow gold, diamond-studded hoops, not ostentatious, but not the sort of thing you picked up at the flea market, either. Twelve grand retail.

Being somewhat baked it had taken me two minutes of staring to accomplish an analysis I'd normally have done with a glance. Tess mistook my interest in her ears for interest in herself and well, one thing led to another, as it will do when both parties are of diminished capacity and one party's hotel (hers) was conveniently right next door.

Tess had recently divorced. Cause of divorce: adultery. Her husband's, not hers – shocking, I know – and she had run away to Amsterdam with a few of her female friends to show the faithless bastard that whatever he could do, she could do and twice as hard.

It turned out that Tess had more than just the earrings. She had a sweet little green velvet-lined jewelry case in her hotel safe. Combination: 6909. I had seen her punching in this number with a bit of purely accidental side-eye, and while she was using the facilities I'd given in to the natural curiosity anyone might have and had opened the safe. And looked at her green velvet box containing – rough estimate again – a hundred and seventy-five to two hundred large in gold, diamonds and emeralds. Her now-tragic engagement ring alone was worth a good fifty Gs.

And I don't want to brag but I took *none* of it. I did not even take one of the diamond-and-emerald pendant earrings despite knowing that a woman who finds herself missing a single earring will assume it was lost, not stolen.

Nor did I photograph the pieces so I could have a paste knock-off made which I could use to replace Tess's jewelry so she wouldn't notice the switch until I was well away.

I didn't even use my phone to make a digital copy of her NFC – that's Near Field Communication – hotel-room key card despite the fact that even I can make the app work pretty well. Mostly.

How virtuous was I? So virtuous I didn't even ensure that her hotel-room window locks were jammed and the blocks removed so as to effect an easier second-story job later.

I did none of those things, which, frankly, was an amazing display of maturity, morality and self-restraint.

For me.

I did shoot front and back pictures of all her credit cards, but that was not for use now, it was for possible use later, emergency use. Only emergency. Taking the credit card pics was pure reflex, and it wasn't really a crime unless I used them.

'Do you need a refill, David?' Tess called to me from the stern where the women were gathered. I was in the bow looking Byronic while also signaling chilly irritation.

A refill? You tricked me aboard this hellish boat, which I, quite naturally, assumed meant a romantic evening cruise preparatory to horizontal (and vertical, if I was feeling energetic) fun later. Instead I am the sole male in a gaggle of women. I am being used as a prop, Tess, dehumanized, treated as an object by you and your drunken friends. Pointed at. Leered at. Laughed at. You're damned right I need a refill. I said none of that.

'I'm fine,' I sniffed.

'Yes, you are,' an unrecognized female voice said, eliciting laughter and even a 'Woo!'

Tess was smart and accomplished, a songwriter of all things, responsible for several lucrative songs in what I think of as the 'mawkish crap' genre of love songs for the sort of women who really need to reassess what actual men are like if they are not to suffer a lifetime of romantic disappointment.

I liked Tess. But I liked her a bit less now that I realized the night-time canal cruise she had arranged involved her friends, and their friends, all female, most British, all divorced or broken up, and all drunk in that rowdy, belligerent-yet-horny way women at the upper limits of the MILF category can be.

It may seem ungallant of me to feel aggrieved, but I was on a boat with seven mojito-powered women, each of whom had excellent reasons to despise my sex. This event was a sort of riff on what the Brits call a 'hen party', which generally involves half a dozen beastly drunk women, one of whom is to be married; they are typically young women at that melancholy point in life when they are still capable of optimism about the hairier sex. Poor things. This party was a sort of alt-hen party with years of real-world experience of men.

And there I was: a man.

Tess of course thought the whole thing terribly funny. Twice I'd heard her say, 'No, David's not like that at all,' which she modified by adding, 'of course, I'm not married to him, hah hah hah.'

To which one of the loutish creatures had said, 'Too right. Your David's not a marrying man, he's the rumpy-pumpy sort.'

Rumpy-pumpy. Those very words. With accompanying seated pelvic thrust.

Also, '*your David*'? I'm not fond of possessive pronouns attached to me by people other than me.

I was in need of more alcohol, especially as the night had clouded up and the temperature had dropped toward uncomfortable, but the on-board selection was heavy on the flavored vodkas (a crime the Hague really must address), gin, the inevitable Bailey's, a lot of rum and a wide array of mixes and garnishes meant to distract from the lousiness of the booze. This bar rested atop the only superstructure, a blocky pedestal amidships which also supported the wheel, behind which stood the boat's skipper, a Dutch woman who I hoped did not share in the drunkenness of her passengers. The skipper could be seen smiling in discreet appreciation of what I can only describe as virulent anti-male bigotry.

One whiskey, just one, decorated the boat's bar, the eternal Jack Daniel's, and that had been dangerously depleted following a round of Jack and cola shots for the harpies in the stern.

'What I would like to know is whether he's actually any good at the rumpy-pumpy?'

That's a translation. The original was, 'Wha ah d'like a know is (hiccup) is he acthly goo at pumply-rumply? Pumply. Rumpy-rumpy. (Giggle.) Fucking.'

This from a woman I knew to be a bank vice president in the City. Compensation package north of three million a year. Better than two hundred employees under her control. Regular appearances on Sky News. God only knew what baubles she had in *her* hotel safe.

Tess's answer was inaudible to me since I was in my bow perch as far from them as I could get without walking on water, maintaining my stoic dignity. But I heard the response: loud, braying laughter with a lascivious edge to it.

'Woo!'

I felt their eyes on me.

I was a conversation piece, an avatar of my sex, a token, a mere object. Worse yet I was a bit of bling, Tess showing living proof that she could still get a man. I was being used.

I was Tess's trophy.

My God, the justifiable outrage I could be reveling in if only I were capable of a greater degree of hypocrisy. But given my life and my career there was really no question that I had it coming. Turnabout is fair play, as either Shakespeare or the Bible must have said, though perhaps more eloquently.

After the first half hour with Tess's gang of ruffians, I had actually thought, *Just kill me*, not realizing that it would turn out to be foreshadowing.

I saw the aspiring murderer in the middle of the Leliegracht (lay-lee-khchkrachkght) bridge, but it was night and what I saw by the lights of the narrow townhouses fronting the canal was shape and shadow without features. I would not have noticed him at all except that he had what I took to be a belt or maybe a bicycle chain in his hand, a serpentine thing, black against the cold light. It was impossible to see his race or features, impossible to judge his height or age, though my first impression was that he was a slight fellow. He was wearing a raincoat with the hood up, though it was not quite raining. That last detail should perhaps have been a warning, but who expects to be attacked while on a boat motoring down a canal? In Amsterdam?

He had chosen his bridge well. There are bridges across the canals roughly every city block, all of them lined with the shabby, chained-up bicycles that are to Amsterdamers what cars are to Californians, but some bridges are busier than others. Some bear the weight of four lanes of traffic and a tramline. The Leliegracht bridge however is not a main thoroughfare, the street comes in from the east tracking a narrow east-west canal, crosses the Prinsengracht and dead-ends. No trams, no trucks, only local traffic.

I was standing on the bow like a disgruntled George Washington crossing the Delaware, a glowing cigar in my mouth, a plastic cup containing the last of the Jack, as exposed as a Central Park flasher.

As the boat's bow reached the bridge I saw the hooded shadow above lean over the rail. Canal bridges are low, low enough that standing in the high bow I was just getting ready to duck. Low enough that the shadow and I could just about have shaken hands, had we both stretched a bit.

I didn't see the noose. I did feel it, though, as something hit the back of my neck. My first thought was that one of the women had thrown something at me. Roughly half a second later I had a different idea entirely because the boat kept moving, doing maybe five miles an hour, and I was just beneath the bridge when the noose tightened suddenly, cutting off both air and blood and threatening to separate my vertebrae.

I cried out in surprise. 'Urkh!' A very nearly Dutch sound.

I dropped my cigar and my drink and clawed with cat-like speed at the rope and was just able to insert my fingers into the noose when the rope went iron-taut and I was yanked back hard, like a stunt man taking a shotgun blast. Yanked right off my feet.

It hurt.

My heels pounded the deck, and then a bench, and then my back hit the center console so hard I thought my spine might have been snapped. I was dragged backward, kicking and flailing over bottles of vodka and tonic water, which made an astonishing noise as bottles fell and shattered on the deck while I made sounds that never escaped my throat.

Over the bottles I went, over the wheel with big knobs that gouged my back, drawn right past the skipper who stepped nimbly aside, made a grab for me, caught me around the waist and instantly lost me.

Then I was hauled right through the mass of Tess's friends, knocking women down, kicking them in my frenzy, holding the noose with my fingers and realizing I wasn't strong enough to stop it cutting off blood and air – two things I find useful in remaining alive.

And all at once I was in the canal. In the canal, in black water decorated by floating debris, beneath the bridge, kicking like mad as the party boat motored on. I saw shocked and angry faces aimed my way.

Tess yelled, 'David!'

One of her friends yelled, 'Hey, arsehole!'

I think they saw it as me spoiling their party. I had, after all, wiped out most of the booze.

The boat moved on and the current held me under the bridge, ancient brick supports on both sides, blank concrete above. The current tugged at me and kept the rope taut. The pressure was so great that my fingers, rather than helping me escape, were pressed into the arteries of my neck, blocking my heart's frantic effort to keep my brain oxygenated. My head felt twice its normal size, a stretched water balloon. My throat convulsed as my lungs became aware that they were sucking on nothing and sent my brain strongly worded signals that it was time to panic.

Panic, right now!

But I've never found panic to be helpful, so I shifted my right hand sideways a bit in the noose and felt a surge of blood through my carotid arteries. No air, but a bit of blood. I saw stars and geometric patterns and my peripheral vision collapsed into the tunnel view that precedes unconsciousness, which would be followed by death.

Oh my God, I thought, *I could actually die.*

The absurdity of it struck me and I might have laughed, if it had been happening to someone else. How many times had I escaped perils in my life, only to be choked out in an Amsterdam canal? It was ridiculous.

I had a sudden flash of what was below me. I'd heard somewhere that 12,000 bikes a year end up in the canals, and I pictured my dying body, trailing tiny bubbles, sinking into a gloomy, submarine bicycle graveyard. Though someone would have to cut the rope first.

My lungs burned. My head was a big balloon full of blood. But the wannabe killer was not hauling on the rope, which would have finished me. No, he must have tied it off to the railing and fled, which is what I'd have done had I been fool enough to think of lynching a man off a boat. It was prudent but also served to undermine his attempt to finish me off because a human body in water is buoyant and the (attempted) murderer had left the rope a couple of feet too long so that I was submerged almost to my waist.

It finally occurred to me that rather than fighting the noose I should lessen the tension by grabbing the taut rope with my freed right hand and pulling hard while kicking to raise myself in the water.

Sure enough, this did lessen the pressure and I was able to gasp half a lungful of sweet, sweet air, instantly coughed up. More trash floated past me, paper sleeves that had held *bitterballen*, cigarette butts, water bottles. On the bank of the canal I saw that some people had begun to point – not do anything useful like cut the damn rope, of course, but they could point.

As long as I could hold onto the rope I could avoid dying, which was rather a flaw in the murderer's thinking. I congratulated myself on that insight and allowed myself a sneer.

Yeah, asshole, that's why when they hang people they tie their arms.

I felt a return of optimism but it went as fast as it came because I noticed something that my wannabe-assassin had almost certainly counted on: Tess's party boat was not the only boat on the canal. In fact there was a second boat, one of those long, low, glass-canopied tour boats that cruise the canals, coming right for me, and when it hit it would either choke me out or snap my neck.

I had maybe eight seconds.

My stronger right hand was pulling on the taut rope, my left was partly inside the noose, keeping minimal blood flowing, but that tactic had seven seconds left before it proved irrelevant. So I freed my left hand and with both arms pulled myself up. This did not immediately loosen the noose and my head was swimming better than the rest of me, but with wild, desperate thoughts bouncing around in my oxygen-deprived brain, I hauled with all my strength until I was halfway out of the water.

Try hauling yourself up by a rope. Try it when you've added the weight of wet clothing and you're feeling the carbon dioxide build up and the current is fighting you. It was not easy. In fact, it was impossible. I got myself out of the water to about the lower butt cheek level, but as I rose I lost buoyancy, which meant I was heavier. I had reached the limits of my upper body strength. My muscles were quivering, a warning of impending collapse.

Four seconds.

Four seconds and I was crotch-deep in the canal. To make matters still worse, the current kept trying to spin me around so that when the boat hit me – about three seconds now – it would catch me mid-spine, a few dozen tons of tour boat moving at five miles an hour, smack, right between the vertebrae.

I kicked madly, trying to walk on water but with my legs submerged. I managed to twist around to aim my exploding tomato face at the prow which was suddenly *right there*, right there and coming at me like a slow-moving bus.

Time's up.

I was all-in on adrenalin and had just one last, desperate heave left in my screaming muscles. I curled my legs up so that I was sort of butt-surfing, and at the last moment thrust my legs forward and . . . contact!

You wouldn't think a boat moving at a little above walking speed would hit that hard, but speed is one thing and mass is another, and there's a world of difference between being hit by a Frisbee moving at five miles an hour and being hit by tons of boat doing the same.

My ankles buckled, my knees buckled, I felt a shock in my pelvis. I was pushed back like a pendulum, then fell forward, and hit the prow with my calves. In rapid succession I snapped a short flagpole, managed to swing wide of a sturdy wooden staff bearing a light and began motoring my heavy, sodden feet like I was auditioning for the role of Wile E. Coyote.

I was up and promptly smashed the crown of my head into the bottom of the bridge. But by this point I was an old hand at maintaining motor activity while the carbon-dioxide-poisoned rational part of my brain was busy thinking, *Oooh, fuzzy lights.*

The bridge was too low to allow me to stand atop the superstructure so I dropped to my belly and crawled like the world's most motivated tortoise, trying to keep the life-enabling slack in the rope, while the boat moved relentlessly beneath me. Tourists looked up from below, formed their mouths into 'o's and pointed. *Look, mommy, is that Spider-Man?* I was about two seconds from running out of canopy at which point I'd fall into the rear well and be dragged over the stern, there to be run over by every subsequent boat.

I felt the noose begin to give. I had maybe an inch of

slack, enough to allow for breathing, not enough to allow me to slip out.

I reached the end of the canopy, grabbed the rope with my right hand further up than I'd been able to do earlier and pulled while using my left to yank at the noose, sliding the rough hemp up over my chin, crushed my nose, dropped from the canopy, bounced from the stern, snapped another staff with another limp flag, banged the hell out of my shin, Tarzaned out over the water, slipped the noose and suddenly I was in the canal again, landing in a wild flailing motion.

But free of the rope.

I sucked every molecule of oxygen my starved lungs could take in, sounding like a hungry seal or Jimmy Carr laughing. The rope dangled harmlessly.

Beyond the bridge and past the tour boat I saw Tess's party boat make a turn to come back and rescue me.

But I was done with that. I swam the other way, invisible in shadow, searching in vain for a ladder or a ramp as the quay-side was too high for me to scale. There was one of the low, blue-trimmed boats that carry a crane to dig debris out of the canal, which would have been low enough to climb onto, but it was in the wrong direction and would mean fighting the current. So instead I swam to the side opening leading to the Leliegracht canal with its lower banks. I rolled onto my back and kicked my way along the smaller canal until I spied a trio of stoned tourists, who giggled as they hauled me up to land on the embankment like a suicidal whale.

'Dude!' one of them said.

'Thanks,' I gargled through my bruised voice box. I was soaked, shaking, nauseous, my face all pins and needles as circulation returned. Hands seized mine and levered me up onto my feet. One of which was still wearing a shoe.

'Want a hit?'

Did I want a hit of weed after nearly choking to death? Of course I did, also much alcohol, but I knew if I did either I'd start coughing and hack up an organ. 'No. Thanks,' I croaked.

I walked away lopsidedly with their collective wisdom wafting after me.

'Gotta watch where you're walking, dude.'

'Yo, man, canals and shit.'

Much laughter.

I was not in a mood to share in their merriment. Someone had just tried to kill me. And I hadn't even done anything wrong. Recently.

TWO

My name at the moment is David Mitre.

Long ago I was named Martin DeKuyper – no relation to the people who bottle Blue Curacao. Young Martin DeK went down a dark path of lies and fraud and theft and more lies. Martin got into serious trouble of the burglary-of-a-business variety, was arrested and jumped bail. I became, and I remain, nineteen, almost twenty years later, a fugitive from justice.

Once you've made the decision to jump bail, you're going to need fake ID. It's easy enough to buy excellent drivers' licenses online and I have a few, but if you want an ID that will pass muster at Customs and Immigration, and get you past the facial recognition stuff they're bringing online, you need to go all-in and build an identity from the ground up. I have several such ground-up identities – David Mitre being one – and other shallower identities that are just drivers' licenses and credit cards.

Under various names I currently have four Netflix subscriptions, four Amazon accounts, two iTunes accounts, two each of the *Washington Post,* the *New York Times* and the *Guardian*, and other bits and bobs of subscriptions, all as a way of keeping my aliases' credit cards active. A small price to pay. And I have five quite genuine passports: three American, one Canadian and a rather less impressive though equally real passport from Peru. Peru, though; well, that's the kind of passport that makes border patrol agents roll their eyes because it's available to anyone with a fat enough bank account.

I am at age forty-two a (retired) thief and grifter, and currently an author. If that seems an unlikely collection of occupations, consider that a grifter is by definition a storyteller. Grifting, writing, pretty much the same thing, only there are no unkind Goodreads or Amazon comments sections for criminals. Prison, sure, but no snotty one-star reviews from people who won't stop telling you how much better a writer Tana French is.

I'd been in Amsterdam for a few days, occupying an AirBnB at the corner of Kalverstraat and the Singel, from which I had a straight-on view of the Munttoren, the rather ordinary red-brick clock tower, and a sidelong glimpse of the flower market where tourists bought suitcases full of tulip bulbs they could buy online for half the price.

Within a few hundred feet of my apartment were a number of decent restaurants and cafés and coffee shops of the sort that serve coffee but not primarily coffee. There were also a number of bookstores including the impressive American Book Center, and a surprisingly large and well-stocked Waterstones where I was due to speak on an author panel in nine days.

The apartment was on the fourth floor (or third if you're European) of a triangular building that had previously been a hotel. It had three bedrooms and was large by Amsterdam standards, with a beautifully updated interior that was all sleek hardwoods and stainless steel and marble. I had the master bedroom with its queen bed and mini-balcony overlooking the canal, and the upgraded but still cramped en suite bathroom. One bedroom was unoccupied. The remaining bedroom, with its own en suite, housed Chante Mokrani, my personal assistant.

Chante – no exact idea of her age, so let's say twenty-three-ish – was an appendage I had picked up while in Cyprus where an FBI legat from the Rome embassy dragged me into a matter involving child sex trafficking, money-laundering, corrupt cops and mediocre beer. Chante – pronounced 'shont' – was French by way of Algeria, and in no particular order a rather good cook, a lesbian, a literary snob who sneered at my work, and a suspicious, ungenerous, demanding, insolent pain in the ass.

My personal assistant: Chante the Unhelpful.

As I battled the keys to the apartment door, she opened it. Not a large woman, Chante, quite small actually though she punches above her weight. She had vaguely punkish black hair and dark, suspicious eyes that never quite looked *at* me, but seemed always to be interested in something happening just behind me. She was pretty in a hostile/gamine sort of way, like a darker-complected Zooey Deschanel maybe, if Deschanel were fueled by spite and resentment and marinated in Gallic insuperability.

Chante took in my wet, disheveled, half-shoeless condition and said, 'If you track mud on the floor I will not clean it.'

'It never occurred to me that you would.'

'Is it raining?' she asked as I brushed past her, making big, wet, mismatched footprints on the hardwood floor.

'No, someone tried to murder me,' I said, expecting this news to throw her off-stride.

'What did you do?'

'What did I *do*? What did *I* do?' I spun to face her and tried out my moral outrage using both points of emphasis, but she was unmoved. 'Some asshole dropped a noose on me and hauled me into the Prinsengracht.'

I made a point of saying *Prinsengracht* (Prince-'n-chghkgraaakhght) because as bad as my Dutch pronunciation was, Chante's was worse.

'You will need to send your clothing to the cleaners. I have several things to go as well, I will put them in a bag and leave it by the door for you to take tomorrow.'

Me? Me? I'm doing a laundry run? Me? The guy paying your salary? The guy paying the rent? Listen here, honey, I am the semi-famous, semi-successful author, you are my assistant, not the other way around. You take the stuff to the cleaners, I don't do your laundry, you annoying troll. I didn't actually say any of that out loud.

What I did say was, 'I'm getting a drink.'

'I'll take one as well.'

Because now I was her launderer *and* bartender. I was outraged, but there's something about standing in wet clothing and a single Ferragamo loafer that makes it hard to strut around issuing pronouncements.

I kicked off my remaining shoe, retrieved my bottle of Talisker 10, poured myself two fingers if you were using gorilla fingers, and a bare, resentful shot for Chante.

'Your date, it did not go well?' Chante asked.

'Nonsense, I like being dragged away by the neck and

dipped like a fucking teabag in the shadow of the Anne Frank house.'

She wanted more detail, but she'd be damned if she'd show interest in me or my activities. 'Police will come,' she warned.

'Let them,' I said through gritted teeth. 'I hope they catch the crazy bastard.'

I managed this with some bravado, but I pulled out my main phone – turned out the new iPhone really was waterproof – and texted Tess.

Hey, I'm fine, went home to sleep it off. Sorry to ruin the party. Seems my sleeve caught on a spike on the bottom of the bridge. It'd be funny if it weren't so embarrassing.

I wanted to add, *don't call the police*, but it was possible that she hadn't and if I made a point of telling her not to, she just might.

I had changed out of my wet things and slipped into sweatpants and a hoodie when she texted back.

Tess: *Are you all right?*

Me: *Sleepy, embarrassed and a little drunk.*

Tess: *Poor baby. Want some company?*

Me: *Nah, you play with your friends. Night.*

And lose my number, lady, I don't appreciate being used. I didn't text that. Instead I did the cowardly thing and blocked her number. She was leaving town in a few days, joining a long list of women I'd disappointed and/or outraged.

I would most likely have survived the minimal scrutiny cops give a victim – and, astonishing thought: I actually was the *victim*, there's a first time for everything – but a man in my position seeks to minimize conversations with people who hold arrest power.

I've been retired from crime these last ten years, give or take. It's nice being able to retire in your thirties. It's a luxury that few criminals ever achieve unless you think San Quentin is a Spanish-themed retirement home. The decision to leave the grifting life came as a result of a realization, and an event. The realization was that the game of cops and robbers was not a game of fox vs. hounds, but rather a game of tightrope walker vs. ground: sooner or later you're going to slip, and the ground is always there. It's a fact of life, any crook not working in banking or politics gets caught, so the only way to win is to cash in your chips, disappear and find another career.

The incident, the thing that finally pushed me out of the criminal life was, well . . . A guy shot himself. Because of me. I didn't pull the trigger, but . . . Yes, I tend to get a bit elliptical when I think back on that.

I went back into the living room in search of more whiskey and Chante said, 'Must we leave Amsterdam now?'

'No! Why?'

She produced one of the many shrugs in the French shrug armory and said, 'We had to leave Cyprus . . .'

'That was different,' I snapped. 'I have things I have to do here. I have a panel!'

'*Pfff*!'

'That's not the only reason,' I said defensively, because I couldn't stand the idea of Chante thinking I took things like author panels seriously.

That cocked her eyebrow.

'I also have an obligation to a guy.'

Cocked eyebrow remained so.

'It's a bit of a story, actually.' I hesitated going ahead, Chante's interest in my life being roughly the same as my interest in particle physics. But she hadn't sneered yet and if I were to pretend that my assistant might actually assist me at some point it would make sense if she knew what was going on.

'Like twelve years ago, give or take, I was in Portugal hanging out with this woman—'

'A rich woman?'

'Of course a rich woman. Why would I be running a con on a woman who wasn't rich? Unfortunately she turned out to have some issues. For one thing she was rather fond of heroin.'

'I will pour you more alcohol while you tell me how you despise drug addicts.'

'I don't despise . . . well, I kind of did, but live and let live. It was an issue but also helpful because, man, when a junkie passes out, they pass all the way out. I could have dynamited her safe and she wouldn't have woken up. But that was not the real issue.'

'No?' she asked an invisible person just behind and to my right.

'No, the thing was she had Hollywood connections and wanted me to accompany her to a movie opening, I assume because I look good in a tux. But walking the red carpet in front of half the cameras in LA is not something the intelligent fugitive does.'

She wanted to make a crack about the insinuation that I was 'intelligent', I could see it in her eyes, but she held her fire, possibly because she was just waiting for a better opening.

'So I did something a bit stupid—'

'No!'

And there was the better opportunity.

'Cute,' I said. 'I emptied her safe but I hadn't yet found a hook-up – a fence.' I was at the refrigerator now, suddenly ravenous. Some ham looked promising. 'So I find this name on the Dark Web and I go see this guy who uses a rare books shop as a front. We do some business, we have some lunch at a local *tasca*, we get back to his shop and the fucking Polícia Judiciária have already popped Azevedo's – that's the guy's name – safe. Some detective is literally holding my loot in his hand.'

'*Your* loot.'

I pretended not to hear that bit of snark. 'At which point Azevedo could have said, "Hey, boys, that stuff belongs to this American, I was just getting ready to call you." Instead he did the honorable thing and ended up catching two years while I walked.'

'Honor among thieves?'

'I live by a code.' I said that just to provoke her. She let the baited hook glide by. 'So last week when we were in Tbilisi he reached out to me and we had a little Skype.'

We'd gone from Cyprus to Tbilisi prior to Amsterdam to confuse the trail. Lovely city, impossible language, not great food. None of which is relevant.

'Long story short, Azevedo has a nineteen-year-old daughter named Madalena who he says is mixed up with some dude here in Amsterdam. Named Milan Smit. He wants me to check on her.'

'So? Have you?'

'I have to find her first. She's gone off-grid. I wanted to settle in for a few days before—'

'We have been here for almost a week.'

'A few days, a week, Jesus, now you're nagging me? What do you care?'

That ended our little tête-à-tête. Besides, I had thinking to do, so I took the Talisker and repaired to my bed and there, alone in the dark, I asked myself the big question: why was someone trying to kill me? *Me?* Granted I was not a candidate for sainthood, but in the great Pez dispenser of people who needed killin' I was nowhere near the top. How did I deserve to be killed while Harvey Weinstein, Bashar Assad and Boris Johnson still lived?

I began to wonder, upon realizing I had been (attempted) murdered, if Azevedo had been indiscreet and an enemy with a grudge and an overly complicated plan had found me. But that didn't add up. Azevedo was a smart old guy and wouldn't carelessly endanger the asset he'd sent to rescue his daughter.

As for people who wanted me dead, they divided into two camps. First there were my victims – I prefer to call them clients – irritated that I had relocated their money to my bank account. Realistically, though, the idea that some oil man from Houston or horn-bedecked husband from Paris would actually attempt murder? Unlikely in the extreme. Even I don't kill people, and I am (was) an actual criminal (retired).

Then there were the bad guys I'd fallen afoul of, a list that included more gangs than I'd have preferred, but gangsters don't go in for attention-grabbing antics involving nooses and canals, they'd shoot me at my front door or cut my throat in a dark street. Then, too, there was the fact that no smart gangster was going to spend the money and assume the risk of a hit in a very law-abiding city like Amsterdam over a mere matter of revenge. Gangsters are businessmen. *Cui bono?* Where was the profit in killing little me?

'This is fucked up,' I informed the small water stain on the ceiling. 'No part of this is right.'

There remained one possibility: that I was not the intended victim, just the dummy who happened to be in the wrong place at the wrong time. That would make it a prank rather than a hit. But what were the odds of that?

It worried me quite a bit since I remain unalterably opposed to being killed, but I found reassurance in sheer improbability. It made no sense, none at all, and it is a persistent weakness of the rational mind to seek reasonable explanations for human behavior.

Chante was not wrong that it might be time to grab a cab to Schiphol and fly away, but I couldn't do that until I had rescued fair Madalena and delivered some bromides to a bookstore audience. So, first thing tomorrow, as soon as I'd had coffee and put a few hours in at the laptop, I had to get serious because if I solved Azevedo's problem I could still always catch that cab to Schiphol. Better still, if I solved the question of who had tried to kill me, I could stay in Amsterdam, land of legal weed and tall, gorgeous women riding bikes.

It all made perfect sense. Really it did.

THREE

'Well, I was pretty drunk, I have to admit, officer.'
'First thing' in the morning had not worked out because first thing was: cops. Or cop, singular. The policeman who knocked politely at my door had been informed of a possible crime involving me. Tess, undoubtedly, given that the cop had my address.

Irritated note to self: WTF is the matter with you, David? No one should ever know where you live.

I was on my second cup of coffee and getting ready to start working, but I was prepared. He was just a uniform taking a statement, an almost too-Dutch kid: appled of cheek, blond of hair, confident despite looking like a nine-foot-tall twelve-year-old. He glanced perfunctorily at my passport and handed it back without even noting the number. A fact which allowed me to breathe more easily.

'It's so stupid and embarrassing, but I . . . wait, you know what? I still have the shirt.' I fetched a blue dress shirt from my bedroom, a shirt with a badly ripped sleeve. I'd hated to sacrifice a perfectly nice shirt – bespoke, fit like a dream – by ripping the sleeve and smearing it with grime, but I'd anticipated this moment and there's nothing like an apparently unplanned prop.

My story was either too ridiculous to believe or so ridiculous it had to be true. I couldn't know what the police officer would conclude, but I felt about as good as I can ever feel upon being questioned by an LEO. This did not strike me as the opening stage of a city-wide manhunt.

'We received a statement that a rope of some sort—'
'A rope? Nah. Whoever said that must have even been drunker than I was.'
'In truth we found no rope.'
Didn't you, just? Well, well, the killer had gone back to

remove the rope. I had to approve of the tradecraft – even a piece of rope can be evidence if you leave skin behind.

'Please inform the police if you have any further incidents,' he said, and was gone.

I don't dance or high-five but I did allow myself a sly, 'Heh heh heh,' as the door closed.

Then I banged out some pages of my latest opus, had lunch, did some research on Amsterdam – basic stuff, know where you are – and wasted some hours on Goodreads, alternately preening or spewing silent bile. So 'first thing' became eight p.m. which meant I'd be starting my search for fair Madalena in places where a drug dealer and his presumably naive love-slave Madalena might go: clubs.

The strobes were seizure-inducing and the music was techno and loud enough to cost me an IQ point for every minute's exposure. I held up my phone. 'Have you seen this girl?'

'Pardon?'

I squeezed into a place at the bar between a young Dutch couple and a seriously drunk Spaniard ranting about housing costs in Barcelona, and swiped between photos of Madalena. 'This girl. Have you seen her?'

'Are you the police?'

'No, I'm just looking for this girl because she's in trouble.'

I had placed a fifty-euro note on the bar. It could be for a drink, it could be a bribe. I slid it toward the bartender, but he was a busy man, the bar was hopping and the bartender, eyes going opaque, slipped off to make cocktails.

At the next bar I showed the bartender my phone. 'Have you seen this girl?'

'Do you want a drink?'

'Sure.' I scanned the bright-lit shelves, running down my mental list of drinkable whiskies. No Talisker. No Lagavulin. No Ardbeg.

'Johnny Black, please, neat. Now, about this picture . . .'

That earned me a shrug, a polite if condescending smile, and, 'I am not the missing persons bureau. You must go to the police.'

Sometimes you know it's not even worth flashing cash.

In preparation for the night's sleuthing I had stared long

and hard at the three photos of Madalena that Azevedo had provided me. I was pretty sure I'd recognize her if I happened to run into her, but equally sure that I was not likely to run into her. No, I would need to ask questions and the first question when asking questions is who to question.

My answers were doormen, bartenders, bud-tenders, bouncers and pimps, in whatever order they came. If clubs came up dry I'd head to the Red Light District for chats with pimps.

'Have you seen—'

'Sorry.'

Nee. No. I see many girls. Nope. Unh-unh. Nee, meneer. Nope. There was even a genial Aussie, *Feck off, mate, eh?* and a less genial, *nyet.*

I had no notion of the Amsterdam club scene, so I had googled, 'hottest clubs in Amsterdam', checked map view and decided to work north to south. I'd already been to a good, old-fashioned lap-dancing establishment, and a cramped place with bad speakers, and a place with speakers so good I thought they might liquefy my kidneys, the club names evaporating in memory as the turn-downs added up.

'I'm looking for this girl . . .'

'She's young for you, no?'

That stung.

A pimp of the furtive variety approached me and offered a girl who looked just like Madalena, only she was Ukrainian and if I would just follow him . . .

By midnight I was deaf, stunned, depressed, foot-sore, frustrated and approaching intoxication. I wandered into the Cave Rock Bar, which was not on my list, drawn by the music of my youth. Green Day's *Dookie* and The Offspring's *Smash* both dropped in 1994 and Rancid's *And Out Come the Wolves* a year later, crashing onto a musical landscape then dominated by Mariah Carey and U2. Someone in the bar was playing Rancid's 'Olympia, WA' and I'd had all the dance music I could stand.

The Cave Rock Bar was not one of 'Amsterdam's hottest bars' rather it was a tiny place just below street level, with a pair of blood-red vomit-resistant plastic booths, a brace of pachinko machines glittering like a pocket Vegas, and a small, low stage at the far end of the long, rectangular room. The Cave was decorated in headbanger eclectic, with paintings of dragons on the crushingly low ceiling, a skeletal Grim Reaper standing in one corner, and various demons posted here and there to make sure no one smiled. Definitely more metal than punk, but the punks never were great ones for interior decorating.

There was a good crowd, some locals, some Germans, some assorted Mediterranean folks, countries of origin uncertain, and a gaggle of Japanese girls in one of the booths, six of them squeezed in together producing rolling, synchronized waves of incongruous giggles. There were quite a few untrimmed beards, a lot of lank hair protruding from beneath stocking caps and denim jackets festooned with identity patches, as well as extravagant tats, body mods and all manner of things I don't much like.

But on the stage was a slight, bald, bearded gnome of a guy who evoked Charles Manson: Tim Armstrong. He wasn't covering 'Olympia WA', it was his song, played with a pick-up band. His voice, never great, hadn't weathered the ages any better than any other fifty-something dude who'd spent decades yelling lyrics over amps turned up to eleven, but he could still play and he could growl and his bass player and drummer laid down a tight beat.

Yes, I fanboyed a bit. It was like walking in and seeing Mick Jagger if you were old. Or Beyoncé if you weren't.

The song ends on a melancholy note about not wanting to be alone. Again. I was several whiskies and a couple of friendly hits of Gorilla Glue into it at this point so I went directly to contemplation of my own solitary condition. Not lonely *again* so much as *still*.

My closest relationship was with Chante, a woman who could barely tolerate me. I think nine out of ten mental health professionals, and a hundred percent of daytime talk show hosts, would call that unhealthy.

The bar selection was not encouraging – way too heavy on the Jaegermeister – but they had Johnnie Black so I stuck with that and held onto it, dodging heaving denim and puffy, down-encased bodies and shouting to the bartender my by-then tedious questions.

I almost didn't know how to react when she nodded her head and said, 'Yes, I've seen her.'

'You're kidding. Really?'

'*Ja*, sure. I recognize this girl.'

She went off to pour drinks but after a while came back of her own accord.

'Is this girl in danger?'

Interesting word choice, 'danger.' Not even 'trouble.' In any other country I'd suspect that a person for whom English was not the first language had simply grabbed the wrong word. But this was Amsterdam, and products of the Dutch educational system speak better English than most Americans.

'May I ask your name? Mine is James. James Lee Burke.' I extended my hand and she shook it firmly.

'Ella,' she said. She frowned. 'Your name seems familiar.'

Note to self: stop using mystery authors' names as aliases, some people still read books.

'Pleased to meet you, Ella. Do you have reason to suspect Madalena's in danger?' I asked.

Ella, a tall twenty-something with a thick brown braid and a sleeve of tattoos that upon casual inspection seemed to have a Tolkien theme, shrugged bare shoulders. 'Is that her name? Madalena?'

I leaned forward into confidential space. 'Here's the thing, *mevrouw* (muh-frow), I'm working with her father who knows about this Milan Smit dude she's with and is very concerned. He's not trying to run his daughter's life, she's an adult of sorts, but he would like to know whether she is entirely . . . free . . . to make her own decisions. Just that: he wants to be sure she is *free*.'

Ella's eyes glittered. Like Americans, the Dutch are big on talk of freedom, and they actually mean it. Ella nodded. She had no reason to trust me, but she'd seen something about the Madalena–Smit relationship she didn't like, so she *wanted* to believe me, and that's half the battle.

'If you can tell me anything . . . anything at all . . .'

'He's a headbanger, a metal head,' Ella said, flipping her

braid back over her shoulder. 'He will come on Saturday. Twan van Geel is performing.'

I sensed that I should be impressed. 'Who?'

'The guitar player for Legion of the Damned.'

'Ah. *That* Twan van Geel,' I said. 'How would I recognize Smit?'

'He is tall, two meters, with long blond hair.' She used a chopping motion to indicate hair down to just below shoulder level. 'He wears a jacket that says *Hells Angels Antwerp.*'

'There's a Hells Angels Antwerp?'

'Of course.' Then, with a disparaging sniff, added, 'Belgium.'

'One more question and I'll fuck off: is there something about this girl or the dude that made you think, "danger"?'

Her eyes stared, unfocused, into the middle distance. 'They had an aura. Sometimes when someone is in danger the normal aura – they were both predominantly orange – can show streaks of a muddy blue, the sign of fear.'

Well, I did ask.

Thankfully she had drinks to pour so I escaped the *prana* lecture that was sure to be on the way.

I walked home from the Cave Rock Bar in a pleasantly weaving sort of way, feeling quite impressed with myself, feeling that detective work wasn't so hard, all it had cost me was some hearing loss, a vague despair for today's youth, and a hefty tip to Ella.

Amsterdam's a great walking town if you avoid the Red Light District. And remember not to be run down by the trams that sneak up on you quiet as a Tesla. And if you don't fall in a canal. And above all, manage to avoid the tinkling menace: Dutch people on bikes. But I'm about as alert as your average squirrel, especially when I've recently been attempted murdered, so I was not too concerned with the various methods of silent death practiced by Amsterdamers. My focus was a block ahead and a block behind, looking for a familiar face I'd need to avoid, as one does. Fugitive Vision is the extended awareness that is rather like aerial combat in that the trick is always to see before being seen, recognize without being recognized. It's not a good state of mind to be in if you're stopping to smell the roses, but it comes with the fugitive lifestyle.

I took the most direct path, straight up the Leidsestraat then hung a right on the Singel and walked along the two blocks of closed-up greenhouses of the tulip market. Past the Starbucks, past the Old Dutch Pancake House and the tourist cheese shops (really, you're going to put a whole twenty-six-pound wheel of Gouda in your luggage?) and suddenly I felt eyes.

I came to Vijzelstraat and instead of crossing I turned hard right into an arched gallery illuminated by the dimmed lights of closed shops. I slipped behind a pillar. I opened the camera on my phone and slid just the lens around the corner to see that yes, someone was coming.

No professional would be caught by such a ruse as simple as ducking behind a pillar, but then no professional would tail a mark down an empty street at night, either, certainly not from just ten meters back.

But I soon discovered that I was wrong, for the guy I thought had been tailing me turned out to be a thirty-something woman in a hoodie. I remained in the shadows and watched her walk past and almost laughed aloud at the release of stress. Not my aspiring murderer, just some woman on her way home.

I breathed a big sigh, had a little laugh at my own expense, and toddled off home.

FOUR

had a day free of obligations to my Portuguese fence. On Saturday I'd go back to the Cave and see whether I could spot Milan Smit. If Madalena was with him I'd try to get her somewhere private and ask her what she was up to. If she wasn't with Smit I'd follow him.

Then there was the Hangman – I'd named him now, like a Spider-Man super-villain. *Beware the Hangman!* And I'd spent more time than I care to admit mentally costuming and equipping my supervillain.

Return of the Hangman!

I imagined various clever ropes enhanced by technology, like Hawkeye with his arrows, but even dumber.

Hangman Be Not Proud!

I had decided the Hangman was a buffoon, a clown, and that, along with the flaccid police response, gave me a sense of security and drew the Hangman's sting.

Some crazy person. Some nut.

That said, my threat level was elevated from yellow to orange. Or Defcon 3 to Defcon 2, because Defcons count down, not up. I wasn't going to full sphincter-tightening alarm, just turning the dial up a notch on my Fugitive Vision.

In the morning I worked for a while with the window open, feet up on the iron railing of the faux balcony, coffee close at hand, a Romeo y Julieta double corona clamped in my teeth, laptop on my lap, and dragged my way through a tedious but unavoidable expository scene that just would not end. Joe Barton, my fictional detective in the fictional-but-Chicago-like city of New Midlands, had an info dump to manage, which is wearying work.

I put in a solid three hours, only half of which was spent going online to see whether there really was a supervillain called Hangman. Turned out, yes, he was a minor Marvel character who started off as a guy named Harlan, evidently a rather brutal good guy like the Punisher, and later became a dude named Jason who went over to the dark side. He favored purple tights, a sleeveless black top, a blue cowl and Robin Hood calfskin boots. And a rope, because you couldn't very well be the Hangman without a rope, but he also carried a scythe, which is impractical, in tight spaces but probably beats a rope in hand-to-hand combat with superheroes.

From there I was of course distracted by the thought that it'd be a hell of a lot easier for law enforcement if criminals wore signature outfits and carried impractical weaponry. And that led inevitably (writers will understand how this happens) to the question of what *my* signature costume would be if I were still pursuing a career in crime. I'd probably look OK in spandex, but only OK as I lacked steroid thighs. I knew I couldn't rock a cape, but maybe something like a stylized tuxedo, black, tailored to emphasize my lean tallness, with a splash of color, a collar or a crest. Turquoise? Something with some yellow or gold? Would a diamond stickpin that was also a high-tech lock pick be too on the nose?

And what would I call myself? The Thief? The Grifter? What if instead of keeping all the money I stole I made contributions to the poor? Say, 50 percent? Too much, too showy? Maybe 20 percent? A 'portion of proceeds'? Could I call myself Robbing Hood then? If I did, would I have to wear the boots and have a sidekick named Will Scarlet?

Sometimes it amazes me that I ever get any work done, but by the time lunch beckoned I had six new pages down.

Chante might be, well, Chante, but she could cook. For lunch she served up some sautéed herring filets with lime and pepper, roasted potatoes and Brussels sprouts with bacon and caramelized sugar.

'Excellent fish,' I said. I don't stint on praise for people who feed me well. Enlightened self-interest.

We ate together, pulling a small round table up to the French doors before the faux balcony. It was early September and had rained during the night bringing clammy humidity, but the temperature still lingered in the low sixties and the street outside was bustling with late-season tourists in North Face down and jeans, or tight leather and jeans, or Ralph Lauren oilskin and jeans. I was glad to note the appearance of stocking caps as the weather cooled. There's no quicker or more portable disguise than a stocking cap and glasses.

Chante did not respond to my compliment; she took it as a given that her food was excellent. 'Coffee?' she asked, meaning that I should make coffee.

'Actually, I'm going out. I think I'll find a nice café and drink beer all afternoon, unless the rain comes.'

I slid my laptop into my battered brown-leather shoulder bag and walked north along the Kloveniersburgwal (Cloven-ears-burgs-val), which back in the sixteenth century was part of the city walls and was now a lovely residential street beside a wide canal.

My destination, the Dam, is the largest of Amsterdam's various squares, divided into unequal portions by a crossing street and further sliced up by tramlines. On one end there's the seventeenth-century royal palace which, if you're familiar with French, British or Italian notions of a royal palace, is pretty disappointing. The Dutch were never big on kings. The underlying ethos of Amsterdam was that of a mercantilist republic devoted to making money, Protestant modesty, and also making money. The palace is half a dozen stories tall, topped by a turquoise dome, and looks like a very nice city hall, which is what the original builders intended, and thus completely lacks the 'fuck the peasants', grandeur of a Versailles or a Kremlin.

Just to the left of the palace and set back a bit is the Nieuwe Kerk, the New Church. New because it was built in the fourteenth century, practically yesterday. The original burned down, as things were prone to do back before the invention of smoke detectors, and was replaced by the current, grandly gothic structure in the seventeenth century. It's not used as a church anymore but as an exhibition space, the outer walls invariably hung with banners advertising the latest show.

Then there is the Ripley's Believe It Or Not! and the Madame Tussauds with its giant, tacky, domineering sign, mute testimony to the fact that the Dutch are perhaps just a little too willing to compromise aesthetics for the amusement of tourists.

At the other end of the square is the National Monument. Here again, people imagining something that is the equivalent of the Washington Monument or perhaps Nelson's Column have failed to grasp the degree to with the Dutch reject ostentation. The Dutch are not big on fancy frills, and lack in great tyrants to build great monuments to their own greatness. So when challenged to design a monument to World War Two, they slapped up something that looked rather like a travertine butt plug with various puzzling symbolic statues and bas reliefs arrayed around the base.

The pillar is their official monument to the suffering of the Dutch under Nazi occupation, and it's fine, I suppose, but the real WWII monument is a Dutch canal house on the Prinsengracht, not far from where I'd gone swimming. Anne Frank and her family were kept hidden by people with good Dutch names: Kleiman, Kugler, Gies and Voskuijl. Those people weren't risking money or career or even three-to-five, they were risking their lives and the lives of their families.

Righteous Among the Nations, the Jews call people like that. I don't pretend to understand the kind of humans who would be so moved by simple decency they'd risk a trip to a concentration camp, but I will readily admit that the world would be a better place with more of them and fewer of me.

My goal on this fresh, gorgeous day was not the palace or the church or even Madame Tussaud's. I was heading to the Majestic, an outdoor café on the Dam. The food was mediocre, the service often absent without leave, but they poured good beer and provided a place for me to sit while eyeballing passersby and making up lurid stories about them.

A phalanx of young women in cowboy boots walking with linked arms – probably foreign art students – became a group of defiant cancer survivors.

A busker waving a huge bubble wand and sending great, undulating shapes skimming across the paving stones, became a former high-tech executive who'd had a nervous breakdown and now sold bubble wands to tourists. He's never been happier, though, sure, there are days when he feels regret . . . but then he meets a pleasant Canadian family and it turns his mood right around.

An old man in a long raincoat was either a flasher or a Nazi-collaborator who'd hidden out in Argentina after the war but was unable to resist coming home. This story had some problems in that the man was old, but he was definitely not old enough to have served in the war.

The sounds on the Dam were gentle, the clip-clop of horses' hooves ahead of a carriage full of tourists; the clink of glasses; the musical tinkle of bicycle bells which the Dutch cyclists are required to ring a half-second before they run you down.

There were clouds in the sky, some forming tall white towers reaching to a pale daytime moon, others, lower, threatening to dump rain. It was pleasantly cool, cool enough that the patio warmers had been fired up.

After about a month a waiter appeared and I ordered a Rodenbach, a strange beer which pours almost red but has a nice white head, which arrived just a few weeks later. I had a table behind the first row and toward the center of the café, the spot chosen because it felt snug and safe from the Hangman. Unless my comic book nemesis was Will Rogers he'd have a hard time lassoing me.

I sat there for an hour or so, progressively squeezed and jostled as people came and went – one surly woman with the face of a DMV clerk very nearly knocked over my beer – the crowd waxing and waning like a tide. I contemplated my situation, particularly the question of why someone might want to kill me, but I kept circling around the fact that there was no evident logic to it. I'd left a trail of slightly impoverished rich people, betrayed women and embarrassed cuckolds in my wake, but none of that justified murder. At least not *to* me, *of* me.

I was drinking good beer, but only beer, and as a rule it's not possible for me to get drunk on beer – I don't like it enough – so I was surprised when I stood up to go in search of the restroom and found I needed to put a hand on the table to balance myself.

'Wha th'fuh?' Tongue and lips were not working quite right, which was surprising. I was more surprised still when the table tipped and my glass shattered on the paving stones and I did a sort of twisting collapse move, looked up at the awning, felt myself accelerating downward and landed hard, flat on my back. Someone should have yelled, 'Timber!' because I was nothing but six feet of toppling flesh tree. My head bounced and geometric patterns confused my vision.

I lay there on the ground noting the cries of alarm and the recoiling of my fellow café patrons. I tried to stand – as one does when one finds oneself flat on the ground – but my limbs were not having it and rather than stand I just flailed limply as my vision narrowed and went in and out of focus like a phone camera video trying for a close-up.

Then a woman wearing a bright-yellow, high-visibility jacket appeared, bent over me and in a loud but unsteady voice said in English, 'Give him rooms!'

I stared at her shoes, right at eye level. They were Adidas sneakers in a complex blue-and-pink pattern. I'd seen them before, of course I had: on the feet of the surly woman who'd almost knocked my beer over, and, it was now clear, had dropped something into my glass.

I tracked up and saw that she was wearing gray yoga pants. Also wrong for an emergency medical tech. And the scoop-necked top was wrong, EMTs and ambulance drivers and such generally being too busy to want to flash cleavage. A whole bunch of wrong was happening and I could not make my mouth work to say anything more than, 'Unh.' I was paralyzed, legs and arms numb as if blood had been cut off. I thought I could move them, should have been able to, but could not.

Frightening, but of course the drug had the effect of damping down fear so that even as my rational mind was screaming, *This is bad!* the rest of my brain was basically OK with being restfully flat on my back in a café.

The 'clumsy', beer-knocking paramedic with the wrong shoes, pants and top bent over me and slipped a hand behind my neck, palm cool on my rope burns. She put her other arm under mine which brought her face to within inches. She was probably younger than she looked, with dark hair that blew in the slight breeze and tickled my nose. She was white but not, I thought, Dutch, at least not by birth. She had an eastern

European look, with Slavic cheekbones and a sad, downturned mouth. Her slightly slanted eyes were so pale the blue was a genuine gray. She avoided meeting my stunned-stupid gaze, nor did she mutter soothing words of comfort.

What she did say was, 'Please, some person to help me get him to wheelchair, yes?'

Wheelchair?

Some big ol' Polish guy with a popped collar and a thin calfskin jacket stepped up like a gentleman and between the two of them they half-carried, half-dragged me through tables rapidly pulled aside, ignoring such cogent remarks of mine as 'Mrh guh' and 'Whuh mh fra', and there, parked just a few feet away, was a wheelchair.

Not an ambulance. Not a gurney. A wheelchair.

My body was paralyzed but my brain was not. I knew I'd been poisoned. I even had a pretty good notion as to the specific poison: Rohypnol. I was familiar with it because I'd used it twice before. Not to commit a rape. I'm not an animal. I only ever used it to ensure that my 'client' slept soundly while I worked on gaining entry to a safe or a laptop or a phone.

The Good Samaritan and the woman I was now forced to suspect was actually the Hangman dumped me into the wheelchair. I noted with embarrassment that I no longer needed the restroom since my very relaxed body had decided not to wait any longer to recycle the Rodenbach. Thus with soaked crotch and a cut finger from my tumble I was wheeled away, rattling across the paving stones of the Dam, embarrassment in my wake.

The nature of the plan eluded me. Why roofie me and drag me to a wheelchair? And why was she now pushing me across the Dam? And down a narrow side street beneath construction scaffolding?

The construction site was closed off by waterproofed canvas tied to an anodized aluminum frame with plastic zip ties. The EMT – no, the Hang*woman* – opened a clasp knife and cut two zip ties. Then she pushed me through the flap.

I was now in a space hidden from foot traffic on the busy street just inches away, surrounded by stacks of two-by-fours, or their metric equivalent, which had accumulated a thick coat of dust. There were bags of cement, also dusty. And a dusty, parked, white van. The dust was not good news: no one had worked here for some time.

We were alone, me and the Hangman, surrounded by debris.

My kidnapper leaned back against the van, breathing hard, then sneezed as the dust got to her. I aimed my wandering eyeballs at her, focus going in and out and never quite coming clear. But I would recognize her if I saw her again, I was sure of that.

I was still not terrified. It was all too ridiculous and I was too high to generate profound fear . . . until I noticed that she had not folded her knife away.

Then I was properly terrified.

It was becoming clear that this crazy woman meant to murder me right there, right then, and there was not a single damned thing I could do about it. Her next move would be a slash across my throat which, if she did it right, would have me unconscious in three seconds and dead in fifteen.

I said, 'Unh uh uuuunh,' to which she did not respond.

I wanted to ask her why. *Why?* For what crime I was I being executed? I wanted to ask her a lot of things. I would have had a nice long chat about Amsterdam's favorite philosopher, Spinoza, anything to stall for time. But brain and mouth were not connected, and increasingly brain was not even connected to consciousness. I could soon be unconscious and miss my own death.

She frowned and bit her lip and sent every signal that she was scared and nervous and uncertain and then she stabbed the knife into my left pectoral muscle.

The knife, a nice, brass-and-bone handled, locking-blade clasp knife with what looked to have a three-inch blade, plunged through my jacket, through my shirt, and penetrated skin and muscle. But only about half an inch.

She drew back, disgusted by what she'd done, alarmed at the blood that bloomed like a poppy on my shirt. At the same time, though, there was a light in those gray eyes, a glitter of excitement. I could see her steeling herself. She licked her lips, nodded encouragement to herself, and drew a deep breath. She was going to stab me again. This time she would mean it.

'Who's in there?'

The Hangwoman froze. She actually put a finger to her lips as if urging me to stay silent. Like I had a choice. Like if I'd had a choice I'd have agreed not to scream, 'Save me, a crazy woman's trying to kill me!'

I heard the sound of the canvas being thrown back.

'Drop that knife. *Now!*' A woman's voice, husky, authoritative. American.

And oddly familiar.

'Go away, you have no permission!' The Hangman protested in an accent with more than a few Slavic tells in it.

The stab wound started to hurt. It would hurt worse if I survived.

The Hangman looked frantic, unsure, glancing from me to my unseen would-be savior. She laid the knife's edge against my throat and had I not already wet myself, this is when I'd do it. Cold steel on neck flesh is dire. But she did not swipe right to end my life, rather she dithered.

Then suddenly she turned and ran, tripping and cursing through the construction debris.

Another woman stepped into my extremely limited field of vision. She was tall, black, around my age, about eighty percent leg, gorgeous and clearly amused at my predicament.

'Well, hello there, David,' said FBI Special Agent Delia Delacorte.

FIVE

I had flashes of rolling back across the Dam. Flashes of being hauled up the stairs to my apartment by Delia, Chante and the Croatian guy I recognized as living in the flat below mine.

I was dropped on my bed and left there.

Sometime later I woke with a huge headache and pee-stained trousers. My limbs worked but awkwardly, like they were the members of a band reuniting after twenty years' estrangement. I had just enough coordination to stand, fighting a tsunami of nausea, and stumble to the shower.

Hot water helped – it always does. I had no memory of being bandaged, but there was gauze and tape on my chest, being made heavy now by water. I peeled the bandage off and looked at my terrible wound, which, OK all things considered, wasn't too bad. A neat, half-inch vertical cut. No stitches needed.

Funny how I'd gone my whole life without being stabbed, but since meeting Special Agent Delia Delacorte? Twice. That was either an omen or a coincidence, depending on one's level of superstition.

Clean and dressed in fresh clothing over fresh bandages, I emerged in search of the remaining vital element of recovery, which was handed to me.

'Black, if I recall correctly,' Delia said as she passed me a mug of coffee.

'Like I like my women: black and bitter.' I grunted and gratefully sank onto the sofa, still very shaky, spilling a bit as I did.

Chante was in the open-plan kitchen busily cooking something that smelled amazing and made my stomach cry out.

'How long was I out?'

Delia Delacorte, FBI legat out of the Rome embassy, Special

Agent of the Bureau, the physical embodiment of danger to my continued freedom, all six feet of her, sat opposite me, feet on the coffee table, a cup in her hand, her sleepy, half-lidded eyes watching me. 'Let's see, it's seven thirty—'

'Is that a.m. or p.m.?'

'It's a.m. You slept all through the evening and night, so call it sixteen hours?'

That explained the ravenous hunger. It did not explain why a crazy woman had roofied me. Nor did it explain Delia's presence here, a presence that brought very mixed emotions: fear, lust, worry, pleasure, resentment, some more lust, some additional fear . . . basically all the emotions of which I am capable aside from greed and self-regard.

The caffeine was kicking in and I had many questions, among which were, *I have this image of a construction site. Was that real?* But I also smelled frying pork and knew that not all of my brain was quite fully engaged with reality, so questions could wait.

'This is my interpretation of a full English breakfast,' Chante said, placing a plate in front of Delia like she was serving the queen. Chante slid my plate across to me as if I was the cowboy at the far end of the saloon bar. We sat like a little family: reprobate dad, responsible mom, and their difficult daughter.

Chante's interpretation of the Full English involved eggs *en cocotte*, not bacon but a slab of good Danish ham, a grilled herbed tomato, a well-browned sausage, a piece of fried fish, quartered new potatoes, a welcome absence of black pudding, a slightly less welcome absence of beans, a fruit salad freshened with mint, freshly squeezed orange juice and straight from the oven scones with clotted cream and orange marmalade.

I try to hate the girl, I really do.

Finally, sated, caffeinated and with a pair of ibuprofen chasing my headache, I looked across at Delia and said, 'So. To what do we owe the pleasure?'

I did not ask how she'd found me. Delia had a snitch. Part of the deal for allowing me to continue to breathe free air was that Delia would have a way to keep track of me. I hadn't hired Chante because I found her charming.

'We can talk about that in a minute. First of all, why are you getting roofied?'

I told her the sad and desperate tale of my near-hanging/drowning, a tale of courage and endurance, quick wit and clear-thinking which the two women found very entertaining.

'If only we had pictures,' Chante said. Or to be phonetic, 'Eef un-LEE we had peek-tures.'

'Not exactly professional work,' Delia remarked after the merriment had subsided.

'No,' I agreed. 'You can tell when it's a professional hitter because you're dead.'

'Mmm.' Delia frowned and tilted her head, looking at me as if I had the explanation. 'It's beyond amateur. It's hard to get a firearm in Holland, but still, there are knives. Why not just cut your throat in an alleyway?'

'Or run you down with a car?' Chante suggested.

'Or push you in front of a tram?' Delia offered.

'Or, if someone is going to the difficulty (dee-fee-cool-tay) of poisoning your beer, why not the belladonna or the strych-nine or even concentrated nicotine? You can make that easily in the kitchen with only two packs of cigarettes or a few cigars. Or, you could grind glass up very finely and in beer the carbona-tion would keep it from settling to the bottom of the glass.'

This by the way, all from the woman whose food I regularly ate. I shuddered to think what Chante's browser history must look like.

'Do you have any idea who might be responsible?' Delia asked.

'I got a very good look at the fake paramedic and she's no one I know. She was not a past . . .' I hesitated to try floating the word 'client' past Delia and 'victim' was so harsh – 'a past, um, dalliance.'

'She drugs you then pushes you into a construction site to stab you ineffectually? She could have cut your throat in the Dam and just walked away,' Delia pointed out.

Chante chimed in with, 'An icepick in the ear . . .'

'Or she could have dipped me in a fucking vat of acid,' I said. 'Gee, this is fun. Let's think of more ways I could have been killed.'

'The question is not how you could be killed,' Delia said sagely, 'but why someone wants you dead, and why the attempts were so bizarre.'

'No one even knows I'm here in Amsterdam, outside of a few book nerds and you, Delia, as well as Chante, and your old pal Agent Kim, and whoever else you told at the Bureau.'

I rubbed at my stab wound. It ached.

'By the way, Delia,' I said, belatedly. 'Thanks for saving my life.'

She accepted it gracefully. 'No problem, David. And FYI, you are listed as a confidential informant with an assigned code name and number. Your various names never appear, and I have not included details about you. Besides, the Bureau does not leak.'

'It feels personal,' I said, reflecting. 'At least the motive if not the means. Someone – some perfectly average-looking Slavic woman – is sincerely trying to kill me, just doing a lousy job of it.' Then I shook my head, realizing I still did not have an answer to a rather important question. 'Um, Delia? What the fuck are you doing in Amsterdam?'

'It's almost like you aren't happy to see me,' Delia said.

'I love seeing you above all people, Delia, but you showed up while someone was trying to kill me, which means you already had eyes on me. So I kind of have to wonder just what the hell is going on, Agent D.'

'My business with you is not connected to you being targeted for a hit.'

'Sure of that, are you?'

'Reasonably.'

'Because I have to tell you, it seems like a hell of a coincidence.'

'Coincidences do happen,' she said.

'Oh? TV cops never believe in coincidences.'

'David, you of all people should know that there's no such thing as TV cops; there are only writers for TV cop shows and they're a bunch of twenty-something Ivy League kids who've never so much as met a real law enforcement officer except when they got drunk on spring break.'

'Which takes us right back to, WTF? You're here and you had obviously been looking for me. Why?'

Delia pushed back from the table, stood, stretched, and started to pace. 'I'm deciding whether it is time for Chante to leave, and I think, sadly, that it is.' She smiled sympathetically at Chante. 'I'm sorry, but it's for your own legal protection, Chante.'

Chante nodded and without so much as a sneer, marched off to her room. She could have cleared the dishes on her way, but no, so I used my ancient waiter skills to load the dirty dishes up my arm, then walked them all to the sink.

I scraped plates into a can – Europeans don't do garbage disposals – and said, 'All right, spill, Delia.'

Delia loaded the dishwasher. Her expression grew serious. Mine grew worried.

'You know the phrase "it takes a thief to catch a thief"?'

I answered with a suspicious drawl. 'Uh-huh.'

'Wait . . .' Delia dried her hands on a towel and retrieved an iPad. She lit it up, satisfied herself that she had the right document, and handed it to me. 'That's a non-disclosure agreement. I need you to sign it. And David?'

'Yes, ma'am?'

'We are not playing around. This is a very serious NDA, we will absolutely arrest you and prosecute you if you violate it. I will not be able to protect you. Do you hear me?'

'Yes, Delia, I hear your pointed threat.'

'I hope so. Look me in the eyes, David.'

I looked her in the eyes. She imagined this moment as me recognizing just how serious she was. In reality I was mostly thinking that she was gorgeous and forbidden and I knew from past experience that any attempt would be rebuffed. Still . . . but I also got the whole, 'this is serious' thing. I am able to multitask.

I used my fingertip to sign the document. 'Cross my heart and hope not to die.'

'OK,' Delia said.

I drizzled dishwasher detergent and hit the right buttons. We moved to the shallow balcony with drinks in our hands and a cigar in my teeth.

'Nice location you have here,' Delia said. 'The wages of sin?'

'It's an AirBnB. The Wi-Fi is excellent, but the master bathroom could use another fifty square feet. I practically have to stand in the shower to take a leak, but that's kind of not the point, the point is you're worrying me, Delia. Should I be worried? Because you're worrying me.'

She sighed and took a moment to organize her thoughts, while gazing out of the window at the crowds passing the Munttoren. 'The last time we worked together, as you recall, I was not officially on duty. This time I am. I've told my supervisors that I may have a way to solve a problem they, we, have, a big problem with serious political and international relations implications.'

'Oooh, implications.'

'Yes, implications.' She found that word less absurd than I did. 'A very wealthy man, a very, *very* wealthy man, a man with deep political connections, a man who owns a controlling interest in a major defense contractor, is preparing to do something extremely stupid.'

'Sounds like the kind of guy who could get away with it. Whatever *it* is.'

'This man is old and sick, in late stage COPD, gasping for every breath. Like a trout in the bottom of a boat. He'll be dead within a year.'

I had my phone out and was busy googling.

'This man,' Delia went on, 'we'll call him USP One, United States Person One, has essentially unlimited assets. We know he's planning to commit a crime but—'

'But arresting Daniel "Chip" Isaac would be a huge political mess?' I winked coquettishly. Hearing about upstanding citizens who are secretly scumbags always makes me happy.

Delia's left eyebrow rose an entire two millimeters, mute evidence of the depth of her surprise. I held up my phone. 'Arms merchant with COPD. Doesn't take major Google-fu.'

'USP One,' Delia insisted pointedly, waving away a cloud of my cigar smoke, 'is of Jewish origin—'

'Daniel Isaac? I'd have thought Buddhist, but OK.'

'And as he's neared the end of his life, he's become more pious.'

'That's the trick with God,' I opined. 'Be as much of an asshole as you like then, right at the end, when you're impotent and reduced to gruel and chamomile tea, you discover faith. Ta-da! Heaven!'

'This will go quicker without the snide asides.'

'Yeah, but it won't be as much fun. So what is USP *numero uno*, Danny "the Chipster" Isaac up to?'

'USP One has come to believe that a recently discovered Vermeer – that's a painting—'

'A Vermeer *painting*, you say? Not a Vermeer brand cheesesteak?'

'Belonged to his family before the war—'

'Which war?'

'World War Two.'

'Ah, that one. I've heard of it,' I said, with a cheeky smile. I was still trying to charm Delia, still wanting her to like me. It's both a strength and a failing of mine that I want women to like me. Men I can take or leave, but I want women to like me, to be charmed. Someday I should go to a shrink, just to see what a professional makes of a guy who wants to be liked by women . . . and then takes their money. I am not a mental health professional, but I'm guessing that's not 'normal'.

'Anyway,' Delia said, grating a bit, 'his family owned the painting – *Jewess at the Loom* – here in Amsterdam before the war and it was, according to family lore, looted by the Nazis during the occupation. Also, according to that same family lore, the *Jewess* in question is an ancestor of USP One's family. So now he wants the painting back. It's become an idée fixe. An obsession. I suppose he sees it as some sort of penance, a balancing out of things he may not wish to discuss with Saint Peter at the Pearly Gates.'

'Saint Peter? You said he's Jewish.'

'So was Peter.'

'Pretty sure that's not how it works. I think he'd be talking to Moses not Peter. I don't suppose you want to save me some Google time and tell me just what Chip's done that Moses wouldn't approve of?'

No, she didn't. 'The current owner of the painting denies

USP One's story and claims it was legally purchased by his great-grandfather before the occupation.'

'At a steep "the Nazis are coming" discount?'

'Exactly. Early on the Nazis went easy on the Dutch seeing them as fellow Aryans, but everyone knew it wouldn't last. Everyone knew that sooner or later the Gestapo would roll into town and start deporting Jews to slave labor camps. Or worse.'

'OK, so Isaac's great-grandfather—'

'Just his father, actually. USP One is eighty-seven years old.'

I glanced down at my phone. 'By amazing coincidence, so is Chip Isaac.'

'But the courts,' she plowed ahead, determined to ignore my interruptions, 'have decided for the owner, who handed it off to the Rijksmuseum. In fact, they're adding it to their Vermeer display next week. In six days.'

'So . . . more lawsuits?' I suggested. I did not yet know where this was going, but I was already having a bad feeling about it.

'USP One doesn't think he'll live long enough for a new round of lawsuits even to reach a court. He's decided on a different path: he's going to steal it.'

I very nearly did a spit-take. 'The fuck?'

'He's hired a gang of thieves, a professional gang called the Ontario Crew. He's hired them to steal it from the Rijksmuseum and bring it to him.'

This made sense if you stretched the word 'sense' far enough. It's easy to steal art, any clown can do it. The problem is that the art cannot then be sold because the internet is always watching. If *Starry Night* shows up at Sotheby's auction house no one is going to doubt it's stolen property. The only people who turn a blind eye to stolen art are the Chinese – if said art is itself Chinese and ends up in a Beijing museum. Theft, repatriation, it all depends on where you're standing, I suppose.

Even a bespoke theft made sense only if the collector meant to keep it hidden away, which I suppose seemed like a solution to a dying old man who wouldn't have to cope with the FBI kicking the door in with a search warrant.

'OK, so call up the Dutch cops and warn them.'

'How?' she asked, and leaned back, the better to poke holes in my answer.

'How? Pick up the phone. Dial 112. Hello, officer? Hey, guess what? Someone's going to hit the Rijks.'

'And they ask: who? Who is calling with this helpful tip? And who is doing the stealing?'

'FBI and the Ontario Crew, respectively.'

'So you want us to lay our cards on the table for the Dutch? Pray tell, master criminal, what do the Dutch cops do next?' Now Delia got to be the smart-ass.

I shrugged. 'They demand more information.'

'Which we cannot give them without implicating USP One.'

'Which you don't want to do because of politics. And the arms business. Which are pretty much one and the same.'

'Mmm.'

'OK, so you tell the Dutch cops about the Ontario Crew and leave it at that. They run a search, see if they can turn up crew members in the city. If they can, they mount surveillance. They want to catch them in the act, that makes for a better headline and promotions.'

'Yes,' Delia agreed. 'The Dutch lay a trap, the Ontario Crew are arrested, and they are questioned. What do you suppose question number one will be?'

I shrugged. She waited, knowing the answer I had to give. 'OK, so Dutch cops offer them a deal if they give up their employer, US Person Isaac. But that goes nowhere unless the Crew have something on Isaac.'

'Unfortunately, there is something on USP One: FBI electronic surveillance intercepts.'

'Yeah, but that's what *you* have, not them. It doesn't mean . . .' I petered out, knowing what she would say.

'The Dutch cops will ask us if we have anything.'

'And like idiots you'll tell them?'

'We are the Bureau,' Delia said stiffly. 'We do not conceal evidence. Especially not if this case gets anywhere near a court, in which event we can be legally compelled to produce evidence. And, by the way, the crew know we have it on tape because the surveillance was on a whole different matter, for which we questioned them and, well, we didn't have enough to—'

'Whoa.' I held up the appropriate, out-turned 'whoa' palm. 'The Ontario Crew are coming to Amsterdam to steal a painting for the Chipster, and they know you know about it? And they're still going through with it?'

'Mmm.'

'They think they're protected. They think they're untouchable by US law because of Isaac. They know you know and they're so sure you can't do anything about it, they're going through with it?' My usual baritone hit a soprano squeak by the end of the question.

'USP One,' Delia said, the words bitter, 'is offering to pay the Ontario Crew fifty million dollars.'

'Jesus! I'll steal it for half that. Wow. That boy wants his painting.' I was confused. 'So, Delia, this is all very interesting, but what does it have to do with me?'

'I need you,' Delia said, giving me her slow, sly, disconcertingly predatory smile. There are times with Delia when I feel like a field mouse being eyeballed by a hawk.

I like to think that I'm pretty quick to catch on, even in the face of the unexpected, but in this case there were simply too many absurd ideas to process. I had heard all the words, but since those words included *gang of professional thieves*, *Rijksmuseum* and *I need you*, all spoken by an FBI legat, it did not immediately make sense.

'After all,' Delia went on, 'it takes a thief to catch a thief.'

'Yeah, that's bullshit. For a start, I'm not an art thief,' I protested. I realized I was unconsciously backing further into the tight corner where balcony railing met wall and forced myself not to retreat further.

'My list of available consulting thieves did not include an art thief. It did, however, include you. If there is anyone who can figure out how they're doing it, and stop them without getting them arrested, it's you.'

I'd like to say I'm immune to flattery. I'd like to say lots of things that also would not be true.

Only you, Batman, only you can save Gotham . . .

'Before we go any further, and bearing in mind the last time

I helped you, I have to ask: is the Russian mob, or for that matter any other mob, likely to make an appearance in my life?'

Delia has an array of smiles. There's the skeptical one, the amused one, the one that's more of a sneer than a smile. Her smile now was the patient, 'explaining to the slower students' version. 'There is no mob, Russian or otherwise, involved. Unless you're worried about tangential Nazis.'

Tangential Nazis.

It was a good forty feet to the cobblestones below and I wondered, if I were to throw Delia off the balcony, whether it would kill her or whether she would just brush herself off and come back at me like that liquid-metal Terminator.

'Tangential Nazis?'

'Calm down, I just meant the painting was stolen by Nazis. Tangential Nazis. Let's not get bogged down in semantics.'

Oh, no, no, no and a hearty fuck you, Delia, I did not say but instead beamed via my white-hot glare. 'Semantics? You could say the same about *almost dead* and *dead,*' I shot back. 'Semantics.'

She just waited then, watching me, infuriating me because I knew she was tracking the workings of my mind, which went something like:

1. She can pack you off to San Quentin if she decides to.
2. Who the hell steals art nowadays?
3. She did kind of save your life.
4. Tangential Nazis?

Was this why someone had tried to murder me? Had Delia or Delia's office leaked information about me? Was I already being threatened for something I was only just now finding out about?

'What do I get?' I asked bluntly.

'The continuing blindness of the Bureau as pertains to a certain fugitive from justice? And the warm glow of knowing you've done something good and useful?'

'Ah, the glow. Of course. My balls in your pocket and the glow. Swell.'

'Was there something else you had in mind?'

There was, but I wasn't going to tell Delia because I'm not that kind of toxic male, I'm a whole different kind. Also in a physical fight my money would be on her. She knows things.

Plus . . . something. Something was causing the back of my head to tingle. My subconscious had heard something intriguing, it just wasn't sure what.

'How's this for a *quid pro quo*,' I said. 'I do my best to figure out if there's a way to stop the Ontario Crew without anyone knowing, and in exchange, you find out who's trying to kill me. Like you, I can't exactly involve the Dutch cops.'

Delia had to think about that. 'Without local law enforcement there's not much I can do.'

'You have computers. You have data. You can tell your bosses that your confidential informant has a price, and that's it.'

She nodded. 'Fair enough.'

'Also, I'm looking for someone. I have a name for you if you can run it without attracting attention.'

'A name?'

'Madalena Azevedo. Oh, and Milan Smit. She's Portuguese, I think he's Dutch or maybe Belgian.'

Delia favored me with a dubious look but she tapped the names into her phone and nodded acceptance of my terms.

'Let's start with what you have on the Ontario Crew,' I said.

'Not much,' Delia admitted. 'We only have one name, one guy, this character Willy Pete. He may be the head man, or not, we don't know.'

'Interesting name.'

'It's an alias. His real name is Carl Willard. Willy Pete is military slang for white phosphorus, something Willard used in an early bank robbery.'

She picked up her phone, swiped around a bit and a moment later my phone dinged.

'That's the only photo we have of him and it's eight years old.'

I opened my phone and looked at the mug shot of a white guy, late twenties, skeletal, with eyes sunk so deep the pupils were invisible. The scale on the wall behind him measured him at 5'10". And he was wearing a uniform.

'He's a soldier?'

'He was. Army. Special Forces, actually. And the picture may not be much use. Carl Willard was injured, burned, perhaps ironically. The report said extensive tissue damage to chest and neck, some facial damage. We don't have a shot of him post-burn.'

'OK, that's yours, now find mine. Did you get a good look at the woman who poisoned me?'

'I did,' Delia nodded.

'Tit for tat. I stop your Crew, you find that crazy murdering woman and Madalena.'

'Deal,' Delia said. 'After all, I can't have a valuable CI murdered in the middle of helping me on a matter of national security.' She was practicing, I suppose, for the likely inspector general's inquiry that would follow if this thing blew up in her face.

I relit my cigar and politely blew the smoke over her head. I wanted time, time to listen to my instincts and see whether they were making sense. But the clock was ticking, both on Delia's concerns and mine.

'I may need to do things you can't know about, Delia.'

She took her time thinking through the implications of that. Then she sighed and shook her head in disbelief at the words coming out of her mouth: 'Just don't kill anyone. And, David? Don't get caught.'

'Delia,' I said, sounding more weary than proud, 'my whole life is about not getting caught. I am the living god of not getting caught.'

SIX

n six days the Vermeer would go on display.

Delia had offered some additional details, to whit that it was arriving from London the next day in the hold of a KLM passenger jet, guarded by both private security and Dutch cops. It would be taken from Schiphol to the Rijksmuseum.

If I lived in a movie rather than reality, the Ontario Crew would organize some elaborate heist which, despite all their planning, would inevitably devolve into a wild shoot-out in which tiny machine pistols would spray ineffectual bullets by the hundreds.

This was a possibility, I supposed, but it would be fantastically stupid. And the Ontario Crew were supposedly professionals so, no, that wasn't going to happen. The object would be hanging on a wall in a week, why would you take on armed guards?

When *Jewess at the Loom* arrived at the Rijks the experts would go to work verifying, cleaning, mounting for display and all that, during which time the Vermeer would be in a basement or attic room somewhere in the bowels of the museum. If the Ontario Crew had an inside man the painting would be vulnerable during that period.

Thing was that finding and corrupting a compliant inside man wasn't something to be done over a long weekend. The Crew had very little more lead time than I had, and while it was possible they'd quickly find and exploit a staff vulnerability, it was very unlikely. And in any case, what the hell was I going to do about it?

Delia repaired to whatever hotel had a discount deal with the US government. And I knew what I had to do: enjoy some art. Six days was not a lot of time to locate and somehow neutralize a gang of professional thieves.

Obviously Thing One would be to visit the Rijksmuseum (Rikes-moo-see-um) and get the lay of the land. Just as obviously

I wasn't going to go there looking like me. If a theft went down the cops would be looking at video from the security cameras, and I planned never to appear on those cameras. It was Captain Louis Renault who first explained basic police methodology when he said, 'Round up the usual suspects.' Fugitives are always 'usual suspects.' A fugitive who'd been a thief? Hell, that's not a suspect, that's your perp, case closed. So it was going to have to be fun with disguises.

'All right, Chante, I'm giving you a free shot. Tell me: if you just saw me walking around on the street and had to describe me afterward, what would be the main things you noticed?'

That invited a stare. I believe it may have been the first time Chante actually looked at me rather than around me.

'I would notice different things in different countries. In France you are tall, here in Holland you are only average height. Your face . . .'

'What about my face?' I said, trying not to sound vain and defensive.

'It is symmetrical and some might say handsome . . .'

'Some.'

'But it is also average in a way. You have no outstanding features, though you have good hair.'

'Uh-huh.'

'But what is most noticeable is not something one sees, but something one feels. You stand apart. You are at a distance from life around you.'

It was too late to stop her, now. She was circling me, examining a specimen.

'You are at once wary and predatory. Like a cautious fish who wants the bait but senses the hook.'

Wary and predatory, OK, that sounded kind of cool. But cautious fish?

'I prefer to see myself as a wise lion.'

Chante squinted at me. 'No, the lion is majestic.'

'So glad I asked.'

Chante has a face she pulls, a sort of wry, condescending, implied-eye-roll thing. 'If you are asking how best to disguise yourself, I would say that you must conceal your hair, your eyes and your arrogance.'

The thing was, she was basically right. An effective disguise is as much about acting the part as looking it. But looking the part is the starting point so, shopping first.

If I were teaching a class – Crime 101 – I would stress the fundamental importance of evidence. A) Don't create it, and B) If you do create it, don't let the cops find it.

I never had a wise mentor in crime myself, I had to figure things out the hard way, but right from the start I'd known to avoid creating evidence. In my first second-story job I'd had to cut my way down through a restaurant's roof crawlspace. To do that I needed a sheetrock knife and a small wood saw. I bought the sheetrock knife along with five other, unrelated items at a hardware store twenty miles from the scene of the crime. I bought the saw at a yard sale as part of a box of random tools. I paid cash for both. I dropped fake names and misleading details. When I was done with the job, I took the cutter apart and removed the handle from the saw and scattered the bits in random dumpsters and handy bodies of water.

The cops could deduce that I'd used a cutter and a saw and they could search for a year and never prove that I had ever owned either.

Tradecraft. If you're going to enter the exciting world of crime, boys and girls, work on your tradecraft.

Don't. Create. Evidence.

If you absolutely can't avoid creating evidence, and if you suspect the cops are going to get their hands on it (and you should definitely suspect that), make sure your evidence trail is as confused and contradictory as you can make it. Never forget that juries are made up of people who lacked the imagination to get out of jury duty. Salt-of-the-earth folks, or, as we learned from Gene Wilder in *Blazing Saddles*, morons. Presented with any explanation requiring more than one step a moron will dismiss it out of hand. This fact also explains most of politics.

With all that in mind, I went to the mall – but not the Gelderlandplein, the big mall south of the city center. Instead I walked to the train station and bought a ticket – cash, from a machine – to Rotterdam, about a one-hour ride with trains leaving every half hour. Once at Rotterdam Station I walked

a few blocks to a Hilton and caught a cab. I directed the cab
to an Asian restaurant I'd googled which was a few blocks
from the Alexandrium Mall. *Then* I walked to the mall.

I'm aware that my fellow criminals might find my tradecraft
a bit extreme, overly imaginative, bordering on obsessive-
compulsive and well into advanced paranoia, but I'm aware
of something else as well: most of the guys who'd call me
obsessive have done serious time, and I have not. I have an
arrest record (well, several under various names), but zero
convictions.

Zero.

My clothing choices usually run from Ralph Lauren to Boss
and Canali with a side of Tommy Bahama. I dress like a guy
with some money because people with money are much happier
giving money to a guy who looks like he already has some.
And I follow the David Mitchell Sartorial Dictum: that my
appearance should be in no way noteworthy, but not so
un-noteworthy as to be in itself, noteworthy.

But that was not the look I wanted now. I needed to look
not like me, distinctly not like me. So I spent some money
which was perhaps not technically mine since the credit card
wasn't technically mine, either, and came away with enough
gear to look like a guy who probably fixes air conditioners
and is taking a vacation in Amsterdam so he can get high and
go to a hooker.

On the way out of the mall I spotted a rucksack and bought
two in different colors, then, with my shopping complete I
reversed direction, returned to Amsterdam, and walked from
the station to my apartment.

'You have shopped,' Chante said, making it sound like an
accusation.

'I have indeed. I looked for a flying broom for you, but
they didn't have any.'

It was still just early afternoon, plenty of time for a preliminary run at the Rijks. But first I went to my annoyingly narrow
bathroom where I applied instant tan – at least I hoped that's
what it was, the label was in Dutch – going for a 'probably
lives-in-Arizona' tan and used my fingernail scissors to cut
half an inch of hair from the nape of my neck. Crouching to

peer into the articulated make-up mirror I applied spirit gum to my upper lip, then spent a very long, very boring time carefully seating hairs to form the kind of mustache Tom Selleck probably had by age ten.

I stepped back to admire my work, using my scissors to trim the ends. It would work so long as no one stared too closely or I started sweating.

I added body weight – a towel over a small throw pillow, secured around my waist. I added some more weight by stuffing the back of my underpants with toilet paper, like an insecure high school girl stuffing her bra before prom. The effect was lumpy though, so I slipped on a second pair of underpants to compress and smooth my padding, and decided the net effect worked well enough.

I took a small temporary tattoo of a cannabis leaf and applied it to my neck, just below my right ear, and emerged at last from the bedroom as a corpulent, granola-crunching, carbon-neutral, blue collar, hiking type of creature with a neck tattoo, a sleazy mustache, a well-tanned complexion and cotton balls in my cheeks both to distort my face and the sound of my speech.

'You like the new look?' I asked Chante, serving up a slow one for her.

'Have you changed something?'

I walked to the Museumplein to soak up some art. It was raining – not a downpour, more of a sullen drizzle – and I had to use an umbrella to keep rain off my mustache. As I walked, the extra clothing and padding added to the humidity made me sweat, and rain and sweat together are not good for fake facial hair. So I slowed my usual New-Yorker-with-a-twenty-minute-lunch-break pace, willing myself to be cool.

What the Red Light District is for guys who've never learned to masturbate, the Museumplein (moo-say-um-plane) is for parents and couples and, I suppose, a few genuine art lovers. It's moo-say-ums and green spaces, a fabulous concert hall and a couple of nice outdoor cafés.

You arrive at Museumplein via the Rijksmuseum's central arcade, a tall passageway as wide as three cars abreast, that cuts through the middle of the building. The Rijks is about as grand a structure as the Dutch will allow, a late-nineteenth-century, dark-brick behemoth built around two courtyards. It's a bit like a squared-off number eight, with the cavernous arcade as the crosspiece, and the courtyards as the holes. There is almost always a classical group playing in the arcade, often Eastern Europeans, doing rather good renditions of classical bits and bobs. On this day it was Vivaldi's 'Summer' from *The Four Seasons*, and the ensemble included two violins, an accordion, a tuba and a balalaika the size of a surfboard, which I don't think was quite how Vivaldi would have arranged it, but it worked with the accordion and tuba coming together to sound surprisingly like a pipe organ.

I walked through the arcade energized by the frantic violin, squeezed around the bulge of music lovers which inevitably spilled off the walkway onto the center lanes meant for bikes and the rare official vehicle, and passed out of shadow into the damp overcast of the Museumplein.

The first thing one notices is a very large red and white sign/sculpture forming the words 'I Amsterdam,' with the 'I' and the 'Am' in red, the remaining letters in white. This is irresistible for tourists who climb all over it like clumsy monkeys and strike poses for the benefit of their Instagram followers, who would, I assume, see the photo and think, *douche*, which I suppose makes people happy. It was both wet and chilly and there were nevertheless seven people in or on the sign, including a terrified toddler propped in the hole of the lower-case 'd'.

Beyond the sign/sculpture was a fan-shaped open space with the efficient name of Art Square. Art Square featured at the northern, Rijksmuseum end a long, ovoid pool, which in winter became an ice-skating rink. There was a large and usually busy outdoor café, not so busy on this day, and just a bit further on kiosks selling hot dogs. Beyond that point (the hot dog latitudes) the *plein* becomes a vast lawn extending to the concrete lozenge of the Van Gogh (Fon-CHGHKOKGH) museum ahead and to the west, and the Concertgebouw (con-SERT-gay-bow), a great pile of limestone and red brick with classical Greek pretensions. Inside the Concertgebouw is where they keep the giant pipe organ the breezeway accordion wanted to be when it grew up.

The *plein* is too large ever to be called crowded, it manages to swallow even the largest tourist horde, and on this day, with gray clouds not a hundred feet off the ground, and with peak tourist season fading, there were only a few dozen people, families with kids mostly, wandering around the pool, tossing coins, trailing fingers, yelling at children who believed the word 'pool' implied 'wading'. Individuals or small pods of people walked the gravel pathways heading to and from cultural touchstones. They walked beneath umbrellas, many emblazoned with a hotel's logo, some with Van Gogh's sunflowers or irises, booty of the souvenir shops.

I kept an eye open for the Hangwoman, but I was in disguise and in the open and not drinking spike-able beer or motoring down a canal, so not very concerned. I kept an eye open for Madalena and Smit as well, but given what I knew of them they didn't strike me as museum people. I also kept an eye out for Willy Pete whose interest in art would be quite as avid as my own.

I stood there by the pool for a while with my phone open and my umbrella sort of resting on my head to free my hands, and compared the overhead satellite view with my horizontal real-world perspective. *Mise en place* is the useful French phrase, a culinary term which translates as *putting in place* referring to the chef's arrangement of foods and garnishes, spices, herbs, pans, spoons, ladles, strainers and knives required to prepare an evening's meals.

This was my *mise en place*. Where were the major buildings? Where were the walkways and streets and canals? Where did people cluster? And the always important: where are bathrooms, trash cans and places where one might duck out of view or dump something incriminating?

With the essential pieces of the exterior setting clear in my head, I walked back to the musicians who were now at work on one of the Brandenburgs, shook my umbrella and entered the Rijksmuseum, following the stairs down into one of the museum's two great courtyards. It's a covered courtyard, all lovely light gray marble, with red brick rising

as the backdrop and blanked side windows looking down.
Tasteful, restrained, but also a bit generic.

Ahead and down more steps was the gift shop. I went there
first because that was what a not-very-artsy tourist might do.
Also the various printed museum guides were a good way to
get a preview of the building itself. I studied maps, struggling
to make sense of the long corridors and the exhibit rooms,
which ranged in size from suburban master bedroom, up to
great echoing hangars housing the larger and gloomier works.

From the shop I wandered upstairs into the actual art.
Room by room, floor by floor, doing my best impersonation
of a rube who thought he should at least put on a show of
loving art.

And the embarrassing thing was that I do enjoy art. Maybe
embarrassing is the wrong word. *Unexpected* might be
more apt. I'm mostly uneducated, a (retired) criminal, and
worst of all, an American – not the usual CV of an art lover.
But I'm also a writer, a guy who creates what might very
loosely be called art, of a sort, and I respect guys who do
create art, whether with paint or chisel or words on paper.

'You're good at this. Don't look at me.'

Delia. Standing to my side. Giving me a heart attack.

'Agent D? I'm casing this place,' I said, staring resolutely
at a small self-portrait of the young Rembrandt.

'I know. I've been watching you. You look very average,
very much the tourist. Sometimes you almost seem to care
about the art you're looking at.'

That slighting crack didn't bother me at all. If it had I might
have said something like, 'It's a peek into another person's
epistemology, what they see, what they think about the things
they see, how they digest what they see, how religion and
ideology figure into it.' All that first-year art student stuff.

'Unexpected depths, David. You never cease to surprise me.'

'And yet I managed to miss that I had a six-foot tall,
African-American tail.'

I glanced at her. She winked at me. 'FBI, baby. F and B
and, also, I.'

'Uh-huh. That and Chante told you where I'd be and what I
was wearing. Why are you following me?'

'I'm not following you. I'm seeing whether anyone else is following you.'

'Ah. And?'

'You're clean.'

'Did you happen to make any plainclothes cops cruising the area?'

'There was one possible, but not probable.' She made a dismissive snort. 'Not exactly Fort Knox, is it?'

Delia drifted away, playing the art-lover, same as me. It was not a problem having her watch me, in fact, it was reassuring – on *this* occasion. But I did not at all like the fact that I hadn't spotted her before she spotted me.

The Rijks has some very famous paintings – Rembrandts, Vermeers, Van Goghs – but I found myself staring for the longest time at a Lucas van Leyden, a six-foot-tall triptych altar piece of the Last Judgment. The center panel was Jesus sitting on a rainbow with his feet propped up on a cloud because recliners had not yet been invented. There were apostles and shadowy camp followers floating around with him, while below various folks freshly risen from the grave, and looking well-preserved for all that, were divided into the faithful and the sinners. The sinners were herded off to the right side panel, there to be beaten by demons and tossed into a flaming animal mouth.

The faithful were escorted to the left panel and included a statuesque blond woman with a very nice bare bottom being eyeballed by an angel in blue who was catching the full frontal denied to us viewers. But my favorite part showed a young, good-looking, very naked dude being shepherded toward heaven by an angel in red, who unabashedly grabbed the young man's naked ass while shooting a defiant look at the viewer. The thought balloon would have read: *Yeah, I'm grabbing some ass, why do you think they call it heaven?* Sadly the thought balloon also had not been invented at that point in history.

Everything I was doing was performance art for the video cameras and the bored guards and the possible-not-probable plainclothes cops. I was making a movie for them, a movie about a brightly dressed, too-tan yahoo of a tourist doing his lonely best to appreciate culture, complete with eye-rolling, dismissive head shakes, admiring nods and occasional prurient leers.

One thing above all else caught my eye: they appeared mostly to have security cameras in the larger rooms. These cameras were mounted about a dozen feet up, set in the corners, aimed toward the center of the room. I did not know how wide their field of vision was, but there were certainly blind spots if only I knew where they were. It was theoretically possible that there were cameras in the smaller rooms and that they were concealed, but that would be silly: the point of cameras is to intimidate and unseen cameras don't do that. No, the more likely explanation, the Occam's answer, was simple: a given security guy can only really watch so many monitors at one time, and security guys have to be paid.

I assessed the guards I could see, a mix of retirees and students, all in blue blazers and neutral gray slacks. They had spiral wires behind their ears, but no guns. Not even billy clubs as far as I could tell, which made them essentially a non-factor, excluding some reckless hero leaping where he should only look.

I noticed other useful things as well. There were hatches placed irregularly in the hardwood floor. They did not have handles but I imagined I could pry one up with a screwdriver and gain access to electrical conduit or switches or something not worth taking a risk for. There were also ventilation panels set in the walls at an accessible height, plenty big enough for a man to hide in, but I didn't like those at all. Nope. Definitely not. I don't trust things that look too easy, too conveniently *Mission: Impossible*. The panels could be alarmed, or they could have motion sensors inside and the Rijksmuseum might not be quite Fort Knox, but surely they weren't *that* stupid.

Was the Ontario Crew careless enough to want to look into those vents? I suspected not, not if they really were professionals.

I managed in my wandering to get a good sense of how the paintings were hung. The larger ones like the massive *Night Watch*, cantilevered out from the wall, hung by wire. The smaller ones mostly rested on brackets.

The museum also featured bits of ornate furniture, carved wooden chests and desks and cabinets, some of them quite tall, a detail that interested me.

There was loot taken from the Dutch East Indies, modern Java, including some excellent spears. And as a national brag they'd mounted the bulky, carved stern transom of the English flagship, *Royal Charles*. The Dutch had captured it in 1667 right in British home waters, then towed the *Royal Charles* to Amsterdam where the ship was broken up. They held onto the stern, the nautical equivalent of antlers.

The question I faced was simple: how would the Ontario Crew steal *Jewess at the Loom* the museum? But, as I'd suspected, the answers were mundane. They could do a simple snatch 'n' run, grab the painting and beat feet for the most useful exit. Or they could do a basic B&E. Bash in a window at night, grab what they wanted and run before the cops could get there.

Then there were the usual subterfuges: enlist a guard or security person as an inside man. Or hide in some dark corner (say a too-convenient vent) until everyone had gone home.

I supposed if the Ontario Crew were flush with funds and wanted to seem cool rather than merely effective, they could climb the roof, cut through a skylight and drop down using a motorized winch like every dumb heist movie ever, but why? Why would anyone go to that trouble when all you had to do was grab the painting and run? The challenge was almost never stealing the art, it was always in fencing the damned stuff once you had it, but because the Ontario Gang were working under contract they had made that issue irrelevant. They could buy tickets, walk right up to the Vermeer, yank it off the wall, run for the exit and almost certainly make it out before security could call a lockdown. Risky, maybe, but for the money they'd been promised?

I mean, damn, were people in the art theft business making that kind of money nowadays? No. No, surely not. I supposed it was nothing to a war-profiteering billionaire sociopath like Isaac maybe, but still . . . Good God. Maybe I'd retired too early.

Take the *Jewess* off the wall, run away, hide from the

inevitable manhunt, then get the Vermeer to Dan-o 'The Chipman' Isaac and get paid. That was the Ontario Crew's remit, and for that kind of payday I'd take a shot at the British crown jewels.

The problem with me stopping the Ontario Crew was obvious: unless I knew the 'when', the 'how' didn't much matter. The museum had unarmed guards. They probably had plainclothes floaters. They clearly had remote lockable doors between many of the rooms, blank gray and as out of place aesthetically as a Lego brick in a Tiffany egg. And they had cameras.

What was I supposed to do, buy a blue blazer and become a guard? And anyway, then what? I yell, 'Stop, thief?' And, somehow they're stopped but with no impolitic police involvement?

Delia had said it takes a thief, but that was nonsense. What it took was cops, LEOs – Law Enforcement Officers. Cops to lay on added security, cops to squeeze informants for information, cops to search hotel registries for the Ontario Crew. I was one guy, one guy who couldn't stay half an hour in any one spot in the museum without being asked to state my business.

There was a coffee shop (a real *coffee* shop) tucked into what amounted to a wide stairway landing on the north side of the Rijks. It was illuminated by a big, clear, pedestrian-height window looking out onto Stadhouderskade, the busy avenue separating the Rijks from the old city. That window was one way out if the lockdown had been instituted too quickly for exit by front door. Grab the painting, bash the window out, and you had street, tram and canal, all right there. Of course it was double-pane glass, which meant a nice, heavy sledgehammer, which would not be subtle because, as every good burglar knows, breaking double-pane glass makes an unholy noise.

I sat in the little coffee shop beneath graceful, echoing arches and focused with great seriousness on the problem of stopping the Ontario Crew. I really did. But there was a tingling in the back of my head and a sly voice whispering, *you know how to do this.* That sly voice was not referring to stopping the Ontario Crew. Sly voice had a whole different idea in mind.

No, David. No.

I shook my head, dismissing that seductive satanic voice, and refocused. There were exactly three sensible ways to stop the Ontario Crew from stealing the Vermeer.

1. Call in the cops.
2. Locate the crew before they struck, and dissuade and/ or kill them.
3. Wait until the theft was complete and try to grab them as they exited, or when they reached a hideout.

Delia vetoed option Number One. Option Number Two? Setting aside dumb luck I was not going to be able to find the crew before they struck. That would require police resources, see Number One. Number Three had the same problem.

Funny how useful cops are in catching criminals.

There's another way . . .

My mind sang that phrase, turned way into *way-ay*. *There's another way-ay, David. Martin knows there's another way-ay . . .*

As a criminal I'd been a competent craftsman. I was good. But I had never been an artist. That's what Hangwoman was trying to do, I had decided: turn murder into art, which was probably giving her too much credit, she was most likely just an idiot, but I preferred to think I was being targeted by a clever bunny who I would outfox, rather than a cretin I could only hope would accidentally hang herself with her own rope or poison herself with her own roofies.

I had always been too results-driven to dabble in art. I was a master criminal – a judge during a bail hearing once called me that – but I had never seen crime as a creative outlet; rather, I had used, improved upon, even perfected, tricks that had been around since the days of whoever Paul Newman and Robert Redford were supposed to represent in *The Sting*. I knew what I was, and I respected who I was, but I had never been the crime world's Picasso or Van Gogh. I didn't revolutionize anything.

Which is why the taunting voice in my head was so hard to ignore. It wasn't just that I'd figured out a clever way to do a job for Delia, thus ensuring my continued freedom from FBI attentions. That part I'd already worked out: simple, efficient, probably safe and I knew how to make it safer. That was all just craft and experience. But what I had just begun to conceptualize would be art. Criminal *art*.

It would be brilliant if I could make it work. *If.* Huge if. Without even having gotten into the weeds of detailed planning yet I sensed layers of complication and risk. But if . . . If, if, *if* . . . I would revolutionize art theft. I would singlehandedly redefine the genre, like Le Carré with spy novels, or Ferran Adrià with haute cuisine. The world of art theft would be divided into pre-Mitre and post-Mitre. Though, hopefully, my name(s) would not be attached.

What also occurred to me, along with visions of a place in the criminal pantheon was the dollar sign, as well as the euro sign and that squiggly L-looking thing that denotes a British pound. All those lovely symbols danced in my head. Because if, if, *if* . . . I would revolutionize art theft, while doing a mitzvah for the FBI and simultaneously take down the biggest score of my life.

The word *irony* did occur. Also the word *hubris*.

But I wouldn't do it if it was hubristic. I would only do it if I knew I could. If I had worked through every detail. If I had minimized every possible risk.

If I could do this . . .

I sat there sipping an Americano in the Rijksmuseum coffee shop and I had chills. Because I knew now exactly how I could stop the Ontario Gang: Option number 4.

I was going to steal the Vermeer myself.

SEVEN

Once I'd thought a bit more I walked back through the Rijks, this time with an eye not to stopping the Ontario Crew but with my own plans in mind. I was looking for something specific and I found a couple of possibilities.

First was a massive, very ornate dresser that stood a good seven feet tall and was outside camera view but not far from the spot where they'd be hanging the *Jewess at the Loom*.

And I found a second, more desperate answer in one of the back stairwells. There was a little hatch in the wall concealing a water main shut-off. The hatch was not locked. I spread my hand in front of the hatch for scale and took a picture. It would mean doing a bit of damage to the paintings frame, and I didn't want that, but in an emergency it'd do.

My scouting expedition to the Rijks had convinced me of something I didn't want to accept: I was going to need help, human help. Whenever possible I fly solo in my criminal enterprises and avoid crime partners like the plague, because there's a synonym for crime partner: *witness for the prosecution*. But just the shopping, let alone the operating of various devices and a bit of DIY construction, would mean many days if I tried to do it all, and if I was going to do this it had to be done very soon after the Vermeer went on display in just six days. Any more time and the Ontario Crew might make off with my painting.

That's right, *my* painting.

There was a guy I knew, and he was probably not far away, unless he was in stir, which, in his case, was a distinct possibility. His name was Ian McSweeney. He was an Irishman, a lousy thief, a mediocre grifter and rather more violent than I am comfortable with. But he owed me and he was almost certainly broke and best of all, when he worked – which was seldom – it was in construction, so he was good with his hands. Presumably. Anyway, better than me.

I searched my memory for the name he knew me by. I keep useful contacts I don't want anyone to find in my One Password file, all nicely encrypted and hidden behind a computer-generated, sixteen-character password I dare the NSA or GCHQ to crack.

I opened the latest, updated end-to-end encryption app and texted:

Me: *It's Jimmy C. I have profitable work for you.*

I didn't expect an immediate response, but unless Ian had changed his number he'd get the message and he would respond. Ian could no more ignore me than I'd been able to ignore Azevedo, because I knew things about Ian.

The rain stopped in late afternoon, and by nine that night, when I again ventured out, I could spot occasional stars through breaks in the overcast sky.

Twan Van Geel turned out to be a thin dude with long, stringy blond hair – rather like what I'd been told to expect of Milan Smit. Twan was a decent thrash metal axe man backed by an excellent drummer, with Cookie Monster lyrics growled by a front man who sounded as if he dined on raw flesh.

Headbangers do love the dramatic.

My bartender Ella wasn't on duty, so I wormed my way to the bar, hand on wallet the whole way – crowds and pick-pockets go together like bacon and eggs – and ordered a Johnnie Black which I carried around but did not drink.

My immediate problem was finding Smit, if he was there. The crowd was thick, on its feet and obscured by the band's smoke machine. It was a sea of bobbing heads lit by strobes punctuated by frequent air-punching. I pushed my way around the room, beset on all sides by jumping, thrusting, heaving bodies, largely male given that the music was metal. The crowd was different from Tim Armstrong's crowd on my initial visit – no gaggle of giggling Japanese girls, more dudes who looked like trouble, some of whom did not like the look of me: I was a well-dressed guy lacking interesting hair, extravagant beard or other visible evidence of rebelliousness. Also, I looked like I probably had some cash in my wallet. When I left I was going to want to make sure no one was following me.

Two hours I stood and occasionally sat and milked that one Scotch. I was offered sex three times, twice straight, once gay; I was offered drugs once, and sex plus drugs once. Two different junkies thought I'd be an easy touch and started to regale me with their life stories, so I gave them each a tenner and they disappeared.

All through the band's first set, a break, then the start of their second set I endured, and finally, there he was. Possibly. Anyway, he was tall, blond and looked like trouble. When I managed to get closer I confirmed the presence of a Hell's Angels Antwerp jacket. *Bingo*. I had my guy and I was pretty pleased with myself.

And . . . now what?

I could try to cozy up to him but a 42-year-old, conservatively dressed, expensively coiffed guy vs. a metalhead in an Angels jacket was not the basis of friendship, it was grounds for suspicion. He'd make me for a narc or a perv.

Which left following Smit when he left, and that was not going to be soon.

The Cave Rock Bar is on a block with a bakery (closed at that hour), a schnitzel-themed restaurant and not one but two coffee shops of the Amsterdam variety. All three had outdoor seating but the restaurant was shutting down, so I went into the adjacent coffee shop, bought an eighth and some papers, ordered an orange juice – coffee shops are not allowed to sell alcohol – plopped down at a tiny empty table on the chilly street and idly chopped my purchase up with the edge of a metal American Express card. I edged my chair sideways a little and had an excellent line of sight to the below-grade entrance of the Cave. There would be at least one other exit, but in theory at least, Smit wouldn't take a less-convenient way out unless he thought he was being followed, and he wasn't. Yet.

I sat and did not smoke the weed I'd bought, but did drink three orange juices and was then faced with a desperate need to pee, which could result in losing Smit if he chose that two minutes or so to leave. So I went back over to the Cave, spotted Smit chatting disinterestedly with some girl who was clearly not Madalena, did the necessary, and re-emerged just in time to see Smit heading for the door.

I followed him from the door of the Cave Rock Bar all the way to where he'd chained a bike to a rack, twenty feet away. A bike. Not a motorcycle for this wannabe Hell's Angel, a grubby Amsterdam bike.

He rode off and I watched him, helpless. But fate lent a hand in the form of another bike whose chain lock had not quite caught. I stripped away the unlocked lock and for the first time in probably thirty years swung a leg over a bike seat and saw that I was observed. The observer in question was a thirty-ish hippie-looking dude, replete with rainbow-striped Peruvian poncho, torn jeans and sandals despite the intermittently wet weather. He was too young to have been anywhere near Haight-Ashbury and I had a thrilling moment of fear suspecting he was an undercover cop. But he also had a rather gruesome tattoo up the left side of his neck, a dragon that looked as if its artist had been in the throes of a delirium tremens shakes. Undercover cops do not typically have lurid, poorly done tattoos.

I pulled out my wallet and held a twenty-euro note out to him. 'You're not seeing me,' I said and smiled conspiratorially.

He took the money but said nothing. He had clean hands. Clean fingernails even. That stuck out to me, that and the blond hair that had not been professionally barbered in the last few weeks but had been at one time. Again, absent the tat I'd have made him for a cop.

'Oh, you can have this, too.' I tossed him the eighth of an ounce I'd bought at the coffee shop. He caught it in mid-flight, nodded, did not smile and turned away.

Amsterdam bikes are Dutch modesty squared. I am convinced that in the entire city of 847,000 bicycles – that's not a made-up number – there are not three bikes with a street value over thirty bucks. It was almost not stealing to take this bike, certainly no more than petty theft. The challenge was that while I had all kinds of tradecraft when it came to tailing someone on foot or in a car, I had no idea at all how to tail someone on a bike. But I had seen the Dutch way of bike riding and did my best to mimic it: I sat tall and straight and looked rigidly ahead with an expression of smug belligerence on my face. Bike riders in Amsterdam do not wear special outfits, no spandex, no helmets, just the armor of righteousness, so it was not unusual that a grown man wearing business casual should be biking along at one in the morning. Stranger, perhaps, was a man wearing a Hell's Angels (Antwerp) jacket on what was definitely a girl's bike.

I was able to ride reasonably well as it turned out, helped by the fact that I was sober. My biggest problem was avoiding outpacing and catching up to Smit, because he was in no hurry and not overly devoted to straight lines. We were heading south by east along bike paths that sometimes ran beside large, multi-lane boulevards and in other places ran past patches of woods.

I googled as I rode, checking out the landscape ahead. We were almost certainly headed for the Bijlmermeer (Bale-mer-meer) district, which I had never before visited. It was a landscape of big, modern buildings, bigger sports stadiums, and what the Brits would call council housing and Americans would call subsidized housing. Bijlmermeer looked like the boxes that dainty central Amsterdam had been packed in. It was an intimidating place, especially at night, with vast open spaces and closed big box stores, parking lots with a single random car, a cross between an industrial park, a community college campus and a working-class ghetto.

On the plus side the openness of the terrain allowed me to keep falling back gradually, while still maintaining visual contact. I took an opportunity to veer off, to disappear from any rearward glance, race around an electronics store and follow Smit on a parallel track. I was learning the bike thing.

Finally, after half an hour, Smit slowed and dismounted before a gate in a chain-link fence which ran between a three-story red-brick apartment building on one side, and an eight-floor building that I guessed was also apartments and which accommodated at street level a tailor, a lawyer's office and a tattoo parlor. The fence that connected the two buildings protected a short, dead-end street that had been made into a closed courtyard.

Facing this fence from across the street was a wide greenway with well-spaced trees, where I was able to dismount behind a trunk and watch without being seen. Smit unlocked

the gate, pushed his bike through and locked the gate behind
him.

I flitted from tree to tree like Elmer Fudd sneaking up on
Daffy Duck but could not get close without stepping out
into plain view beneath street lights. But I was able to see in
which backyard he parked his bike and that gave me the
location of his apartment, five doors down. I walked around
the back of the building and looked up at Smit's residence.
Facing the street was a door, metal frame but with curtained
glass panels. A tall window stood beside the door on one
side, standard double window to the other side. Turning my
gaze upward I saw that each townhouse was three floors, with
the top floors having two windows per level, one of which
had a waist-high iron railing as if it was a balcony. It was
not. But I guessed that the windows with the iron railings
could be opened while the others could not.

There was a light in the top-floor window and the curtains
were not drawn completely, but at this angle I could see nothing
but the ceiling light fixture in that top-floor room.

I returned to my borrowed bike, feeling pleased that I
now had Smit's location. Tomorrow or the next day I would
return better prepared to mount surveillance, discover whether
Madalena was in the townhouse, and ask her why she was
upsetting her poor father.

I was not very worried about Milan Smit as I pedaled
away. In my experience real threats almost never ride bikes.
I made it almost half a block before a little Nissan hatchback
went roaring past, skidded to a screeching stop just ahead,
and disgorged three men.

They did not look happy to see me.

EIGHT

'Good evening,' I said politely as I mounted my bike. 'Not for you,' said a fellow who looked like he'd been a frog, kissed by a princess, and had the transition to human stopped halfway.

Grunted laughter from the men.

Like all humans, indeed like all animals who've been at some time in their evolution subject to predation, I have a fight or flight instinct. Mine is weighted heavily in favor of flight. This was not a time to argue against that predisposition.

Three of them. One of me.

Their turf, not mine.

Car vs. bicycle.

No, there was nothing encouraging in this scenario. Then I noticed the clubs hanging by the sides of two of the men and electric fear shot right up my spine. I twisted my bike around, stood on the pedal and began to flee at a speed best described as leisurely. I was doing a good, oh, three miles an hour when Toad Man plowed into me from the side and knocked me over.

I hit the pavement hard but rolled away and managed to avoid the first swung club, which hit the pavement too near my head.

'Hey, what the fuck?' I yelled. Because thugs faced with an interesting question will stop beating on you in order to . . .

Wham!

Right on the crown of my head. Sweet Jesus it hurt! Like I'd bitten down hard on a live power line. My eyes rolled around in their sockets causing the world to look as if it were being shot by a jittery handheld camera. There was a fire alarm in my ears.

A blow hit my right shoulder. I was trying to stand, managed to get up onto all fours and took a boot toe in the solar plexus, which was the end of any fight coming from me. I collapsed face down, wrapped my hands as well as I could over the back of my head, and just lay there being beaten. I didn't count the blows, ten, twenty?

I lost consciousness, blank, then drifted part of the way back to reality, noting hands in my pockets, a hand reaching inside my jacket and some angry talk followed by another few blows and the next thing I knew I was in a bed with starched sheets and an IV needle in the back of my hand.

I had a raging thirst and turned my head to look for water. How to describe the stab of pain in my head? Like someone had it clamped in a giant vise? Like someone had broken a glass bottle inside my skull? Both of those things at once. Nausea rose in a tidal wave and I rolled onto my side and retched, producing nothing but a trickle of spittle from my empty stomach.

My eyes hurt and closing them didn't help. My back and buttocks and thighs hurt. My arms hurt. I hurt everywhere, but after a few minutes at least the nausea passed and I pried open one eye to take in my surroundings. I was in a hospital bed in a room with five other beds, some concealed by drawn curtains, some empty, two with patients I could see, a white-haired old man and a woman who had to be a hundred years old and looked like a plucked turkey.

I had a plastic bracelet with a bar code. To my left was a steel table and yes, hallelujah, there was a carafe of water and a plastic cup. Reaching for the carafe was amazingly unpleasant, pain plus nausea, and only my desperate thirst gave me strength to persist. I drank a cup of water and immediately felt my stomach rebel. I was afraid I'd lose it all, but was able to keep it down, probably because the water was immediately absorbed. I was a wrung-out sponge.

I knew what had happened to me, my memory had not been affected: I'd taken a serious beating. But I recalled thinking even as it was going on and on and on, that it had not been a beating meant to cripple or kill. They'd searched me, so presumably my wallet and phone were gone which meant I'd need to cancel all my credit cards, get a new license . . . damned thieves.

A nurse in dark blue uniform and a cheerful floral pattern

hijab saw me gulping, came right over and took the carafe from me. 'I will get you ice chips if you are thirsty.'

'Thanks,' I said in a husky, Alec Baldwin voice.

'Are you having discomfort?'

'No, but I'm having a hell of a lot of pain.'

That earned a tolerant nurse smile. 'I will inform the doctor that you are awake.'

I was awake but not sure for how long, as a bone-deep weariness moved like liquefied lead in my veins, sapping my energy, forcing my eyelids to half-mast. A doctor arrived with surprising promptness, a sturdy woman in late middle age, with pursed lips, white hair and the kind of authority that comes with the medical diploma.

'I am Doctor Visser, how are you feeling?'

'Like I got beat up.'

No smile. 'You suffered a great deal of bruising but, surprisingly, no broken bones and we see no evidence of serious concussion, though if you develop headaches, dizziness, blurred vision or a ringing in your ears you should immediately tell your doctor. Fortunately it seems in your case that a policeman was able to intervene before more serious damage was done.' She pulled a pen from her pocket and held it in front of me. 'With just your eyes, follow the end of my pen.'

I did that. I also had my blood pressure taken and lights flashed in my eyes and a stethoscope pressed here and there. I lay there in my flimsy hospital gown as Dr Visser pulled sheets aside to show me some angry-looking bruises, then I gave some blood to the lab, and took some ibuprofen.

The doctor took off and the nurse came back to tell me that I had a visitor. I was hoping for Delia, what I got was Chante. She drew the curtain around my bed.

'Delia asked me to come,' Chante said.

'Kind of her.'

'She asked me to discover your condition.'

'My condition is that my entire body is one big bruise. Fortunately my innate cowardice caused me to cover my head as I was weeping into the pavement, so my head and face weren't bashed in. Though there's an impressive bump under my hair.'

'I see you have all your limbs.'

Impossible not to hear a small note of disappointment. Impossible as well not to ask myself the question: how did Delia know I was in the hospital?

'Yes, I can still count to four on my limbs,' I said peevishly. 'I have all my fingers, too. I am operating in base ten.'

Chante unslung her backpack. 'I have . . . Delia sent . . . some things.' She pulled out a pair of socks, underpants, a clean shirt and a pair of jeans. Then a brand-new laptop and a phone, along with the appropriate chargers. 'Delia says they are clean.'

That was not a reference to the clothing. Delia was making nice, offering me 'clean' tech to play with.

Clean tech. From an FBI agent. I mean, I like Delia, but no.

'And this, but she says you must use common sense.' She glanced over her shoulder – silly given that we were surrounded by beige curtains – and slipped me a flask.

I unscrewed the lid and inhaled. Hello, Scotland my old friend. I took a test swig. God was that welcome. Hospitals would be so much less depressing if they served cocktails.

'Thanks, Chante.'

'Do not thank me,' she said, looking down as if embarrassed.

She left. I took another swig, slipped the flask under my pillow and fell asleep and from there into a lurid and disturbing dream.

My subconscious mind remembered details forgotten by the cleverer bits of my brain, for in the dream I saw an Amsterdam cop in bicycle gear standing over me and talking into a radio. And I noted that the clubs my attackers had used were cut-down wooden baseball bats – better than full-sized bats for concealment, better for rapid swings, worse for inflicting serious injury. I saw the arriving ambulance only as a vague cloud of dancing lights, a hallucinogenic cross between Smarties and popcorn.

And an interesting detail. A tattoo on one guy's arm, the letters *BBET* surrounded by death's heads and a symbol that was not quite a swastika but was meant to evoke one.

When I woke next the privacy curtain was open and night had come. I'd been in the hospital for twenty-four hours and asleep for all but about two of those. I felt around and with deep relief found that my flask remained undiscovered. I took a judicious swallow and looked at what were now three sleeping people, my fellow patients, one snoring so loudly I thought the noise was some kind of malfunctioning machine.

Eerie light came from bedside monitors constantly checking blood pressure, pulse, respiration and oxygen saturation – primitive Dutch medical tech. In the US a hospital monitor would also have shown the state of your health insurance, your bank balance and your credit rating.

White light came from the nurse's station just beyond the open double doors of my ward and I saw blue-clad medical folk carrying compact iPad-like objects which I assume they use for playing *Call of Duty*. Then I bent down – oh, so very painful – and lifted the laptop Chante had brought. I considered using it to look up BBET – the tattoo – but decided against it. The laptop might be clean*ish*, but I had to consider the strong possibility that Delia had loaded some spyware. So, for her benefit I spent the next twenty minutes searching out the very best fetish porn websites. Enjoy my browser history, Delia!

By the way: wow. There are people into some very odd stuff.

I felt positively paralyzed without secure access to the internet, but I have certain skills, and a certain insouciance regarding petty crimes, and I had noticed that Captain Snores over there had a smart phone by his bed. I decided to borrow it.

This turned out to be much harder than I'd anticipated. Swinging my legs off the bed? Not good. Very much not good. Standing up? Well, in my misspent youth when I would frequently combine various intoxicants I used to suffer from head rush. This was like that but with a nausea undertow added in for kicks. When blood had returned to my head and my fortunately empty stomach had quieted, I gamely advanced toward my target at a speed that would have embarrassed an arthritic ninety-year-old stroke victim. I doubt this is accurate but my subjective sense was that it took me most of an hour to cover thirty feet. A single human step requires many more muscles than one might think unless a beating has made one acutely aware of every single muscle cell.

I reached snorer's phone. Password, thumbprint or facial recognition? Facial. Swell. Snorer's face was aimed away from me, which meant walking all the way around his bed, a good eight, ten steps. I reached snorer's face, got the phone positioned and . . . the son of a bitch rolled over.

So. I did some more pain managing and some more sotto voce cursing and this time got the phone looking at his face. It opened obediently and I typed *BBET* into the browser.

Behavior Based Ergonomic Therapy.

Yeah, not that. I added the word '*Dutch*'. And got beets. As in the vegetable.

I added quotation marks around *BBET* and added *Dutch* plus the word *slogan*. And we had it. BBET: *Bloed, Bodem, Eer en Trouw*. Which translated as Blood, Soil, Honor and Faith.

Great. Just absolutely great. Fucking white power skinheads. *Tangential Nazis.*

This did not rise quite to threat level of, say, a Chechen gang, or some former mark recognizing me on the street and screeching like Donald Sutherland at the end of *Invasion of the Body Snatchers*, but it was not good, not good at all.

I hobbled back to my bed and considered the next crisis. A cop had apparently saved me from a worse beating, which meant that cops would be by in the morning to question me. Which was the greater danger: attracting attention by escaping the hospital against medical advice? Or risking a second conversation with Amsterdam cops?

There was a drawer in my steel bedside table. I slid it open and to my astonishment found my personal effects – watch, phone, cigar torch, my original flask and my wallet. My wallet, which had held about two thousand euros, was now empty of cash, but they'd left my credit cards. And my phone.

They'd found my wallet, had taken the cash, then what – just dropped it next to me as I lay there blowing red snot bubbles? Interesting. Cash is not traceable. Cards and phones are, which suggested my Blood and Soil boys were A) being cautious, and B) had resources and discipline enough to pass up the few euros they'd have made unloading said phone and cards. There was another possible explanation, that they'd been searching me for something specific, but I dismissed that.

So much in my life at the moment was making so little sense, which is not the state of mind to be in when confronted by cops. And given that I now saw two serious-looking people being led my way by the nurse, it was clear I'd have to do it anyway.

NINE

'Hello, Mr Mitre, I am Lieutenant Martin Sarip, and this is Wachtmeester . . . sorry, Sergeant Olivia DeKuyper. We are from the Koninklijke Marechaussee.' (Koning-click-uk Marsh-ka-say. Something close to that.) Not a cop, a pair of cops; one male, one female. The female was classic Dutch: tall, pale, thin, blond and blue-eyed. Olivia DeKuyper, possibly a long-lost relative, a possibility I would not be mentioning. She wore a pale blue uniform and a jaunty blue beret.

Lieutenant Sarip was of Javanese ancestry, short, slightly built, with a dark goatee and mustache that made him look piratical. He was in plainclothes, but the kind of plainclothes you wear when you normally wear a uniform.

I am not remotely superstitious, but did I lose a few heartbeats when I realized that between them the two cops had my actual birth name? Yes, I did.

I'd done the necessary peek into Dutch police organizational structure upon arriving in the country, not something most tourists think to do. Turned out all their cops are basically federal outside of some glorified meter maids. I'd checked out the matter of rank and questions of specific units and sub-divisions, many with fantastic Dutch names, like Dienst Koninklijke en Diplomatieke Beveiliging, which handles diplomats and was not my problem, and Koninklijke Marechaussee, which was the name I had not wanted to hear because they were, apparently, the *serious* cops, the gendarmerie, the military police, the guys who handled things like terrorism and organized crime.

I extended my mouse paw to the two hungry cats and winced manfully as they shook it in turn.

'I'm afraid there isn't much I can tell you, Lieutenant and Sergeant. I was riding a bike and out of nowhere some dudes jumped me. That is literally all I recall.' Abashed smile, shrug, wide, innocent eyes. 'But I'm told that a police officer rescued me, so I hope I get a chance to thank him. Or her.'

The piratical lieutenant nodded understandingly. The sergeant did not. She was doing the dead-eyed stare, probably something she picked up binge-watching *Law & Order.*

'We are very sorry that you have suffered this incident,' Sarip said. 'We know you are in some pain and will make this is brief as possible.'

'I appreciate that. I am . . . well, there is some pain.' I was suffering stoically and making sure they knew it.

'The first matter we must clear up is what you were doing riding a bicycle in Bijlmermeer in the middle of the night.'

I shook my head, embarrassed. 'This is going to sound absurd, especially to a Dutch person, but I was testing my skill with a bicycle before I risked riding one around Amsterdam.'

'I see. You are not a cyclist?'

'No, I'm American. We have cars.'

'But surely you have ridden bicycles before this?'

'Well, yeah, thirty years ago. But let's face it, riding a bike in Amsterdam is like driving a car in Rome: you need to bring your A game.'

'Your . . .'

'A game. Emphasize the "a". Your best game, your highest level of skill.'

'Ah, yes, of course. You are intimidated by cyclists.'

I laughed which reminded me of every single muscle in my chest and stomach. 'You're lovely people, you Dutch, but you're dangerous on two wheels.'

'So you did a practice ride that took you half an hour away from your hotel. At one o'clock in the morning. And the bike?'

I shrugged, yet another lesson in the details of the human muscular system. 'It had two wheels, that's all I know.'

'Yes, but where did you get it?'

I had a choice here. I could either lie and say I bought it, which they could disprove. Or, I could confess, but only to stupidity. Which would work so long as they had not come into contact with my well-manicured Jesus Hippie friend.

I frowned, puzzled. 'It was on the street.'

'Yes, but it was not yours, yes?'

'Yes. I mean, no, but everyone says if you see an unlocked bike it's for anyone to use. That's the law.'

'What law?' the sergeant asked.

'*The* law.' I winced through another shrug. 'It's Dutch law.' Allow a shadow of doubt to appear (frowns were pain-free) and . . . 'Isn't it?'

'It is not. If you took a bicycle, it is theft,' said Olivia with my last name.

'No fucking way! Seriously? I swear, like, three people told me that. This dude at the coffee shop . . .' I let that trail off into deepening embarrassment.

Were these two going to bust me for stealing a bike? No, of course not. But it had the appearance of what is called 'an admission against interest', an honest guy confessing to an honest mistake. And I was a recognizable 'type', the clueless tourist smoking weed and acting stupid.

Sarip went into the protracted silence mode. Two kinds of people keep talking when a cop plays the quiet game: guilty newbies trying to fill the air with bullshit, and honest people protesting that innocence. Only one kind of person will sit there stolidly silent: a professional criminal who knows the game.

So I babbled. 'Oh, man, I am really sorry. Was the bike damaged? Because I'm happy to compensate the owner, I mean the bike can't be worth more than what, a hundred euros? Tops? But that doesn't matter, I apparently stole a bike and if there's a fine or some kind of compensation . . .'

Now I played silent. DeKuyper was perhaps not the sharpest knife in the Koninklijke Marechaussee's kitchen drawer, because she only seemed to have the one look: disapproving. But Sarip was smart. I could see it in his twinkly brown eyes. I could practically read the doubt as if the word *twijfel* (Dutch for 'doubt', possibly) was lasered onto his eyeballs. He knew, in the immortal words of Madeline's Miss Clavel, that something was not right.

Ah, Lieutenant Sarip, you feel something's off, don't you? A disturbance in the Force? Well, too bad, pal, because cops aren't allowed to beat confessions out of suspects let alone crime victims, at least not in the Netherlands. You need evidence, and you don't have any, do you, hot shot? I said none of that, not being suicidal.

What I did say was, 'Do you mind if I summon the nurse? The pain is getting worse.' I added an apologetic wince.

'Of course, Mr Mitre. Of course. We will leave you now.'

Sarip turned away and so did the brigadier. Then he pulled an actual, textbook Columbo.

'I almost forgot,' Sarip said.

Sure you did, I did not say.

'Yes?'

'I just felt I should apologize on behalf of the city of Amsterdam. You've had very bad luck to be both accidentally dragged into a canal and set upon in this way.'

'Hah!' I said, shaking my head ruefully as my internal organs dissolved at the realization that they'd connected the two events. 'I sure have.'

Had I tried to explain it away he'd have been ready with a follow-up, but my blank Bambi innocence disconcerted him.

'I also have one last question.' This from the sergeant. Her 'Columbo' was clumsier. 'You are an author?'

'Yep. In fact, that's why I'm in Amsterdam: I have a panel to do. At Waterstones. An author panel. You know, questions and answers? Kind of like what we're doing now?'

'Yes, I saw that you have written novels, but according to the Wikipedia, you did not publish before eight years ago. May I ask what you did before becoming a writer?'

It was a perfectly innocent question on its face, but the timing was everything. She'd saved the question up to watch my reaction, hoping to throw me off-stride.

Because I'm a fucking amateur who doesn't know how to look an LEO right in the eye and lie like a Republican promising to fight for the middle class. 'I owned a small office cleaning business in Tampa until the immigration crackdown made that unprofitable. But honestly that business failure pushed me to get serious about writing, so in the end it was a good thing.'

Try finding records for a failed small business that was probably, given the mention of undocumented workers, a bit on the shady side to begin with and thus might not have a business license. Or a tax ID number. Yes, I was quite proud of that lie – it sounded like another admission against interest – and I had to remind myself not to reveal a look of triumph as I watched the light die in the sergeant's eyes.

Sarip left me his card. I thanked them.

Had my body been fully functional I might well have fist-pumped as they disappeared from view. I contented myself with a raised middle finger salute held discreetly beneath my sheet.

Mouse 1; Kitties 0. And fuck you both.

I was at a crossroads. My general rule is to abandon any project that attracts police interest before the commission of said project. But in this case I couldn't just walk away because of Delia, Madalena and the stupid panel.

Bullshit, David. That's not why you won't walk away. You've fallen in love with your own plan. Your own . . . art.

As I always say, though not out loud: lies are for others, you tell yourself the truth. But the other truth was that if I was to make opening day of the Vermeer, I had four days. Four. In which to move mountains.

In the morning I was checked out of the hospital with a frankly disappointing haul of painkillers – in the US they'd have given me enough Fentanyl to hook a whole West Virginia mining town. Chante was out when I got home, so I did not have to chit-chat but got right down to business: examining my Personal Security (Persec) and my Operational Security (Opsec), terms I had learned from the internet but understood intuitively.

Persec: avoid the Hangwoman; avoid another beating or worse from Milan Smit's skinhead pals; and avoid getting in the path of the Ontario Crew in such a way that they noticed and I ended up dead. Also: try not to run into the jilted Tess or the cops. Or anyone who might recognize me. Time to turn the paranoia up another notch. Fugitive Vision to maximum.

Opsec was Priority Number 2. Opsec had five major components:

Identification of critical information
Analysis of threats

Analysis of vulnerabilities
Assessment of risks
Application of appropriate countermeasures

The 'critical information' was that I was seriously considering – indeed, actively planning – the commission of a number of felonies. That was the info I needed to keep secure.

Threats? Oh, that was a long list, but included every law enforcement agency in or near the city of Amsterdam, including Delia, also the Ontario Crew and Chip Isaac, Smit's Blood and Soil guys and the lunatic Hangwoman.

Vulnerabilities? Let's see. I was already walking the fugitive tightrope. I had no real backup aside from Delia and possibly Ian if he showed up and stayed sober. And I'm not Jack Reacher, not very impressive in physical fights, as witness my less-than-Reacherish performance with the skinheads.

Assessment of risks? Prison. Death. Prison plus death. Yeah, that covered it.

Application of appropriate countermeasures? I'd gotten Delia to look into both Milan Smit and the Hangwoman. I doubted she'd accomplish much, but it was better than nothing. In a more reasonable country I might start spreading some cash around where it would do the most good, but the Netherlands is the eighth least corrupt nation on earth so there was a near-zero chance of me bribing anyone.

I emerged after a while to find Chante unloading groceries and wine in the kitchen. She didn't bother looking at me, just said over her shoulder, 'Delia is coming for dinner.'

'Is she?' Said with a strong implication that I should have been consulted.

'Yes.' Said with a finality that denied the need for consultation.

I spent the remainder of my day planning, both the beats of the caper, and the shopping and DIY that would make it work. I have a lawyer in the Caymans who I instructed in setting up some new shell corporations. When those were established I'd have a second lawyer – in Panama this time – have those shells subsumed into other shells. And once that paperwork was done I'd have lawyers separately set up bank accounts for the shell corporations. This was all fantastically expensive involving not just lawyer fees, but 'gratuities' would also have to be paid given my short time frame.

Reluctantly I also traveled the Deep Web trolling for credit cards. It's not easy, you can't be sure that you're not buying from some sting operation. But it wouldn't matter too much, I'd pay in virtual currency and of course it was all done via VPNs and a burner phone.

My intention was to make the money flow so hard to follow, it would take the law enforcement version of the moon shot to track it all down in the time I intended to allow.

Next it was a deep dive into nerd country as I assembled a list of ways to stream video. The opposition would do its best to shut down any streaming venue I used, so I intended to use a different one for each 'broadcast'.

When I emerged, blinking owlishly after so much of what I still think of as paperwork even though no paper was involved, I was startled to discover Chante was done up. She was wearing an actual dress, a clingy black thing with an angled hem and a spider web open back, sort of haute goth. And make-up! I was so amazed I almost didn't notice the tray in her hand or that our guest had already arrived.

'Hello, David,' Delia said, rising from the couch. 'Chante has been cooking things that smell amazing.' She offered Chante a dazzling smile to which Chante responded with a twitching grimace that might have been an attempt at a grin. *Note to self: check Chante's face for cracks.*

I sipped the cocktail that Chante had made: a rum drink, essentially a daiquiri I supposed, not my thing at all, but it was of course delicious. Then there came a tray of hors d'oeuvres, including a chevre crostini with figs, a tiny brioche bun topped with crab meat, and grilled oysters which – and I vowed never to say this to Chante – shifted my entire world view on oysters being anything other than raw and ice cold.

The two women chatted about Amsterdam and world affairs, Chante with her bared back to me, Delia occasionally glancing my way with her knowing looks, mocking me as if she could read my inner monologue. An inner monologue, which at the moment ran, *How am I going to get Chante to make these oysters again?*

The apartment came with a small, round, glass-topped wrought-iron table now set elegantly, and placed before the open French doors of the shallow balcony. Delia was invited to take one of just two matching chairs with the view of the city. Chante was to her right in the other matching chair. I was to Delia's left in a low-slung living room chair, which left me a head shorter than either of them. Was this a subtle but deliberate insult? Of course it was. Was I going to say anything while one oyster remained? Of course I wasn't.

'This wine is wonderful,' Delia commented.

Chante blushed and dipped her head like an awkward teenager. 'It is a humble *Vin de pays* from Gascony, where I was a child.'

'You were never a child,' I muttered, ignored. 'If no one else wants that last oyster . . .'

Chante excused herself to the kitchen to finish the starters – apparently the three hors d'oeuvres were mere *amuses bouche*.

'So, Delia. Any progress on our Mr Smit and his skinhead friends?' The question was somewhat garbled by the passage of the final mollusk.

'Some,' she said.

'And?'

Delia shrugged. 'Milan Smit, aka Walter Werner, aka Piet Mueller, has a record. All three names. Low-end stuff: B&E, MDMA dealing, fraud, street hustles, little stuff.'

'Violence?'

She shook her head. 'Not that shows up on a search.'

I said, 'Smit, Werner and Mueller? Isn't that the equivalent of Smith, Jones and Anderson?'

'You mean three very common surnames? Yes, I noticed that. It's possible none of the three names is legal.'

'Don't you just hate people using aliases? Any pimping-related charges? Or hard drugs?'

'No.'

'Huh.'

'You expected something else?'

'I try not to expect anything, Delia, it's bad for analysis,' I said rather pompously. 'But yeah, I figured him for a real bad guy. Instead, he's selling molly? Kicking a door in to steal the silverware? Fraud? Street hustling? Like what, three-card monte?'

Delia's face revealed wild surprise, as expressed in a slight movement of one eyebrow. 'Exactly like three-card monte, actually. And he's really good at it, if you believe the Hamburg police. They say he's a pickpocket, too, but they never got the goods on him for that. So if this Smit character is a low-end hustler, why is your Portuguese friend so worried about him?'

'Because he's a protective father who doesn't want his little girl hanging around with Nazis?'

'Maybe,' Delia allowed. 'But I also ran a check on Madalena Azevedo.'

'And?'

'And she was on the game while her father was in prison.'

I frowned and sipped wine. 'Math isn't my strong suit, but she'd have been, like, eight when her dad went down.'

'Not the second time. Azevedo senior, your buddy, caught a second beef and did three years in a Tunisian prison for stealing and exporting antiquities. He just got out last month. Madalena was picked up soliciting and it must have scared her because after that she seems to have gone legit. In fact she became political. A green group. Also an anti-fascist group.'

I frowned but did not share with Delia my puzzlement that a girl who had skinhead friends should be Antifa. The bigger surprise was that Madalena had been on the game. Madalena, a corruption of Magdalene? A bit on the nose if she was hooking, wasn't it?

Chante returned, bearing plates. The starter course turned out to be foie gras three ways. God only knew what that had cost me, I was relieved it was not yet truffle season. Good? Melt-in-your mouth, fall-to-your-knees-and-thank-God-for-inventing-geese-and-ducks good.

'Not bad,' I allowed.

'Yes, almost edible,' Delia said with a droll look to Chante who beamed.

'When I was growing up in Bayonne I never realized how rare such things as foie gras and truffles are,' Chante said. 'My mother (muh-ZEHR) would serve them often.'

'I thought there was a chance you had a mother,' I snarked, 'but it's hard to imagine.'

'Yes,' Chante said, 'I suppose it would be difficult for you to imagine unquestioning love.'

Delia covered her mouth to avoid laughing out loud.

With the foie gras Chante served small glasses of four *puttonyos Tokaji*, sweet but not cloying. By my rough calculation this meal was on-track to cost me five hundred euros.

'My mother made grilled cheese sandwiches and Campbell's bean soup,' I countered.

'And was your home also a place of unquestioning love?' Delia asked.

The question should not have caught me off-guard, but it did. It was not specific memories of events that flooded my unready mind, but rather the distillation of my childhood, the executive summary. Many, many people have had worse childhoods, far worse, but few grew up amid so much rootless chaos. I had never met my birth father, that sensible fellow had bailed out on my teenage mother. At age four I'd been adopted by my mother's new husband, a soldier. We had moved a lot. I was the new kid in school every year, which would have been a problem for most people, but I welcomed it. It meant I could reinvent myself at each new school, leave behind enemies or too-cloying acquaintances, pop up in a new place with a whole new . . . Pretty much the way I still lived, come to think of it.

It took me too long to answer. So I forced a smile and said, 'Not quite,' and offered no follow-up.

Delia looked down, conscious of a gaffe.

Chante sensibly followed the lushness of the foie gras with the simplicity of perfectly grilled plaice filets set off by a pleasingly austere vinaigrette and garnished with leeks and potatoes.

The food was great, but Delia's information was not sitting well with me. I had not asked Azevedo if he'd been in prison subsequent to our joint adventure, so he hadn't lied about that except by omission. But it was a pretty big omission. That he had probably exaggerated Smit's hardness and perhaps overstated his daughter's innocence was almost to be expected. But none of it soothed my paranoia.

'Anything on the Hangwoman?' I asked.

Delia waited until she'd chewed a bit of fish and made appropriate noises to Chante. We were on to a new bottle, and it appeared I had purchased an excellent Château de Targé, Les Fresnettes, a surprisingly inexpensive Loire wine. Now I thought we might yet come in under five hundred.

'You know, something useful,' I prompted, 'like a way to keep her from murdering me?'

'No,' Delia said.

'Swell.'

'Perhaps a break before dessert?' Chante suggested.

It was the cue for Delia and me to squeeze out onto the narrow balcony and half-close the doors behind us to avoid incriminating my alleged assistant with more detail than necessary.

'So?' Delia asked without preliminaries. 'What have you learned?'

'My tour of the Rijks just confirmed what I already guessed: anyone with big enough balls can walk in and walk out with any painting they can carry.'

'Big enough balls,' Delia repeated dryly. 'I can't tell you how many times I heard that phrase coming up at Quantico and in the Bureau. The funny thing is that as organs go vaginas push out entire humans, while balls shrivel at the touch of cold water.'

'Hey, I meant to ask: how big is the Jewish Lady with Loom, or whatever it's called?'

Delia pulled out her phone, swiped around a bit and said, 'Sixteen inches by thirteen and three-quarter inches. But bigger with the frame.'

'OK, call it what, twenty-two-ish by maybe eighteen?'

'Close enough.'

'Easily carried. You'd need a forklift to get *The Night Watch* out of there, but something the size of a seat cushion? Isaac could have hired any random street punk; he didn't need the Ontario Crew. At least not for the snatch.'

'USP One doesn't know that.'

'Of course not, he's clearly a crazy old fuck. Fifty million? That's madness. That's a man who has lost all track of the value of money.' I drew out a cigar, cut it, popped it between my teeth. 'Do you mind?'

'No, as always, I enjoy your rancid carcinogens.'

'Good,' I said and fired my cigar torch. I saw her eyes glitter and focus a bit too long on the glowing cherry. I laughed. 'I never noticed before: you're an ex-smoker.'

'Three years,' Delia said through gritted teeth.

So, just to be insolent and show that she wasn't the boss of me, I blew smoke her way. I'm mature like that.

'You're telling me that anyone can steal the painting during regular hours,' Delia said, not deigning to admit irritation.

'Hell, any hours. Pop a window and in and out. Literally all you'd need is a ladder and a crowbar. I mean, I'm sure the Ontario Crew filled Isaac's oxygen-deprived brain with Tom Cruise and George Clooney movie caper bullshit, lasers and silenced machine guns and black boxes that magically open locks, and whatnot, but it's a ladder and crowbar job.'

'So? How are you going to stop it happening?'

I puffed. And I did not answer.

'You're a sphinx suddenly?'

'Delia, back when we first met, you drew some lines. There was the law, and you were sworn to uphold it. You made that very clear.' *Also you made it quite clear you were never going to sleep with me.* That part I kept to myself.

'And?' Now the irritation came out. 'Don't smirk, just tell me what you're thinking.'

'OK. What I am thinking, Delia, is that you can't know what I'm thinking.'

It was her turn at the long silence. I didn't interrupt it. Delia desperately wanted to know what I was planning, but she also knew that if I said she shouldn't know, well, she shouldn't know. *Couldn't* know, not without perhaps making herself an accessory.

At last she shook her head in disgust. 'Fuck you, David.'

'So . . . you're calling this off?'

'No, I'm just saying fuck you. Just tell me whether you can stop the Ontario Crew from stealing the painting. Yes or no?'

'Yes.'

'And can you do it without incriminating USP One?'

'Yes.'

I puffed. She bit her lip, which is about as conflicted and unsure as I've ever seen her. But then Delia's gaze shifted and she focused with a degree of intensity on the street below. She saw me noticing and without moving her lips said, 'Don't look. It's your friend. The Hangwoman.'

TEN

knew the lay of the land and Delia did not, so I made the call.

'You go first. Out through the door of this apartment, into the stairwell. Go down one landing you'll see a door to a separate stairs leading down into the back of the gift shop. They might still be open, it's not quite eight and tourist shops keep late hours.'

'Got it. Then what?'

'You'll exit out onto Reguliersbreestraat. Go left. You'll see a Subway – the sandwich place, not an actual subway. One more left, down that alley and it brings you back to Amstel. I'll give you a couple of minutes and then follow. When she spots me she'll either make a run at me or bolt, but if she bolts she'll most likely be coming your way.' I looked at my phone. 'Seven forty-seven. I'll go at seven fifty-one.'

Delia nodded and with a quick smile to Chante she left.

'Why is she leaving? Did you offend her?' Chante demanded.

'Quiet, harpy, we're catching bad guys. In fact . . . go out onto the balcony.' Then seeing stubborn recalcitrance, I added, 'It's for Delia.'

I hugged the wall out of sight as Chante stepped out.

'OK, see down there a young woman in a blue hoodie?'

'I see a striped hoodie.'

I peeked out. 'No, that's just some hippie burnout. In the blue! In the blue! That is Hangwoman. Be subtle!'

'A Frenchwoman is to be instructed in subtlety by an American?' She rolled her eyes, but she complied. 'I see her.'

'Good. Get your phone ready because we'll want video. But not until I am—'

'She's leaving.'

'What?'

'She is walking toward the Muntplein.'

'Fuck!' I raced from the room, pounded down the stairs

and burst onto the street in time to see the blue hoodie a
hundred yards off. I hurried after her while fumbling with
my phone, trying to text a warning of a change in plans to
Delia. Then I dropped my phone, bent to pick it up, breathed
in relief that it was not shattered and had to break into a trot
to keep up as Hangwoman was hurrying not down
Reguliersbreestraat but along the Singel.

Across the river was the flower market but this side of
the river was closed-up store fronts along a pedestrian and
bike way.

She turned, saw me and broke into a run. So did I. I wasn't
tailing, I was chasing, no concealment required. I'm not
the action-hero type, we've established that, but despite the
fact that this woman had tried twice to kill me, she was still
a woman and I was bigger than she was by a good fifty pounds,
so I wasn't too worried.

She ran but I had longer legs. I caught her, grabbed her
by the back of her hoodie and spun her into a shallow store
entrance alcove just a few yards from a café with a few tables
out on the street.

'Let me alone!'

She struggled, flailing, and managed to land a noticeable
kick to my shin, but I caught her arms and pushed her into
shadows and looked her right in her furious face, our eyes
inches apart.

'Why in the fuck are you trying to kill me, you goddamn
lunatic?' I demanded.

'Let me go! Let me go!'

'Like hell, I will! Why are you trying to kill me?'

She went limp, stopped fighting, and said, 'You must not
think is personal, is for money only. Housing is very expensive.'

Wait, I was being targeted for murder so she could make
her rent?

'Money? Someone's paying you to try and kill me?
Who?' Then I made a mistake. I spotted a cop biking by on
the other side of the canal and I lowered my voice. 'Who is
paying you?'

She noticed that. Like I said, she wasn't dumb enough to be
doing what she was doing. (Though, I suppose the same could

be said about me.) I saw it in her eyes, the dawning realization that I was not going to call Five-0. She waited a few seconds till the policeman was well out of range and yelled, 'Let me go! Let me go! I am attack! Help me!'

She had started squirming again and got one hand free to land a weak smack to the side of my head.

'Let you go, hell!' I yelled, but the thing was, what was I supposed to do with her? I'd caught her, now what?

I did not have long to ponder that conundrum when I heard, 'Oi! Leave the lady be!'

A large, middle-aged man wearing an England jersey, red with three heraldic blue lions, followed by a smaller, younger guy wearing shorts despite the damp chill between rain showers, were coming from the café.

'She's trying to kill me!' I explained.

This would have been much more credible if I were not six inches taller than she, and male.

'Is this man bothering you, missus?' the soccer fan asked.

'He is hurt me!' she cried.

'Not to worry yourself, missus. And you, you best bugger off before I kick your teeth in for you.'

This was addressed to me. To me! The clear victim. Well, clear to me, at least. But I still had her wrists in my big man hands.

It didn't look good.

I tried the patient approach. 'Gentlemen, I know you're just trying to be chivalrous but—'

'He want rape me!'

'Oh, fuck you, you murdering—' I began.

And that's when soccer fan number one placed his knuckles against the side of my head at high velocity. I saw stars. I staggered. I released my grip and weaved back and forth like a drunk as the Hangbitch ripped away, paused to spit at me, and took off down the street without so much as a polite thank-you to the meddling knights of the round table.

The one part of me that Milan Smit's skinhead pals had not bashed was now bashed, but fortunately the England fan had put brain-scrambling but not concussion-level force behind the blow.

Delia arrived a few seconds later as the two Englishmen were berating me with advice like, 'That's not how you treat a lady,' and, 'Go sleep it off, ya fooking pervert.'

'I'll take charge of him,' Delia told them in her authoritative FBI voice, and seeing a tall black woman must have confused them because they promptly let me go and headed back to the café, having done their good deed for the day.

'That went well,' Delia said.

'I think he loosened a tooth!'

'And the Hangperson got away.'

'I noticed that.'

'You should have followed her at a distance and texted me.'

'Oh? Is that what the FBI manual says?' I was not ready to be rational. My shin hurt and my cheek hurt and my head was still not properly seated atop my neck.

I marched away, not toward the apartment but toward a tavern down the street that was warmly lit and cozy. They had both the sound system and a TV (the inevitable soccer, of course) playing, the digital noise adding to the international murmur. They didn't have much in the way of decent whiskey, so I ordered a beer and a double shot of Jack Daniel's, neat, which I poured straight down my throat.

'I'll have a sparkling water, and a lime if you have it,' Delia told the bartender. Then, to me, 'Are you all right?'

'Have you noticed how every time you show up I end up taking a beating?'

'Coincidence,' she said, not batting an eye. 'Seriously, are you all right?' She leaned closer to get a look at my jaw. She smelled of soap, sandalwood and Chante's oysters.

'I'm not great, Delia,' I admitted angrily. 'Hangcreature is under contract. Someone is paying to have me killed. There is a contract out on me!'

Delia blinked. 'She told you that?'

'Like it was an excuse. Like I'd say, "Oh, all right then." It seems the rent is too damn high, so she has to take contracts.'

'Who would spend money to kill you?' She placed the emphasis on 'you', realized that sounded bad and repeated the sentence emphasizing the 'who.'

I covered my face with my hands and tried to settle but I

was rattled. The crazy woman was not giving up. She was still intent on murdering me, and the third time might be the charm.

Delia was less emotional. 'Who gives a contract to an amateur?' she said and frowned. She sipped water. I gulped whiskey. Then I ordered another. Big, tough ex-criminals aren't supposed to admit they're scared, but I was. The near-lynching hadn't quite done it. The poisoning hadn't quite done it. The idiocy of those attempts had waylaid my fear into contempt. But a *contract*? Now the fear came.

A contract? On *me*?

My hand trembled as I raised the second shot. Someone serious was seriously trying to kill me, albeit by employing an imbecile, but sooner or later a motivated buyer would find a competent killer.

'This is no longer funny,' I grated, and downed the whiskey.

'*Cui bono*, that's the question.'

'I asked her that,' I snapped. 'I asked *cui bono*, you crazy bitch? And she said I don't speak Latin, asshole.'

'Another?' the bartender asked, nodding at my empty shot glass.

'No,' Delia answered for me.

'Great, now you're my mother.'

'Enough, David, *enough*. You're upset, I get it. So, take some deep breaths. You're alive and aside from that punch . . . Bartender? Do you suppose we could get some ice wrapped in a towel?'

I touched the side of my face and felt a cheek larger than it normally was, and tender. Like some chivalrous Englishman had socked me.

I was distracted then by a man entering the bar. A man who did not see me or Delia despite our being just about the first thing any new arrival would see. Probably just a guy looking for someone specific . . . but no, he wasn't. Still, I wouldn't have paid him another second's attention were it not for the fact that I was morally certain he was wearing a wig. A shoulder-length, dark wig. And a turtleneck sweater, something I'd not seen in years. Did they still make turtlenecks?

'You need to focus, David. It is not possible that you're

being targeted by someone who you don't even have a connection with.'

'And *yet*,' I snapped. Then, in a more defeated tone, as the whiskey dampened my outrage, 'I don't have a clue. Really. I'm not being coy, Delia, I just don't know. Who would want me dead enough to pay the world's least competent hitwoman?'

'If this were a regular investigation I'd have someone taking statements from the people at the café, including the man who sucker-punched you.' The ice arrived and Delia pressed it against my jaw. 'Hold that in place.'

I felt the door open bringing a welcome gust of fresh, cold air. Then Chante was with us.

'I followed her,' Chante said without preamble.

'The girl?'

'Yes, your Hangwoman. I followed Delia and then I followed her.'

Delia and I were both a bit agape at that.

'Bartender, get this young woman a drink,' I said.

'As soon as she was away from you she began texting. She went to the train station and boarded a train for Haarlem. After that, I returned to search for you, Delia, and when I found the apartment empty I assumed Mitre would be looking for alcohol.'

'There are a lot of bars,' I said suspiciously.

'Yes, but fewer nearby where an older man would be comfortable.'

'Older man? I'm fucking forty-two!'

'Yes,' Chante said, as Delia laughed too much.

'Did she seem to meet anyone?' Delia asked.

'No. In all I only followed her for five minutes. I did not wish to be spotted.'

Delia sighed. 'Well, that's good and bad. Bad in that it expands the possible area in which she might be at any given moment; good in that we have a choke-point – the Haarlem train.'

'Yeah, get some agents to watch the trains,' I said with angry sarcasm to which Agent D reacted by not reacting. But I was getting so I knew Delia's expressions pretty well, limited as they were, and it was probably just paranoia, but there was something just a little too blank. So I poked again. 'I'm starting to see just how helpless you Feebs are without your armies of agents and your helpful local cops. God dammit, now I'm going to be burned in Amsterdam and I really like this city.'

'You're not burned; not yet,' Delia said.

That's only because you have not yet figured out what I'm planning, Delia, trust me, in the end I will be burned in this city. Thanks to you I lost Cyprus and now I'll lose Amsterdam. Amsterdam, where approximately half the population are gorgeous tall blond women on bikes! Beautiful, dainty Amsterdam with its tall, narrow houses like so many cereal boxes stacked side by side. Amsterdam, a city with ten Michelin-starred restaurants, eight of which I had not yet visited. I said none of that, it wasn't even entirely true, Delia wasn't the reason for Hangbitch. But I was in the mood to be resentful and irrational. Resentful, irrational and paranoid, because my eye was drawn again to Mr Wig. He was one of those people you're sure you don't know, and are sure you have not seen, and yet . . .

Delia attracted the bartender who had decided to ignore me, and Chante ordered a Cognac. No one talked for a while, probably because I was giving off volcanic vibes.

'She couldn't be related in any way to USP One . . .' Delia mused, breaking the silence and thinking out loud. 'Extremely unlikely.'

'Well, let's hope she's not related to the Chipster because you gave me an impossible job to do, Special Agent. What you've handed me is a police job. It's a job requiring manpower. I cannot be on watch 24/7/365, in fact if I tried the cops would spot me and assume I was casing the place myself.' I was being elliptical with Chante within earshot.

'So . . . You're giving up?' She put a subtle sneer into that.

'Really? You're going to try and shame me?'

Delia turned to give me the full face with the eyes and the mocking lips. 'David, believe it or not, I don't want you to get hurt.'

'We're not talking about "hurt", we're talking about "dead". Don't play word games with a writer.'

She had nothing to say to that, just silence.

'I'm not giving up,' I said after a while. 'I didn't say I was giving up.'

'No? Because honestly, David, you can. If you want to. This does change things, someone trying to kill you.'

'I said I'm not giving up!' I snapped. 'You have succeeded in guilting me into it. Besides, I have an author panel . . .'

'Right. Author panel. And that's sacred to you, is it?' Delia's laugh drew the attention of Mr Wig who was at the far end of the bar working on a beer, and he did a clumsy job of pretending to be looking at something else. That was a bad move because Delia laughing would draw anyone's attention; there would be nothing suspicious about looking her way.

'Agent D, do you have people watching me?'

She frowned. 'Do you see something or are you just being you?' Which an acute observer might have noticed was not an answer.

'Look in the mirror. Guy in the wig, past me, down the bar.'

'Turtleneck? Really?'

'I know, right? Fashion has taken a strange turn . . .' I snapped my fingers. 'Jesus Hippie!' That required explanation. 'Saw a hippie-looking dude eyeballing me the other day. Same dude was in the street when I spotted Hangbitch. I'd swear it was him but he had a massive, ugly ass tattoo on his neck.'

'A tattoo that might be hidden by a turtleneck?'

'Mmm. Yeah.' I made a point of looking Delia right in the eyes. 'Tell me, yes or no, and no bullshit, is he one of yours?'

'No.'

'Not one of your agents?'

'Don't play games, David.'

She looked at Jesus Hippie's reflection in the mirror. 'A turtleneck and a long wig? He's hiding something. What side of his neck was the tattoo on?'

I thought about it, and then had to resist the urge to curse at myself. The tattoo had been on the left side. And it had extended further north than the edge of the turtleneck.

'Fucking fake tattoo,' I said. 'Just the kind of thing you might apply to disguise a burn scar.'

Delia said, 'Chante? Is there any way you could . . .? Never mind.'

But Chante, eager as a puppy to please Delia, insisted. 'What is it?'

'Nothing,' Delia said. 'Shall we settle up and—'

'Delia wants to know if you can follow the guy in the wig. But she doesn't want to be responsible for getting you in trouble. I, however, have no such qualms, mostly because we don't so much need you to follow him as stay behind and watch to see if *he* follows *us*.'

I met Delia's gaze and she silently acquiesced. We paid the tab and exited the bar. A minute later I got a text.

He follows.

I pulled the selfie trick, drawing Delia close as if we were a couple and taking the shot from a high angle. Chante was of course correct: Jesus Hippie slash Turtleneck Wig, was a block behind us.

I looked at Delia. She looked at me. And as if we'd rehearsed it, we both said, 'Willy Pete.'

ELEVEN

I n four days the Vermeer would be hung on a wall at the Rijksmuseum. In four days it would be vulnerable to the Ontario Crew.

Which meant I had four days – four! Four days to plan, prepare and execute an art theft. Way too much time had been taken up being almost murdered, beaten up and recovering from same.

Also, I should probably think of something clever to say at my bookstore panel on that same night, but that was a lower priority.

Part One, stealing the Vermeer, was complicated, but only because I wanted to raise my eighty percent probability of getting clear of the building to more like ninety-five percent. That extra margin would involve a lot of moving parts, some of which I'd already set in motion.

Part Two would be even more complicated. Because I wasn't just going to steal the damned thing, I was going to commit a whole different crime at the same time. And also make a great deal of money.

Complicated.

The synonym for *complicated* in the world of crime is *vulnerable.* Each new complication was another moving part that might fail. And the odds of failure had risen dramatically with the realization that the Ontario Crew was watching me.

It wasn't hard to figure out where they'd gotten the idea to watch me: the initial leak had to have come from a government source, and it was probably about Delia, not me directly. A lot of Feebs and Spooks are ex-military, and USP One, Daniel 'the Chipster' Isaac, sold weapons to the military. It would not be a surprise if he had connections in the CIA certainly, and probably in the Bureau as well. Politically connected billionaires facing imminent death by COPD had ways of deploying their cash.

Several thoughts occurred: if someone in the FBI had leaked word that the Bureau was onto the Ontario Crew, how had that led to me? I was supposedly nothing more than a CI file number. The answer was mundane, of course: the leak had been about Delia, Willy Pete had followed Delia and Delia had led him to me. And I was an unknown property, someone the Ontario Crew would want to know about.

The more startling realization was that the Ontario Crew knew the FBI was onto them and yet they were still active. The fact that someone in the Bureau had leaked didn't alter the reality that rational crooks did not commit their crimes while aware that the Feebs were on to them. You know, unless someone had basically buried them in a pile of money. Fifty million buys a lot of initiative.

The Ontario Crew had presumably done the same math Delia had. They knew we couldn't rat them out to the Dutch. And they knew as well as I did that in the absence of wall-to-wall, 24/7 surveillance, they were pretty safe. But there was that wild card: me. I bore looking into.

I left Delia and Chante and walked off by myself, down through the Red Light District, De Wallen, the roughly two acres of bars and coffee shops and sex workers sitting in red-lit windows. I was not enticed by the several offers aimed at me, the most direct of which was from a scary hag who sang rather than said, 'Fucky-fucky, let's go fucky-fucky.' This had the unfortunate effect of reminding me of rumpy-pumpy, which in turn made me wince as I remembered the abrupt way I'd shut Tess down.

My phone dinged. It was Delia.

Hey: Located Hangwoman.

Cool. Bit late tonight.

Yep. Tomorrow. Night. I'll get a vehicle.

I checked the time. I'd left Delia an hour earlier in the café, so how had she suddenly discovered the Hangwoman's location when all we had on her was a train and a terminal?

The explanation was inescapable: Delia had agents in town. Goddammit, she had people watching me. Professionals, too, or I'd have twigged them. Agents who must have watched from the shadows and followed either Hangwoman or Chante to the train station and then onto the train, leaving me in something of an emotional quandary: was I more angry at the presence of Feebs? Or more relieved that they'd followed Hangwoman to whatever rat hole she lived in?

I watched creepy dudes and prurient tourists eyeball the ladies until depression threatened and I headed for the apartment. Chante was asleep, a relief, because I was still too jazzed to sleep and wanted to work on my plan.

I sipped Talisker and fleshed out the details of my shopping list and contemplated the nature of my fucked-up life. I fell asleep on the sofa at some point and woke to the aroma of coffee and the sounds of Chante in the kitchen.

This time around at the Rijksmuseum I was not the corpulent, sporty dude with the bad mustache, I was the slow, stooped, gray-haired pensioner in a tan canvas jacket, worn thrift-shop shoes and a plaid flat cap. I established a pattern of taking lots of pictures, lots of video, even pics of things clearly irrelevant: lockers, steps, signs. The idea was to look like an easily dismissible old fart who didn't really know why he was taking pictures of security cameras, guards, the mounting of various paintings, sight lines, distances, crowd concentrations, bathrooms, stairwells . . .

I retrieved my backpack from the coat check, plopped down in the museum café, ordered an open-faced sandwich and a Pellegrino and opened my newest (non-FBI) laptop. I opened Pages and started to walk the plan through, once again, step by step.

The museum was not going to be the problem, the problem was going to be a bunch of technical issues having to do with tracking Wi-Fi connections, stacking up alternate sites to use for broadcast, and the complex issues around money traveling over the internet. Also there would be some DIY construction work, not a strength of mine.

US Person Isaac lived in Las Vegas. That was a nine-hour time difference from Amsterdam. My ten a.m. would be Isaac's one a.m. No good. My five p.m. would be his Pacific Time eight a.m. That was better – not much point in my plan if the Chipster slept through it all.

Five p.m. would be H-Hour. Six p.m. would be the first

broadcast. Six p.m. here would be eleven a.m. in the media centers in New York. At that time the media would light up with the news while Isaac was eating his corn flakes in Vegas.

Plus, five p.m. would be rush hour, lots of people on the streets and canals, fewer in the museum and no school groups I'd have to worry about trampling.

I went over it again. And again.

1. *The diversion(s).*
2. *The snatch.*
3. *The camera walk.*
4. *The dump.*
5. *The cameras again.*
6. *The exit.*
7. *The exterior diversion.*
8. *The boat.*
9. *The twelve-hour tick-tock.*
10. *The banking.*
11. *The reveal.*

I groaned inwardly at the thought of the work still to be done and I shuddered at the thought of all that could go wrong. I had an exit plan in that event, but I wasn't thrilled with it as it involved a great deal of bike riding, at the very least.

Could I build an alibi? If so, was that just gilding the lily? Should I line up a patsy? And would that be a case of buying trouble? Anyway, who was my patsy going to be, I didn't know anyone in Amsterdam.

The old saw holds that armchair warriors talk tactics, while professional soldiers talk logistics. In the writing world, the corollary is that wannabes talk inspiration, while pros talk deals and options. A stick-up artist only thinks about the seventy-two dollars he'll get from a liquor store and the meth he can buy with that money, but armed robbers are lazy and reckless. The professional thief does his homework, and his prep work. The professional plans for problems.

But so much prep work! And so little time.

And as to time, I was to meet Delia at six. Three hours.

In the intervening time I could start acquiring addresses. I typed in *airbnb.com*, checked map view and began to list properties that fronted the canals here in Amsterdam. Then a pair of properties, one in Antwerp the other in Düsseldorf, as safe houses in case it came to that.

The cost was getting ridiculous. I was spending money like water, burning carefully constructed identities along with their credit cards and passports, and, I reminded myself, it was not as if any of this was my idea. I'd been bullied into it.

I nurtured these grudges as a way to rationalize what I hoped would be an impressive payday. How impressive? That would depend. My net worth was right around two million in various accounts in places where banks didn't ask questions. I might well double that. This could be a seven-figure score, and in real money, not discounted by a fence.

The FBI is regrettably pretty damned good at following the money, which meant I needed a way to discourage, slow down, even abort FBI interest in tracking my profits. Well, later for that. First, I had to get together with Delia and find my would-be killer and figure out just who wanted me dead. And how much they were offering to pay.

It was going to be humiliating if the price on my head was too low.

TWELVE

'I have bitterballs.'

I twisted sideways and looked at my friendly, neighborhood FBI legat. 'Are you aware that when you say things like that you put a huge strain on my maturity?'

'Just trying to keep you awake, David.'

Surveillance is boring. We were staring at a building. Delia and I were in Haarlem, a city west of Amsterdam that functions as a bedroom community, though it apparently has a charming downtown, I wouldn't know, I was a long way from the charm.

Delia had rented a small Toyota SUV for the mission and we were parked in a wide cul-de-sac that formed around a bleak, quarter-sized concrete soccer pitch. I imagine, this being the Netherlands, that in winter they hose it down and turn it into a hockey rink. But at this moment no one was playing anything. It was eight thirty, just after sundown in this northern city with a latitude closer to the pole than any of the lower forty-eight states.

The cul-de-sac was formed by three-story apartment buildings and ended in a taller, seven-story red-brick building with generous balconies. Delia and I were parked on the street, facing the tall building, which, according to Delia, was where the Hangperson lived.

'So, these *bitterballen* . . .'

She turned and rummaged around in the back seat and came back with two cardboard clamshells which, when opened, revealed five eyeball-sized, deep-fried balls.

'One set is coconut curry, the other is, um, I think shrimp and . . . something. I also have this sauce which is, well . . . It's green is what it is.'

I snagged one of each. *Bitterballen* are the essential Dutch bar snack, but as with Valentine's Day chocolates, you can't tell from the outside what's inside. They were still warm.

'Nothing sweet?'

'I have a package of *stroopwafels*. Also cold canned coffee.'

Between us we finished off the *bitterballen* and half the *stroopwafels*, and we drank the coffee.

'Aren't you going to sneak a drink from your flask?'

'Is that your way of asking if you can have some?'

'You're not?'

'Not at work, Delia.'

'Work.' She didn't find the word appropriate.

'It's work when you do it properly,' I said, mostly out of boredom and a desire to pass the time in argumentation.

Delia was behind the wheel, I was riding shotgun, with the seat pushed all the way back and declined to a forty-degree angle. We each had a bottle of Evian. I had suggested smoking a cigar and Delia had threatened to punch me out if I did, so, no cigars. But I wasn't actually going to indulge anyway – great clouds of blue-gray smoke rising from a parked car is not subtle.

Night was coming on fast.

'Lights on in, what, nine, ten of them?' I jerked my chin toward our target.

'Mmm.' She sat there, wrist draped over steering wheel, drinking cold coffee. I studied her profile. She was less guarded when she was looking away. Delia Delacorte claimed to have been born in Muleshoe, Texas, a fact I had not checked because if there was no such place I didn't want to know.

If I were unaware of who Delia was, and simply had her profile to judge, I don't think I'd have made her as police, but I'd have made her as smart and forceful. I'd have noticed her. But of course I did know Delia, I had seen her in action, I'd been privy to her thoughts, I'd even noticed that for brief moments she was capable of emotion. God help me, I liked her. I liked our relationship, if you could call it that. And that was a startling thing for me to recognize: I didn't hate working with Delia. I didn't hate what I'd done for her in Cyprus. I bitched about it, I whined, but I had come away from that clusterfuck with this one, tiny little thing, this one mitzvah, this one time when I had done something . . . *good*.

I had stopped a child sex-trafficking operation. Me! Martin

DeKuyper aka David Mitre and a whole long list of names. I
had actually rescued abused children. Me! At great risk. Me!
But only because of Delia.

'I'm going to tell you something, Delia, and if you ever
remind me of it, I'll . . . I'll do something. Something bad.'
I took a deep breath, and to my horror my voice was actually
hoarse with emotion that must have been a result of my beating
or stress or . . . something. 'Agent D, if by some miracle there
really is a supernatural being I have to justify myself to, I'll
have exactly one thing to offer to counterbalance the bad things
I've done. I mean, I give money to street people sometimes,
I hold doors for people, and I have never killed anyone – well,
except that one time in self-defense. And I haven't stolen from
anyone who couldn't afford it, but as to something that took
some effort, that required some degree of courage and was
actually good? The sum total of good I've done has been
because of you, Delia.' I laughed in surprise at myself. 'If
there's a path to some kind of redemption for me, it runs
through you.'

In profile I saw her nod very slightly.

'Anyway, I'm tired of camping out here. See the big gray
rectangle just inside the lobby?' I handed her my Carl Zeiss
Victory compact binoculars and pointed. 'Buzzers and presumably name tags beside them, and mailboxes, but those are
locked and I don't think they have names listed.'

'We don't know Hangwoman's name,' Delia pointed out.
'And we don't even know if the apartment is in her name, she
could be staying with someone.'

I nodded. 'Yep. However, we do know she's Eastern
European. If she's crashing with someone it's likely they are
also not locals. So, you run down the list and eliminate all
Dutch-sounding surnames, all Muslim-sounding surnames,
anything Javanese, etc. . . . . You look for names ending in the
letter "v." Or patronymics. It's not exactly foolproof. But I've
heard her voice and I might recognize it.'

'Well, it's dark,' she said.

Amazingly the lobby door was an unlocked slider so I was
able to pop in and study the names. The first thing I noticed
was that I'd overestimated the number of apartments, there

were just fourteen. That was good. Five of the fourteen had distinctly Dutch names, three were Middle Eastern, one looked Italian. Of the remaining five, two were unlabeled, and none were notably Slavic.

I made note of the two apartments without nametags and went back outside to gaze up and try to connect location to number to name. I walked around to the back of the building and from here the layout was clearer: a central stairwell and elevator shaft, apartments to left and right.

I made note of illuminated windows, compared it to what I'd seen from the front, then ambled back to Delia and leaned in the window. 'I'm going to try buzzing. If she's a pro she could be scared, but more likely she'll assume it was a mistake or kids playing around. However, if she bolts it'll be on foot or bike, so we should be ready.' I pointed out my targets and added, 'Watch the windows.'

I went back into the lobby and buzzed the first of the un-labeled doorbells. Nothing. Again. More nothing.

I pressed the other buzzer. Nothing. And I was just about to press again when a voice crackled from the speaker, speaking Dutch, but even a non-Dutch speaker could hear that the voice was female and not a native Dutch speaker.

I said, 'Sorry,' in a thick accent. I waited for a few minutes to avoid having Hangwoman look out of her window and spot me exiting the building, then sauntered back to the SUV. 'See anything?'

'I saw Hangwoman looking out of her window,' Delia said and pointed.

'Hah! Well done, me. And on just the second floor, too. Or what the locals would call the first floor. Excellent.'

'Now what?'

I considered the building before me. Hangwoman lived on the second floor, so I could climb to the balcony easily enough and creep her apartment when she went out, but—

'Look! That's her, isn't it?'

It was. Hangwoman was walking out of the lobby and heading down the street, on foot not bike, and fortunately not toward us.

'We can front her now, or follow her,' I said.

'I'll follow her,' Delia said. 'And you?'

'Don't ask. Leave me the keys.'

She handed me the key, waited until Hangwoman had turned a corner, and took off on foot after her. I started the SUV and eased it around the circle until it was directly beneath Hangwoman's balcony. I turned on the flashers so I'd look like a delivery person, or maybe a friend of one of the residents doing a quick pick-up. I wasn't too concerned with the Toyota being traced back to Delia – some miscreant had swapped the plates with a Kia. *Note to self: remember to swap the plates back before Delia hands it in to Avis.*

I opened the moon roof, took a careful look around, and climbed up. I'm six foot one or two in the morning before gravity and the weight of my sins drag me down, and the car stood about five and a half feet high, which put my head about eleven feet from ground level. I could see into the apartment past partially closed blinds. The lights were low. No sign of anyone or anything.

So, I hauled myself up and over – easy – painful as bruises take a long time to heal completely, but easy – and paused, waiting for noises from inside. Nothing. I touched the handle of the slider and applied gradually increasing pressure. I was almost convinced it was locked, but then it moved.

I stepped into a living room, surprisingly well furnished for a criminal lair. There were all the little touches – throw pillows, fashion magazines and a local guide fanned out on the coffee table, old advertising posters, professionally framed.

I moved quickly. Some random civilian might have seen me climbing and in this irritatingly upright country they might well call the police.

The only light came from the stove hood. The kitchen was open-plan, and it, too, was empty. I opened cupboards and the fridge, just to reassure myself that someone did actually live here. Yes, it seemed, the flat was occupied by someone who quite liked tinned fish, muesli and vodka, presumably not all together.

This left the bedroom or bedrooms. I saw two closed doors. I tiptoed to the first and pressed my ear against the hollow-core door. Silence. I turned the knob noiselessly, slipped inside and shut the door just as silently behind me. I was confident the apartment was empty, but one must observe the proprieties of tradecraft.

Pro tip: It's better to risk the small noise that comes from turning a doorknob all the way than to risk the more attention-getting click if an insufficiently withdrawn latch touches the strike plate. One must never hurry those things.

The bedroom was also nicely furnished, with a single bed, neatly made; a dresser with one drawer partly open and spilling a scarf; a side table and two lamps. And in the corner two suitcases. I pushed them gently: empty.

I went first to the closet. Clothing. Yep. Women's clothing. But not much, and the sparseness seemed at odds with the rest of the apartment.

Of course, dummy, it's an AirBnB or something like.

I carefully rifled the dresser drawers, taking note of the exact placement of every item I touched, which wasn't much. A sweater and a lacquered yellow box filled with weed, a pipe, papers and a rolling machine.

In the bedside table's only drawer were condoms, a vibrator and lube, as well as a handful of receipts. I shuffled through the receipts – groceries, books, and oh, hello there, a receipt from the phone company, Vodafone. Was her phone number on the receipt? Of course not, that would be too easy.

On the table was an off-brand iPad. Password protected and the answer was not 1-1-1-1-1 or Q-W-E-R-T-Y or any of the dozen obvious passwords. It remained unprobed.

Brilliant. I had discovered that Hangwoman wore clothing, ate food, owned a phone and an iPad, and was staying in a temporary rental.

I almost didn't notice the flyer. It was green, with black print, and it advertised a Waterstones literary event: me, along with three other authors. My picture was only the second largest and I was half-obscured. I almost didn't resent that.

A door led from the bedroom into an en suite bathroom, and a closed door leading beyond to the second bedroom. Careful sleuthing revealed that Hangwoman suffered from seasonal allergies. This was not life-altering news.

A noise!

I froze. Tapping. Someone on a keyboard. In the second bedroom. Someone was in the apartment and it wasn't Hangwoman. I cursed myself for taking for granted that she lived alone. Amateur!

Moving by millimeters I carefully, so very carefully, turned the knob and the door was yanked from my hand and flew open.

He was a bit shorter than me with stringy brown hair that fell to his narrow, sloping shoulders. He had an intelligent face, thin, colorless lips, a nose that someone had broken at some point, and wide, frightened, but clever eyes.

First impression: I could take him.

Second impression: No, I couldn't, because he was holding a meat cleaver.

Third impression: he recognized me. I was able to deduce this just moments after he yelled, 'Mitre?'

I said, 'Sorry, wrong apartment. I don't know how I got so turned around; this isn't my mother's apartment at all!'

This baffled him for a few seconds during which time I saw past him into what was clearly the most important room in the place, because there was a good bit of expensive-looking tech – three monitors facing a black leather ergonomic swivel chair. Definitely not typical of an AirBnB.

'Get out of this place!' the dude yelled, sounding a lot more Slovak or Polish or Russian than Dutch. He brandished the cleaver clumsily.

'So sorry!' I said, backing toward the door. 'I'm just going to leave right now.'

I saw the hesitation on his face. Should he let me leave? Or should he chop parts of me off with that cleaver? I chose not to wait and find out. I turned, shot through the first bedroom and ran for the front door. But he knew the layout better than I did and managed to reach the door before me. I spun away and raced back the way I had come in, via the balcony.

I reached the slider, saw the SUV was still flashing away on the street below, started to climb the railing and the bastard swung the cleaver at me. It missed me but flaked paint from the iron railing. I had one leg over and if I could just . . . but now he was on his knees, hugging my leg to his chest with one arm and brandishing the cleaver.

'Do not go or I will cut you. With this!'

'I thought you wanted me to go away!'

'No! I will cut you!'

As a rule the ratio of threats to actions is about ten to one, but if he swung that cleaver he could carve a filet out of my thigh, so I stopped, one leg still over the railing.

'Who the hell are you and why is your roommate trying to kill me?'

'Go back in!'

'Dude, if you cut me I'll go over the side and you'll be explaining to cops why there's a guy bleeding out on the sidewalk beneath your balcony.'

A pretty good argument, I thought, but I could see that he was running a whole different script. The crazy son of a bitch actually meant it, I was morally certain of that. So I sagged my shoulders in a gesture of collapsing will, raised my empty palms, shifted my weight and fell over the side with gravity yanking my leg free of his grip.

You know how in the movies a guy can fall ten floors but so long as he lands on a car or in a dumpster he'll just walk it off? This fall was maybe seven feet and when I hit the SUV's roof it did not give an inch. I might as well have fallen on concrete. Every molecule of oxygen exploded from my lungs. I was able to protect my head, but I landed on my back and my rear end sagged right down through the moon roof, leaving me stuck with my legs in the air like an overturned tortoise and my hands pushing desperately to right myself, and goddamn if he wasn't getting ready to jump off the balcony and come after me! He was climbing over!

Really?

This was outrageous. I hadn't hurt him and I was fleeing as you're supposed to do when caught in the act, and in those circumstances the proper and correct thing for him to do was to stay on the balcony and shake the cleaver menacingly as I motored off with a middle finger salute extended out of the moon roof.

I hefted myself up on my hands, exquisitely painful with

old bruises welcoming a whole new set. I freed my butt, squirmed around till I could drop my legs down through the hatch and half-tumbled, half-slithered down onto the center post which caused a particular impact I was going to feel really badly in five . . . four . . .

I hit the starter just as Mr Cleaver steeled himself for the jump. He jumped, I hit the gas, and he bounced off the back end and fell to the pavement. I pulled way, my middle finger salute raised, and as soon as the slow-build agony in my nether regions passed, all was right with the world.

'Hey, Siri? Text Delia.'

'What do you want to say?'

'What I want to say is how come when I get involved with you I end up in pain?'

'Ready to send?'

'No, Jesus! Text: Delia I am fleeing in the fucking car. Need a ride?'

Siri sent, *'No cheeses text daily I am feeling in the ducking car need a ride?'*

Good enough.

Delia texted back. *Just a grocery run.* I picked her up outside the Albert Heijn where Hangwoman was buying sausages, and we drove off into the night.

THIRTEEN

an's train was due in at eleven p.m. sharp and I'd been worried I might not make it and he would make a beeline for the nearest bar, but Delia had rented the SUV at the train station so, conveniently we arrived at Amsterdam Centraal twenty minutes early. And then, conveniently, I ditched Delia telling her I was heading straight home.

Once Delia was gone I spent the time trying to flush out tails. I did not see Jesus Hippie aka Willy Pete. But I was pretty sure about one guy, a too-fit, too-alert, decidedly large guy with a shaved-head. He sat reading his phone and sipping coffee and doing the no-eye-contact, pretend-to-be-looking-elsewhere thing.

I walked past him, heading in the direction of the exit. Once out of sight I nipped into a tourist shop and watched as Mr Bald 'n' Fit passed, peering ahead. Turnabout being fair play and all that I followed him out of the station, out onto the square where he spent some time looking all around with mounting frustration until the crowd thinned. Then he made a call.

So tail number two. But for whom was he working? Delia? Or Willy? Or God forbid some third party, like *tangential Nazis.*

There are times when the fugitive life can be a bit wearying. Maybe someday I'll be able to walk through a train station without paranoia. I'd hate to think I'd have to grow old still having to view the world through frightened gerbil eyes.

I went back into Amsterdam Centraal, a conventional European train station with platforms beneath a high, arched, lattice canopy. The Dutch had cleaned it up quite a bit since I'd first visited the city many years ago when I was nineteen and drawn to the city by legal weed and tall blond women on bikes. There were fewer street people, fewer beggars; the burnouts and junkies hadn't been driven off completely but

you no longer had to plot a careful path through the station
to avoid them. And there was a great deal more by way of
shopping opportunities, though I remained baffled as to who
exactly shops for lingerie at a train station.

The train slid up to the platform almost silently, exactly one
minute late. That made it on time by Northern European
standards, hours early by the standards of American trains,
while in Japan that kind of laxity would be a national humili-
ation which might bring down the government.

'Jimmy C!'

How to describe Ian? If you cut his hair he'd look a little
like me: tall, long-limbed, moderately attractive if you liked
bad boys who'd only break your heart. He had gnarled large
hands missing a ring finger on his left. (I knew the story behind
that, one of the reasons Ian would do as I asked.) He was in
his thirties but had the air of a younger man or older boy,
lots of fidgety nervous energy, lots of nervous tics and habits.
He touched himself a lot, reassuring himself that his trousers
are still on, and his sleeves are just so, and his white dog
collar was nicely framed by his black cassock.

That last was one of Ian's little quirks. He sometimes
preferred to dress as a priest. Other times he might be a brown-
clad UPS driver or a mail carrier. He liked uniforms.

'Hello, Ian. How was the trip?'

'Had to change trains twice, and you, you cheap bastard,
you didn't even go the extra for first class. How you doing,
Jimmy?'

We shook hands.

'I'm fine. I rented a place for you, an AirBnB. I want you
isolated as much as possible.'

He had interesting eyes, Ian; they were not entirely level,
the left one drooping a good half inch lower, which made
him one of those guys who, if you want to look them in the
eyes, you have to choose left or right. I preferred the right
eye. It looked less crazy.

'Out of sight, so? Fuck me! Out of sight in Amsterdam, by
God?'

'You'll like the pay,' I said. Spotting a look of shock on
a passing woman's face, I added, 'And most of your better

class of priest doesn't yell, "fuck me" in train stations. Just a thought.'

'No, they yell for the next altar boy. Bring me little Johnny Bunghole!' Of course he shouted that, of course. 'Don't tell me about priests, the bastards, I know about priests. Almost as bad as the fucking nuns, or maybe I should say those non-fucking nuns, right?' He pivoted to leer at a young Dutch woman and mimed the movement of her rear cheeks with his hands. 'What a ride she'd be!'

Ian was a fool, but in the past he'd proved reliable, and he had the advantage of being so obviously full of bullshit he'd probably never make a good witness. Plus, like me, he'd done honest work at times and had some skill with mechanical things.

'Shall we get a drink then, eh, Jimmy? Get properly snattered?' He did a sly look-around as if expecting to be overheard – now that he wasn't leering, miming sex or cursing. 'What I've been at lately, I haven't had a night in a pub for some time.'

'Been inside, have you?'

'No, no.' He shook his head forcefully and crossed himself. 'Just a bit of trouble over a horse.'

'A slow horse I'm guessing?'

'Pitifully slow, Jimmy, and me telling some punter she was a sure winner . . . Ah, well, no point dwelling on it.'

'How much did you bet? Wait, wait. Let me revise that. How much money that you don't actually have did you bet?'

He blushed. He'd never make a poker player. 'It was nothing two grand wouldn't cure.'

All told I don't think I'd spent twelve hours in Ian's company, but he had conceived a strange, almost worshipful admiration for me. I was 'posh' but not a tosser; I had money and was not cheap with drinks; and he knew that I was something other than what I appeared to be. He would play it palsy with me and would gently take the piss, but he was leery of me as well, probably a good thing. He worked at impressing me.

'So what's the gig, then?'

'Mostly shopping. And some DIY construction.'

'Sounds dull.'

'Crime is dull when you do it properly. Try to keep it that way: properly dull.'

'Low profile, eh?' He tapped his nose wisely, then hitched up his trousers and patted his front as if checking to make sure everything was buttoned up.

'So low you were never here, Ian.'

I handed him a burner phone, then texted him an encrypted shopping list. Then, with much trepidation, I slipped him two credit cards, a slip with just numbers, and an envelope of cash.

'You'll want receipts?'

'Jesus, Ian, no I don't want receipts for items that might be used in a crime. Come on, man. This is the only time we will be seen in public together. Our texts will all be encrypted and via burner phones.'

He shook his head admiringly. 'This is why I like working with you, Jimmy. You're a professional.' He tapped the side of his head. 'I learn things from you.'

I sent him on his priestly way after he made the sign of the cross over me.

I made as if to leave but ducked into, and a minute later out of, the men's room so as to follow Ian at a distance. If he headed for a bar I'd buy him a ticket home and tell him to fuck off. But he went faithfully to the address I'd given him. At the same time I kept an eye out to see if he was being tailed, and was reasonably convinced he was clean.

In the morning after a restless night spent trying to find a part of me to lie on that didn't hurt, it was all prep work. I had two days. Two. Ian, bless him, went right to work, having caught an early train to Brussels.

Ian: *Do you want the toy because for a bit more I can get one that takes video.*

Me: *Get the specific model I listed.*

I'd loaded Ian down with work, but there were things I still had to do myself. I had wondered how one summoned a flash mob but it turned out there were a number of companies who did just that and I could manage it all online. Thank you, Google.

I checked in on a special order I'd placed with a graphic design firm that was printing a colorful corporate logo onto a box of thirty-six-inch art portfolios I'd arranged for them to receive. They were on time and on-spec, even texting me a reassuring photo.

Ian: *Where the bloody hell do I find black felt?*

Me: *Craft shop. Google one.*

I spent quite a lot of bandwidth on the matter of AirBnBs. I needed units on a canal, with good Wi-Fi, and access without the presence of the owner – either keypad lock or a key left under the mat, not that I intended to enter any of the properties I was reserving: I was just after Wi-Fi logins.

Ian: *Motorized wheelchairs cost a bloody fortune.*

Me: *I know. Get the model I asked for.*

Ian: *And how do I get the fucking thing back to A'Dam?*

Me: *You ride it onto the train, dude. You can wear your priest outfit if you like.*

I had to credit Hangwoman for the wheelchair idea. No one questions a wheelchair. Disabled people are as close to invisible as you can get without being a street beggar, and part of any good criminal's game has to be exploiting societal weaknesses. Like the old saying goes: hate the game, don't hate the player. It wasn't my fault people avoided looking at people in wheelchairs.

Ian: *Did you really mean eight burners?*

Me: *Yep. Eight. No more than two at any one shop.*

Ian: *Jaysus wept.*

Me*: So I've read.*

By afternoon my eyes were swimming and my head was pounding from too much time staring at a screen, and I had something more fun to do, something I could perhaps actually wrap up: Smit and Madalena. I knew where they lived, and it was daytime, so even if Smit had mounted a guard I didn't think his skinhead buddies would be able to attack me.

I needed to get Madalena alone somewhere and ask her father's questions. If I got that out of the way I'd have a much clearer path to getting the hell out of Dodge just as soon as I'd done my dirty deeds.

I stuffed some handy zip ties in my pocket, figuring that they might be useful. And I pulled a trick I'd learned from a doomed MI6 operative on Cyprus: I filled a small spray bottle halfway with hot sauce and diluted it a bit with whiskey, the better to spray. Homemade pepper gas. Tabasco works, but I had this stuff that's made with ghost peppers and it was a Scoville-scale nuke compared to Tabasco's conventional bomb.

I walked a bit, grabbed a taxi, walked some more, and once I was sure I didn't have a tail, I trolleyed to Amsterdam Centraal and hopped on the train to Rotterdam. There I went through the same tail-losing maneuvers, eventually reaching an in-town Hertz office where I rented an Audi A4, which I drove to Bijlmermeer. I parked behind Smit's building and, using my binoculars, looked at a shaded window. And saw a shade. Seeing nothing but that ecru shade I drove around to the front side and parked near the courtyard gate. An hour. Another hour. Then a girl appeared: tall, dark hair, pretty, with a nicely confident swagger. I swiped to my photos of Madalena.

'Well, hello there, Maddie.'

Then, Smit followed. Unfortunate. Worse, they were both pushing bikes and I would not be able to follow them in a car. They rode straight toward me, intending to pass me on the driver's side.

Well, when opportunity knocks, you should open the door. So I did just that, opening my door just in front of Smit who took it hard. His front tire hit, he went over the handlebars, bounced off the window of the opened door, and sprawled on the pavement, feet all tangled up in spokes and chain.

'*Debiel!*' he yelled, which was likely a rude word, then groaned a bit as he tried to make sense of what had just happened to him.

I don't do the action-hero thing, but I do have a deep well of learning from horror movies, and if Pinhead, Chuckie and Mike Myers have taught me anything, it's that when the bad guy goes down you need to make damned sure he stays down.

So I stood up on the door sill and jumped on Milan Smit. I landed astraddle, bent my knees in and dropped my weight on the left side of his chest as he rolled onto his right.

'*Schijt!*' Smit cried, which was easy enough to decipher, and, '*rotzak!*' which was less so, but which was unlikely to be a compliment.

I fumbled for one of the zip ties. If you've ever seen a

YouTube of a cop trying to subdue a frantically resisting man, then you know how difficult it can be to handcuff someone. And I am no cop.

'*Pleurislijer!*' Smit yelled. Turned out, when I googled it later, that means 'tuberculosis sufferer'. Which is just odd. Smit thrashed and tried to kick and punch and as he was taller than me, younger than me and stronger than me, he almost got away. I barely stayed on, riding him like a novice rodeo cowboy, but ended up facing his feet. My zip tie was not long enough to go around both ankles, and now Madalena was pedaling back, yelling, '*Monta de merda!*' and, '*Cabrão!*' presumably impolite words in Portuguese. And then a word that translates across so many languages. 'Nazi!'

'Fucking sit still!' I growled at Smit who, unsurprisingly perhaps, refused to do so. I took a chance and leaned forward, which stuck my rear in Smit's face but imprisoned his legs. He beat on my butt cheeks and tried to raise his knees to throw me off.

I got one zip tie around one ankle. I endured the butt-beating and found a second zip tie. I threaded it through the first and took a knee to the chest, but still managed it even though Madalena was now punching my poor, bruised back and biting my ear, heaping Portuguese abuse on me all the while.

'*Olho do cu! Nazi porco!*'

She swung her backpack and something in it was heavy because it hit my shoulder blade like a hammer.

'OK, goddammit, that's enough!' I used my sternest voice. But I had a more useful opportunity: there was Madalena's leg, her foot planted between Smit's ankles.

I rolled away and Madalena charged after me, then stopped quite suddenly and fell to her hands and knees, zip-tied to Smit.

I now had two people tied together by the ankles. In a Dutch street. If cops didn't roll up in the next three minutes it would be a miracle.

'Listen, assholes,' I snarled. 'The cops are coming and if you don't want to talk to them you'd better talk to me.'

Smit had managed to stand up. If he had a knife, or even

a fingernail clipper, he could free himself and Madalena, but I saw a look between the two of them that said, *No, we don't want cops.*

'Then get in the car, I'm not here to hurt you.' I helped bundle them into the back seat. I climbed in the front and turned to face two furious but frightened faces. 'I'm not having one of you choke me from behind, give me a hand.'

I grabbed an unresisting Smit's hand and zip-tied it to the passenger seat headrest. Not exactly supermax, that, the headrest could be removed, but I'd have warning at least. I started the car and drove off. Three blocks away a police car with lights and sirens passed by going the other direction. I watched in the rearview mirror until it was clear they weren't turning around.

I drove without destination, came to an 'A' road and took it north. A few miles on I pulled off into a parking area surrounded by marsh which the Dutch were presumably turning into dry land – they do that. There was one other car in the lot but it was unoccupied. I twisted to confront my two prisoners.

'All right. It's come-to-Jesus time. We are going to talk.'

Madalena tried to spit, but her mouth was dry from fear. She was trembling and that triggered my stunted guilt gland. I don't frighten women, I seduce them. As for Smit, fuck him; he'd torn my left ring fingernail.

'Who are you?' Smit demanded. He seemed the more reasonable of the two, or at least the calmer.

'My name is Dennis, Dennis Lehane,' I lied. 'Madalena's father asked me to check up on his little girl.'

I don't know what I expected. Guilt? Surprise? The sullen act? I did not expect stark terror.

'Have you told him?' Madalena demanded, voice pleading.

'Told who? What?'

'Have you told my father that you find me?'

I frowned, not happy about her tone. 'No. Not yet.'

'You must not,' Madalena said, leaning forward, pleading. 'Please, you must not tell him.'

She had lovely smooth skin and huge, dark, soulful eyes framed by absurdly long lashes, genuine as far as I could tell.

I could see why Smit was attracted to her. The reverse was harder to explain.

'Why not?'

'Because he will get me kill because I will not give it to them! Never!'

That stopped me. 'What the hell are you talking about?'

'I tell you nothing!'

'You tell me nothing, I tell your father everything.'

An exchange of sullen glances. Smit shrugged. Madalena was the one in charge I realized, the brains of the couple.

'I took a thing,' Madalena confessed as a single tear went racing down her cheek. Dammit. Women's tears. I'd always made a point of being well away before the women I gave reason to weep started in.

'Money? Jewels?'

She looked down, ashamed now, finally, and in a low voice said, 'I took the gold *Führer*.'

Tangential Nazis.

'The what?'

'The gold Hitler. It is a bust of Hitler, solid gold, commissioned by Goering and presented as a gift after the fall of France. It is what I beliefed you were after when you attack us.'

I'm usually pretty good at absorbing unexpected facts. Except when the words just don't seem to make sense. 'A gold Hitler?'

'Yes, certainly. A gold Hitler. It is very valuable for the gold. It is almost one and a half kilos.'

'That's . . .' Calculating on my fingers. 'Like, fifty-ish ounces. Sixty thousand euros, give or take.' I had not checked gold prices for a while, but it was sure to be over a grand an ounce.

'Seventy-one thousand euros.' This came from Smit. 'As of this morning's price.' He was eyeing me with more curiosity than hostility.

'And with pure gold you're keeping just about all of that, no split with some greedy fence.' I probably should not have said that, it made me sound a bit criminal. So, I added, 'I write about crime. I know these things.'

The three of us fell silent for a moment and looked at each other nonplussed. We were three strangers, suddenly together. In an Audi. In a parking lot off the freeway. It was awkward.
'OK,' I said. 'Tell me your story, Madalena.'
'And you don't tell my father?'
'I'm making no promises,' I said. 'You tell me your side of things, and I'll see. Why not start with why three skinheads jumped me when I followed you.'
Smit made a puzzled face. It seemed genuine.
'Dude, don't play me,' I said. 'I cased your apartment and as I was leaving three assholes jumped me.'
Still nothing. From either of them. I tried one more time.
'One had a tattoo. *BBET: Bloed, Bodem*—'
'*Eer en Trouw*,' Smit finished. His pale face was paler. '*My Gott* they find us!'
I may be a bit better than the average Joe at spotting a lie, but I've been fooled before and I do not believe myself to be infallible. Still, that said, if these two were lying they were doing a good job of it.
I rummaged in my bag for a clasp knife, intending to cut one of the zip ties in an act of good faith. It wasn't there. I reached into my pocket for my cigar torch. It, too, was absent.
'Well, that's embarrassing. I was going to cut you loose . . .'
'Are you looking for this?'
Smit held my knife in the palm of his hand. The hand that I had believed was zip-tied. Delia had said Smit was a pick-pocket and close-up magic con artist. While we'd struggled, the son of a bitch had picked my pockets and then had cut his restraints.
'Also I have your lighter. And your wallet. And your phone.' He shrugged as if embarrassed. 'Also, I looked at your iden-tification and you are not Dennis Lehane.'
How many times have I seen that exact phrase in a review of one of my books?
I looked at Smit with new respect. I wasn't angry, I appre-ciate technique. 'You're good.'
'Thank you. I worked very hard to perfect certain techniques.'

I nodded. 'Me too. You know, as a writer. But we're still left with the question of what the fuck is going on with you two.'

Madalena took up the story. 'After my father he came out from prison he was a change man. I have always known that he buy and sell stolen things. Yes?'

'Yes,' I said.

'But in prison he became . . . involved! Yes, involved with bad men. They made him to sneak – that is the word? Sneak? Yes, he sneak drugs in for them. If he refuse they beat him.'

I nodded, genuinely sympathetic. 'Prison can be tough.' Which is why I try so hard to avoid it.

'He was broken, you understand. He was not the father I had known since a baby. They break him.' She tapped her too-young-for-me-to-ogle chest. 'Here. Inside.'

She looked sad. Not a girl who hated daddy, a girl who was worried for daddy and worried what he might inadvertently do to her.

I nodded. I knew what she was talking about. There's tough on the outside, and then there's tough in the joint, and that second one is a whole lot harder to pull off.

'They make him to buy and sell for a gang. Those people, like you say attack you. Skinheads. Nazi pigs. They make him to steal this gold Hitler from a man in Valencia. So my father finds a man to steal it. The skinheads say OK, give it to us now, and my father says no, because I must pay the thief who got it and where is the money for that, so he does not give them the gold and they threaten and I find the statue in his office, yes?'

'Sure.'

'And I am Antifa. You know this word? It is an American word, is it not?'

'You're anti-fascist.'

'Yes, of course.'

Smit nodded agreement. He was also opposed to *tangential Nazis*.

'OK, you don't want these Nazis to have the statuette. But you also don't want them trying to take it from your father, so you took it.'

'Also the thief he is angry.'

I'll bet he is. I'd be mad as hell if I went to the trouble of stealing seventy grand's worth of statuette and ended up being stiffed, I did not say. Instead I said, 'I imagine he would be.'

'So I take the Hitler. Because to melt it and then sell the gold and give the money to my father for the thief.'

'Got it. You want to melt the thing down so the Nazi assholes don't get it, and you want to give the cash to your dad to buy off the thief. You figure this plan takes care of everyone. But the Nazis found out and told your dad if he didn't stop you, they'd hurt him or you or both. It's not about the gold for them, it's about the Hitler.'

Madalena shrugged. 'They are very stupid. There is a legend, a story, yes? A story that their *Führer* will come back to life if this gold Hitler is returned to Salzburg.'

'That is in Austria,' Smit interjected, assuming as all Europeans do that Americans know nothing of geography. Generally a smart assumption.

'Yes, I've been. Why Salzburg?'

'Because it is Hitler's birthplace.'

'Ah.' I rolled my eyes. 'Of course, they can't actually believe that. I mean, granted these wannabe brownshirts are proof that evolution has a reverse gear, but they aren't complete imbeciles.'

'Some know better, many others do not and are easily led,' Smit said. 'They can perhaps be convinced to rally to a person who has such a sacred object.'

'So this gold Hitler is a piece of the True Cross?'

I didn't expect either of them to get the reference but both nodded solemnly, in unison.

'All right, so in this scenario, if I pretend to believe you, old Azevedo is getting squeezed hard. And you think your own father would give you up?'

Madalena shrugged. 'I have also a brother and a sister. I am sure they promise him not to hurt me just take the golden Hitler.'

'If he's doing that, why send me to find you?'

'Because as you said, these skinheads are not intelligent.

They did not find us.' Smit looked down, unwilling to give offense. 'You did. They must have followed you. They beat you to discourage you from further interest in us.'

A very clear memory rose to my consciousness, the image of skinhead-looking dudes at the Rock Cave Bar. They'd known enough to look for Smit there and must have seen me following him. They must have thought I had made contact, perhaps suspected I had the gold statuette and beat me down to search for it.

I had been followed. I had ridden a bike and yet I had somehow been followed. That realization did nothing for my self-confidence.

'Where is this gold Hitler now?' I asked.

Neither of them liked that question. Four eyes narrowed suspiciously and Madalena muttered, '*Vai pentear macacos*,' which I intuited was Portuguese for 'go suck eggs'.

'Ah, so that's the heavy object in your bag.' Not rocket science figuring that out.

'You will not tell my father?' Madalena asked and clutched her bag.

'I won't tell your father unless you bullshit me. If you're straight with me, and you really are afraid of him being, um, indiscreet . . . Look, I am not in the business of setting people up.' My mind was searching for ways to exploit the situation, but I had just enough IQ left over to consider how I was going to keep these two idiot idealists safe, what with having led skinheads to their door. That the skinheads had jumped me on my way back without promptly kicking in Madalena and Milan's apartment door suggested they didn't have the exact apartment number. 'First things first, if skinheads know your location you need a change of location.'

Smit made a helpless, ashamed look. 'We have no money.'

'Of course not,' I muttered. I pulled out my phone and opened the Expedia app. 'You know the hotel Amrath? It's a gloomy old monstrosity, but it's better than it looks. I know you've got aliases, Smit, do you have ID to go with any of those aliases?'

He did. I booked him a room. It was €313 a night. I was beginning to wonder if Delia had a secret plan not to arrest me but to bankrupt me. But these two were my problem, not hers.

'If you spend more than a hundred euros a day on room service, I'll hand you over to the bad guys personally, you hear me?'

Madalena and Milan both nodded.

'You're covered for a week. Take your gold Hitler with you, put it in a locked box of some sort and give it to the front desk to hold in their safe.'

'No,' Madalena said, eyes alight with an idea as she re-assessed me and, like so many of her insufficiently cynical sex, decided I was basically a good guy. 'You must take it and keep it safe.'

'No, no, that's fine, I don't really want a gold Hitler. It's not even my birthday.'

'My father he trust you,' Madalena said.

'The man you say was broken in prison and agreed to steal the goddamned thing and then set you up? That's whose judgment you're relying on?'

But she was ignoring me and opening her backpack. I knew what was coming. And there it was.

It was about the size of a large apple, an apple with a mustache that had gone completely out of style right around 1945. The gold looked sweaty. The features were not chiseled to a Michelangelo level, but it was competent work.

What do you say when someone hands you a gold Hitler? What I wanted to say was, 'keep the fucking thing'. But my recently re-awakened criminal instincts were tickling the back of my neck hinting at some potential use. Also it goes against my nature not to take gold. So I hefted the weight of the thing in my hand, looked into *der Führer*'s iris-less eyes and surprised myself and them by laughing.

'Will you melt it, please?' Madalena pleaded. 'When it is destroyed we will be safe.'

'Kid, the melting point of gold is north of a thousand degrees C, and my AirBnB does not come with a forge.'

I turned it, looked at the profile, the fanatic's brow, the iron determination indistinguishable from invincible stupidity.

'We would be very grateful if . . .' Milan said.

'Yeah? Well, I may have a way for you to repay my generosity,' I said. 'And who knows, I may just have a use for Hitler. But if you want my help, let's make something crystal clear.'

'What?'

'You two belong to me. You'll do what I ask, when I ask, and you'll damn well do it properly.'

FOURTEEN

I dropped my new pals off at the Amrath, returned the rental car and grabbed a taxi back to the apartment with gold Hitler in my bag.

When I got home I was surprised to find the place empty. No Chante. The door to her room was open – mostly – so I peeked in and no, she wasn't there, either, which was good because Chante's bathroom toilet had a cistern while the master toilet (to coin a phrase) was plumbed into the wall.

I flitted into Chante's room, went to her bathroom, lifted the toilet tank's lid. Ah, the memories. Toilet lids were my madeleines, I'd sort of killed a guy with a toilet lid once. It had been self-defense and the guy was a scumbag, but it was the only time I'd taken a life, ruining my proud zero-homicides record. I had to fiddle around a bit to get Hitler properly situated in such a way that he would not obstruct the flushing mechanism.

'*Sieg heil*, little buddy, you just sit right there.'

I replaced the lid. Each time Chante flushed, Hitler would displace and therefore save a good cup or so of clean water, making me something of an eco-warrior. Saving endangered penguins, one cup of Hitler water at a time.

I listened for Chante, heard nothing and passed quickly through her room.

And then I stopped.

Her laptop was open. She had a caffeine app turned on and had not manually re-set the power-down timer. No password required.

Just a glance, I promised the wonderfully tolerant God to whom I make such promises, just a glance. Occupying most of the screen was an open email. An email from *Nouvelle Revue Française*, the French equivalent to the *New Yorker*, perhaps. In any event the kind of literary magazine that openly despised genre writers like me.

It was a rejection letter.

I read halfway through before realizing that fact – my French is fine, but lacks nuance. I read it again from the beginning.

'I'll be damned,' I muttered. There was a short story attached. I forwarded the email and attachment to one of my email addresses, then hid my tracks.

I went to my room, closed the door, and opened the email. As rejection letters go, it wasn't awful. For one thing, it wasn't just a form letter; an editor had taken a few minutes to respond. He was encouraging, but not very. There was a suggestion that Chante needed more years on her, more maturity.

'Don't read the story,' I ordered myself even as I opened the attachment. And read it. Of course I read it, I'm just me, not some better man.

It probably wasn't ready for the *Nouvelle Revue Française*, though I wasn't sufficiently qualified in French to judge the prose to a very high standard. But Chante had put some heart into her story. She'd developed at least one interesting character and a couple of thin but competently detailed supporting players. The plot was meh, and it was a good two pages too long, but she was decent. Decent enough to someday be good. She had talent.

I didn't quite know how to process this revelation. I'd always known Chante was intelligent – she was too evil to be stupid. And I'd known she could cook and had a good singing voice but, well, come to think of it, I knew very little else about her. Her dad was Algerian and she was raised in Bayonne and she liked girls more than boys, which was sensible, so did I.

An aspiring writer. In my apartment. In my life. It was horrifying, really, because in all the world there are three groups of humans toward whom I have some fellow feeling: waiters, crooks and writers. I preferred Chante as a simple object of irritation and useful scapegoat, and I didn't want to have to start thinking of her as an actual human being.

I dropped the email in the trash and emptied the trash. I never wanted her to know that I knew. As much as I disliked the girl, Chante was not a mark and even by my moral stand-ards (rated five stars for flexibility) it had been uncool to creep her email. I knew things about her that she didn't know I knew, and that power imbalance was a result of my bad behavior. So . . . wrong, I guessed. Almost definitely *wrong*.

No wonder people never get anything done: trying to figure out right and wrong is exhausting.

I'd long ago realized that my mind works differently. I think in straight lines. There's where I am, Point A, and there's where I want to be, Point Z. I do the math, calculate the shortest distance between those two points, and act accordingly.

Normal people don't seem to do that; they think they do, but they don't. Half the time they can't figure out either A or Z, and if they get that far they then spend enormous energies turning the bright, clear line into a game of Snakes and Ladders, wandering this way and that, trying to parse their own desires, the opinions of their friends and society at large, what would Jesus do, what would Oprah do, what would the parents think . . . It's crazy. Find Point A, find Point Z, whip out your Sharpie and draw a line between them. Then, if you insist, you can consider secondary questions. But first: draw the line. Solution first, rationalizations later, for if you happen to get caught.

But that's me, and I have honestly begun to question whether I am entirely all right in the head.

I left the apartment, grateful that Chante had not returned, and went for a walk, trending vaguely toward Centraal. I had a new toy, a new capability of the human kind, and if Willy Pete was around, I intended to test it.

And there he was, the clever boy, back in his unconvincing Jesus Hippie Rasta gear: Willy Pete. He was on a bench aimed toward the canal, not like he was looking at me, nope.

I texted Smit at the Amrath.

Let's see how good you are. There's a pocket I need picked.

The Amrath is a stone's throw from Amsterdam Centraal and Smit responded quickly, eagerly even. He practically ran out the front door, possibly wishing to be helpful, possibly just desperate to get out of the hotel. Like I said, the Amrath is nice, but it's also the place you'd expect to find Dracula if he were vacationing in Amsterdam.

I did a shop window pause and confirmed that Willy Pete was tracking me, a block back.

Smit spotted me, I spotted him and I texted.

Walk past me.

He did.

See the white hippie dude?

He did.

I want to know who he is. ID. Credit cards. Careful: he might be dangerous.

We were three seemingly unconnected points on a map, Willy the Jesus Hippie, Smit and me. My shadow was behind me, Milan was walking purposefully past, and I was turning south for Prins Hendrikkade.

My shadow plowed right into Milan who did an excellent job of being knocked on his rear end.

I slid into a Chinese restaurant, walked straight toward the restrooms, located the back door and exited into a courtyard rather than an alleyway. Here I faced three doors, two closed, one open. Two weary, greasy-looking cooks from an adjoining restaurant were catching a smoke.

'Do you mind if I take a shortcut?' I asked, and the twenty-euro note in my hand added weight to my request. Through the kitchen drenched in the aromas of curry and turmeric, through the half-filled dining room, and out the door onto Geldersekade (Gchelder-seh-kawduh). I beelined for Amsterdam Centraal yet again, time running short and confident that I was no longer being followed. Then my phone dinged. It was Milan. Starbucks has successfully invaded Centraal, so I dropped in there and took a table.

Smit: *The hippie is American. Edward Fabruzzi. Virginia driving license.*

Smit typed out the home address and date of birth.

Me: *Anything else?*

A photograph popped up in the text feed. A photo of credit cards arrayed up Smit's arm.

Me: *Well done. Order yourself some room service Champagne.*

I was not concerned that Jesus Hippie wasn't carrying ID for Carl Willard, Willy Pete's true name, of course he'd be using an alias. But why a Virginia license? I Google-Mapped the home address on the license and checked Street View. The address was for a fifties-era bungalow in McLean, Virginia, a town which had absorbed another town. That second town being Langley.

Langley, Virginia, an innocent-sounding place unless you knew that it was home to the CIA, and not the Culinary Institute of America CIA.

I ran a real estate search on the property address. Until 1982 it had belonged to its original owner. Then it had been bought up by a corporation that looked an awful lot like a shell company: Libertree Holdings, a Bahamas-based corporation about which Google knew nothing more.

An Agency mail drop and/or safe house.

I've often sneered at Hollywood's insistence that there exist super-hackers who invariably live in some darkened basement surrounded by glowing monitors and *Star Wars* action figures and can, with a few taps on a keyboard, casually hack anyone. Those people do not exist. What does exist, and in abundance, are guys who have access to credit records. I forwarded the picture of Willy's credit cards to one such person along with the enticement: *500 $$$ if you have it in 20 minutes.*

I stood in line to order coffee and by the time it was ready, so was my source. It hadn't taken him five minutes and my email lit up with charge-card spreadsheets. I scanned the list and had to laugh. On the first card, a Visa, was a Netflix account, the $9.95 paid out monthly, just like clockwork. And nothing else over the last eighteen months, then a flurry of charges first at Heathrow, then at Schiphol, and finally various restaurants and bars in Amsterdam.

And, my, oh my, a hotel charge for the Ibis hotel out near Schiphol. I mapped it. Not just near the airport, about as near as you can get to the meeting of the A4, the A9 and the A10 highways. Easy to get to Schiphol, easy to hop on a freeway and scoot for Belgium or Germany. I approved of the tradecraft. But it was also a tell because of what it was *not* near: the port or the train station. The Ontario Crew were planning exfiltration by vehicle or possibly plane, but most likely vehicle, which suggested they intended once they made the grab to drive it from the Rijksmuseum south. I doubted they intended to really stop in at the hotel on their way, but they would want some place to switch cars, a place where they could leave a vehicle parked for a few days without attracting attention.

I texted back to my credit-bureau guy: *Got a bank account for him?*

He did. An account under the Fabruzzi alias with nine hundred dollars and change in it.

A Portuguese dude who'd done me a solid.
Two fools with a Hitler statue.
Some tangential Nazis.
Two Dutch cops.
A 'friendly' FBI agent who knew things she shouldn't.
A gang of professional thieves.
A lunatic trying to kill me for money.
A dying arms dealer in Las Vegas hung up on legacy.
And now the CI fucking A?

And I was going to do a panel and in my spare time steal a Vermeer from the Rijksmuseum and achieve true, criminal art?

Insane. Pulling off a robbery when the local cops already had you on their radar? That was crazy. Pulling off a robbery when an ex-special forces dude with a possible connection to the CIA wanted to steal the same thing you were trying to steal? On the scale of stupid ideas, it was a good eight or nine on a ten-point scale.

On the other hand . . .

On the other hand, what if I pulled it off? What if I pulled it off despite Dutch cops and Willy Pete and Hangwoman and Tangential Nazis and maybe even the CIA?

This was hubris of the worst sort, so I corrected with a dose of paranoia. If Delia had freelance watchers on me, and those watchers occasionally did freelance work for the CIA as well as the FBI, did that mean Delia and Willy Pete were working together? No, even my paranoid lizard brain wasn't buying that. The obvious answer was that a certain group of dudes were for rent. They probably worked as private investigators or bodyguards or security people the rest of the time and picked up one-off freelance gigs.

You didn't keep the freelance muscle job if you forgot who you were working for. If Delia had watchers (she totally did) they'd be discreet at the very least. Which did not mean they wouldn't chat among themselves, but probably within certain professional limits.

I was thirty-six hours out from D-Day, at another go or no-go fork in the road. I had my flash mob and props. I had my toys either in hand or en route. I had my disguises. I had my accounts and my web portals. I would soon have my wheelchair. Ian and I would manage the DIY . . .

'Who are you kidding?' I asked myself. 'You know you're doing it.'

FIFTEEN

Chante got back to the apartment about the same time I did, not looking exactly traumatized by her literary rejection, but distracted, maybe a bit down.

'Hey, Chante,' I said.

'Mitre.'

'Have you seen Delia?'

'No.'

'So . . . were you out on a date?'

'Is my personal life your concern?'

That was just about what I expected from Chante and it went some way to soothing my guilty feelings for having read her story. But then she sagged into an easy chair and shook her head. She looked sad. Not angry or contemptuous, her two default emotions, just sad. And a bit bereft.

'Drink?'

She nodded. I poured us each a Scotch and handed her a glass. Her movement to take the glass was sloppy and I realized this would not be her first drink of the evening. Chante wasn't tired, she was drunk. Good and drunk. I'd never seen her impaired, it seemed odd, unlikely, out of character for a control freak.

I sat opposite her, feeling awkward, feeling that anything I said or did would be wrong. Also, I'm wary of sad drunks, they tend to reveal things they later regret. I'd once had a guy named Sergei – a friend of a friend, actually – kick in my front door, raging drunk and try to beat me up. But in the act of kicking in the door his leg had gone all the way through and a bit of sharp metal had cut an artery.

Sergei had barely survived, and only did so because I applied pressure to the wound and called for an ambulance. Later, at the hospital, he had summoned me to what he believed was to be his deathbed. And he'd babbled on at length, weeping about how he was jealous of me because I was young and clever and had my whole future, and so on, me dreading every word because I was pretty sure when he sobered up, he'd be extra motivated to kill me.

I doubted Chante was up for murder, but I did not want her spilling her guts and then feeling a regretful need to spill mine. And yet . . . the fact that she *wrote*, the fact that she aspired, that she had some talent . . . I was curious about her in a way she had effectively discouraged before.

'Bad day?' I asked.

Silence. More silence. Then, as I was ready to give up, 'It is not one day but the injustice of the world.'

It's especially funny when drunk Frogs try to speak English. *Eet eez nut ze day but l'anh-joo-STEECE du monde entier!*

'OK.' It was the world's fault she'd been rejected. Fair enough, I'd felt the same way many times with equal lack of logic. 'Yeah, the world is unjust. But . . .' I knew the instant I added that 'but' I'd made a mistake.

Chante's eyes flashed, and as proof that she was drunk her gaze actually focused on me. 'But? Do you have some great wisdom to tell me? Mr Thief?' Just as I'd known I shouldn't say, 'but,' she knew she shouldn't have said that last bit. She waved an apologetic hand. She's French, she could carry on a whole conversation with hand-waves and shrugs.

It shouldn't have bothered me, but it did. It was true but no one likes having their entire life reduced to a previous career. Well, maybe some of the minor *Star Wars* actors selling their autographs for twenty-five bucks.

'Yeah, this thief does have some advice, actually.' I set my glass aside, a signal of seriousness. 'Yes, the world is unjust. There are three ways to react to that. You can be a fucking victim and whine till death finally shuts you up.' I probably should have softened that. But I didn't and Chante didn't spontaneously combust, so I pushed bravely ahead.

'Or you can become a crusader who is going to make the unjust world just. Delia would be the obvious example. Or you can say, "Oh, so the system is rigged, is it? Unfair, is it?"' I leaned forward and she did not recoil. She was actually listening. 'And you can realize the injustice of the world justifies doing what you need to do to get what you want. The world cheats? Well, so do I. So you need to ask yourself which you are. You going to whine, fight back, or with a clear conscience milk that unjust bitch of a system for all you can?'

'What I want cannot be stolen.'

'Crime is not the only way to work the system. But it works as a metaphor. You see a wall, right? You go over or around or under it. You see a lock, you pick it or you kick it in. Use everything. Use everyone. That doesn't mean hurt them, but yeah, you use people.'

For instance, despite being a person you despise, your employer knows one or two things about getting published. And better yet he knows a literary agent in London whose heiress wife doesn't know about his mistresses. Plural. I didn't say any of that, I couldn't.

Also the speech I'd just delivered was cribbed from some dialog I wrote for a serial killer in my second book, but fortunately Chante didn't read my stuff. Irony noted. But halfway through delivering it, I realized I was sincere. I was actually trying to help Chante.

Like I said: waiters, crooks and writers. Chante was a writer. One of my people, my tribe.

Tick-tock, no time to spend worrying about Chante's literary future. I had a heist to pull off and I had not yet dealt with the Hangwoman and her Hangfriend with the computer.

I texted Ian.

Me: *remember when I said we wouldn't be appearing together? I lied. Tomorrow will be a long day.*

SIXTEEN

The time I'd set was eight a.m. and Ian was no happier about the hour than I was, despite the fact that I had brought coffee.

'I was barely asleep, Jimmy, and I'm not a hundred percent, I'll be honest with you.'

'You're not here to be the mastermind, Ian, I just need muscle.'

'And where are we exactly?'

'See that window up there? A crazy woman who is trying to kill me, and her equally crazy boyfriend, are in that apartment. We are going to have a conversation. Did you bring something by way of a weapon?'

He was not dressed as a priest, thankfully, but looked exactly like an Irishman who'd stopped drinking just a few hours prior and had not had time to shower or shave.

Ian held his left arm out at an angle and a short crowbar slid from the sleeve of his jacket into his hand.

'Nice. But you don't use it unless I tell you to.'

'Right.'

'Ian? Look me in the eyes. Not unless I tell you to.'

He sighed, a bit disappointed. 'It's your caper, Jimmy.'

'All right then. And your name is Frank. You have the balaclava I told you to get?'

He pulled the knitted object from his coat pocket.

'Good.'

We waited a while on the street, me smoking a cigar, him with a cig, because loitering draws attention but loitering with tobacco is self-explanatory. My messenger bag was heavy and I shifted it from shoulder to shoulder. We waited twenty minutes before someone came out of the building and I was able to grab the door before it shut again.

Up the stairs we trotted, right to Hangpeople's door.

'Got that crowbar?' I asked.

'We're not going to knock, then?' This delighted him, the crazy bastard. He fitted the sharp edge of the crowbar in place, right beside the lock. When he was ready he nodded.

'Now put on the balaclava, Frank.'

'Frank? Oh, right!'

'You take the guy and put him on the ground, hopefully still conscious. Can you do that?'

'*Pff.*'

'OK, and I take the woman.'

'Aye aye, captain!'

I was honestly more afraid of Ian than of the two bargain-bin assassins in the apartment.

'Go,' I said.

Ian pulled back hard on the crowbar and the jamb splintered. A kick knocked the door all the way back and we were in like SWAT.

Hangwoman was at the breakfast table, dressed in a gown and eating muesli. She didn't have time to scream before I was on her. She tried to fend me off with an awkward cross-body punch but I moved behind her, leaned the weight of my left forearm down hard on her shoulders and clamped my right hand over her mouth. She was pinned in her chair.

Her male companion could be heard singing in the shower. Ian raised a brow and I nodded.

In Ian went, smiling happily. There came the sound of water, the sound of a glass shower panel swung back too enthusiastically, a male yelp, and in seconds Ian dragged a very wet, very naked, shampoo-lathered man out into the main room.

Ian tossed the man on the floor and when he tried to scrabble to his feet gave him a tap of crowbar on his shoulder blade.

'Stay down, boyo, stay down.'

To Hangwoman I said, 'If you scream I'll have my friend beat your boyfriend so badly he won't walk again. Is that clear?'

'He is not my boyfriend, fool, he is my brother.'

'OK, then, I'll have my partner beat your brother half to death. Better?'

She was a tough one, Hangwoman, I'll say that for her. She

was scared and she was furious, but she kept her cool and nodded. I let her go. She stood and cinched her robe tight.

'What are you doing, you stupid man?' Hangwoman demanded. 'You cannot do this!'

'And yet I just did.' To the man I said, 'Roll over. Let's see the front of you.'

'You want to see his penis?' Hangwoman said with all the scorn she could manage.

'Not especially, it's ink I'm after.'

And there it was on his right pectoral: the Wolfsangel which was a Viking rune used by the SS during World War II, rendered in red and blue ink. He had other tats as well, a 'T' for Trump, with accompanying nude Valkyries, a triskelion, some random death's heads . . . Definitely not a member of B'Nai B'rith.

'Well, well, the circle is squared. You're tangential Nazis.'

'Fuck you!' said Mr Naked.

'Right. Anything else you'd like to say?'

I whipped out my handy zip ties and attached Hangwoman to the chair she was sitting in, ankles and wrists. Then I squatted beside Ian and zip-tied the tat-betrayed, shirtless brown shirt's wrists together and one foot to the radiator, which I thoughtfully turned up to maximum.

Delia had once explained to me that torture was a moral evil, and I was sure she was right, but I was arguably just making sure the Nazi prick's foot dried properly. Also, he was a Nazi and really, how much courtesy was he due?

I was protecting him against athlete's foot, your honor.

'I don't suppose you're going to talk?' I asked Hangwoman.

She spat in my general direction, but even tough women get dry mouth when terrified. My second time to be spit at by this person.

'Gag them both. I'm going to see what the expensive computer gear in the bedroom is all about.'

'How do you ken what's in the bedroom?' Ian asked.

'Psychic powers, Frank.' I tapped my head and winked.

In the bedroom from which I'd fled only two days earlier, I found the desktop computer powered up but password protected. It had a standard keyboard so I tried the usual passwords, 1-1-1-1 and 0-0-0-0 and QWERTY and then another few before I hit on the obvious. No to ADOLF. No to ADOLFHITLER. Yes to 2041889 – Hitler's birthday, twentieth of April, 1889.

Twenty minutes later I was back in the main room, the radiator was hot, and the Naked Nazi was squirming and turning red in the face. Also the foot.

'OK,' I said. 'I have to admit. It's kind of a brilliant idea.'

'What's that, Jimmy?' Ian asked.

'You know what these assholes are doing? They've designed an app, a web app on Tor that puts up an encrypted kill list and offers a price, complete with helpful instructions on how to prove you've made your kill. It's Uber for murder. You want a guy dead, so you post his details. So and so lives at this address, here's a photo, and the price is ten thousand euros or whatever.'

'Why the fuck?'

I knelt down and pulled the gag from Naked Nazi's mouth. 'You want to explain?'

'Fuck you! Fuck you, Jew!'

I stuffed the kitchen towel back in his mouth. 'I'm not even Jewish, moron. At least I don't think I am.'

I stood up feeling quite pleased with myself. And impressed with the bizarre, unworkable in the long term, but otherwise interesting concept.

'See,' I explained for Ian's benefit, 'the big problem with getting away with murder is that most murders come with a motive. Pissed-off husband, jealous wife, greedy business partner, something. Something that ties the killer to the killed. Motive, means and opportunity, that's the holy trinity of conviction. But this way there's no motive. No connection. It's *Strangers on a Train*, but updated to the twenty-first century.'

Naked Nazi was grunting furiously and trying to get his naked sole away from the radiator. I took the gag from Hangwoman.

'Who put the hit on me?'

'Stupid man, you are still stupid! No one knows who posts the job!'

'Oh, fuck off with that.' I had to laugh. 'What's that, in

your terms of service? Here at Nazi Murder Uber we don't misuse data? Facebook basically does a proctology exam on its users, but you, no, no, you would never abuse data. Right, Eva Braun? You wouldn't keep a database of IP addresses and screen handles and bitcoin accounts, right? And you wouldn't compare screen names with screen names on Stormfront or whatever Nazi cesspool you favor. It's very inventive. Really. But it doesn't address my main question: why me?'

Ian had an actual idea. 'Maybe you're the showpiece. You know what I mean? The first kill, so they can show some success. The shill.'

'I'm the proof of concept?' It was not a stupid notion. Not at all. 'You know, Frank, I think you've put your finger on it. I'm just well-known enough that a bizarre murder involving me would make news. It'd be on the Google where anyone could see it. Proof of concept. But it doesn't entirely answer the question, because if I'm the proof of concept that leaves me wondering who's the beta tester who picked my name out of a hat?'

Nothing from either of my captives.

So far I didn't think giving Naked Nazi a hot foot would qualify as torture, exactly, certainly not under a certain previous administration's rules. I wondered whether the threat of real torture . . .

I pulled out my cigar torch. 'You know, my little skinhead friends, I once became so frustrated by a fellow's refusal to answer my questions that I was right on the edge,' I fired up the lighter, three jets of butane reaching an inch and a half, 'of burning his eyeballs out. I was only stopped – true story, by the way – by an FBI agent. And I don't see any FBI agents here, do you?'

From the floor came, 'We want *der goldene Führer*! Give us the *goldene Führer* and you will live. Or die!'

I felt the grin spread across my face. I was made happy by my own smile.

'The gold Hitler.'

'The gold Hitler?' Ian echoed, understandably confused.

'It's getting a bit stuffy,' I said to Ian. 'Would you mind turning the radiator off?'

It was obvious, now that I thought about it. Well, not the part about these two headcases, but the motivation. Azevedo, my Portuguese buddy, had leaked to the wrong people that Madalena had the gold Hitler and I was after Madalena. I suspected Azevedo had been persuaded by means rather more compelling than the old radiator hot foot.

Had he tried to warn Madalena? How? She'd dumped her phone. Had he tried to contact me to let me know Madalena had been targeted? No. Probably figured if I knew there was gold involved I'd take the damned thing myself.

I'd been targeted for death almost by accident. The Nazis wanted the statuette, Madalena had it and Azevedo had told them he'd asked me to find Madalena. But he'd have also told them what I did for a living back in the day. They'd drawn the cynical conclusion that if I found Madalena I'd take the sacred object, melt it down and bank the proceeds.

So, kill me as proof-of-concept for the Murder App, and ensure that I wouldn't be grabbing Mr Thousand-Year, er, Twelve-Year Reich.

'You do realize every intel agency on earth will be busy cracking the app, right? Half your customers will be law enforcement or spies.' Naked Nazi did not seem concerned. So I added, 'You won't keep that thing up and running more than six months.'

He looked smug, thinking I'd missed the real point.

'Uh-huh, thought so. You two assholes really are as bad as Facebook. See, Frank, it's the data they're after, that was the point from the start. They reveal the app on skinhead sites and right away some eager beavers sign up as wannabe killers. You increase your registrations by pulling off a moderately high-profile hit that goes unsolved. That'd be me. More people sign up. We get a few more actual murders then, a few months later the NSA or GCHQ take the whole thing down, the skinheads blame Jews or black people or whoever, but they keep a database of right-wing nut jobs ready to commit murder. I admit it: that is clever. They recruit an army of potential agents-in-place for whatever batshit plan they have in mind.'

'You don't say,' Ian did say, having nothing better to offer. 'Do me a favor, Frank. Hop on into the bedroom, and using your crowbar see if you can improve this asshole's computer. Once you've improved it enough you should be able to grab the hard drive. Bring that to me.'

As Ian gleefully smashed electronics in the other room, I took photographs of Naked Nazi and his sister, the Hangwoman. I took a selfie with her and surprised her with a kiss on the cheek. She spat, but too late. Then I fanned out a nice stack of euros on the table and played with the angle till I could get a shot of the woman and the money.

Ian returned with the hard drive. I slipped it in my pocket. 'Untie her, not him. If she moves give her a love tap.'

Then I set my bag down and drew out the object that had made it heavy and set it on the table.

I don't think Hangwoman even noticed that I was recording video, video that caught the bright light of fanatic's joy on her face, video that caught her reflexive reaction. Video that showed stacks of cash before her. She took the gold Hitler in her hands.

I stopped recording.

'No, no, no, you don't get to keep it.' I had to pry the damned thing from her. Like trying to get a piece of Christ's robe away from a leper. Like the thing was magic.

'Now, here's what *I've* got, my little storm troopers. I have pics and video of this asshole naked on the floor, obviously distressed. And I have you, you insane bitch, with money on the table in front of you, eighteen carat Adolf in your hands, and a selfie proving we're besties. Now, you may be able to convince your Nazi pals that it's all a frame. But you already have to explain why you failed to kill me, and why you lost the hard drive with maybe not the only, but certainly the latest, version of your app. So my guess is they'll shoot first, ask questions never.'

'You're going to let them live?' Ian was astonished.

'I don't murder people.'

'Well, I do if my life depends on it!'

'You're wearing a balaclava, Frank. Even if their Nazi pals buy their story they won't know who you are.'

'He knows you, Jimmy. And he knows you've got that.' Ian jerked his chin toward the statuette.

'I'm not too worried about it,' I said. 'I have the hard drive. And I have friends who will know what to do with it.'

My 'friends' the FBI. Life has a sense of humor.

SEVENTEEN

One day out. One day.

'I'm less concerned with vibration than with the light, that's the bigger issue.'

'Ah, is that so?' Ian nodded as if he understood, but he didn't. Fortunately he was much better than I with hand tools.

We were in Ian's rental apartment, cross-legged on the floor and surrounded by saw, drill, drill-bit set, hammer, mallet, sanding blocks, tubes of glue, black felt, sawdust and a video camera. A large plastic storage bin with a tight-fitting top was the easy part. Then we had to cut a platform or base that would fit snugly within the bin. The stand locking the camera in place was a nightmare but we (Ian) had figured it out. Then, recognizing that the camera and the small lights to either side might well not last a full twenty-four hours, we (Ian) had added batteries and wires and applied a soldering iron which only burned Ian twice.

Finally we had to place the print. I could not hope to replicate the look of the frame, so we were working on presenting the print in such a way that it looked less like paper and more like canvas that had been cut from a frame. In the end we went with simple thumbtacks and attached the print to a piece of plywood we took the better part of an hour just cutting to size.

Easily six hours of work all told, just for what I was calling 'the package'.

'This is why I don't own a home,' Ian muttered. 'All the mending and the fixing and plumbing and whatnot.'

'That, plus no one in his right mind would ever give you a mortgage.'

He laughed. 'True enough, Jimmy, true enough.'

In the end we had a camera fixed on a length of wood and pointed at a pinned-up print.

'Let's try it out.'

I opened my laptop and went through the inevitable hassle of getting technical objects to obey me, and then, finally, an image appeared on my laptop. Worked on my phone, too. Ian leaned over my shoulder.

'Not bad,' I said. 'But let's lower the resolution a notch on the camera. Fucking HD is too good.'

We adjusted and tried it again.

The image showed the print I'd made of Vermeer's *Jewess at the Loom*. We had a bit of an issue with the lights reflecting too much, despite the fact that I'd ordered a matte print.

'I have a trick that might work,' Ian said. He scrounged in his suitcase and came out with a pair of well-worn underpants. He cut small circles out of the thin seat then used rubber bands to cover the lights. We tried again.

'Huh. Well done, Ian.' The diffused light not only hid the shine, it had the unexpected effect of adding a sense of distance between camera and print. 'Shake it a little.'

Ian shook the plastic bin. On my laptop I saw slight vibration, but the focus held and more importantly so did the framing.

The metadata had been turned off so that observers wouldn't be able to figure out helpful things like the camera setting – we didn't want clever techies noticing that we'd lowered the resolution. Behind the camera and out of view were the batteries and the Wi-Fi signal booster. Everything was screwed or epoxied or soldered down.

'Well, that's done,' Ian announced. 'Time for a drink?'

I nodded. 'Definitely.'

He poured, which meant we were drinking Irish whiskey. I sipped and went over the latest, revised blow-by-blow again.

The smoke bomb
The speakers
The drone
The portfolio(s)
The flash mob
The hand-off
The boat(s)
The route
The panel
The first broadcast

The stream(s)
The accounts
It was hellishly complicated and there were numerous failure points. There were many ways for the forces of law enforcement to try at least to penetrate the con. That was one reason I had set a twelve-hour run time. It'd take hours at the very least to get the intel agencies interested, and even that was probably giving the law too much credit. But once a video went up online ten thousand Reddit users would be all over it, and they, the amateurs, were the greater threat.

I would steal the painting at five in the afternoon. By six we'd have the initial broadcast. At that time I intended to be in the green room at the Amsterdam Waterstones doing my humble author act for store personnel and getting ready to do some panel.

'OK, let's do another practice run with the drone,' I said.

'Let me get that vase down off the mantel first, eh?' Ian said. I'd so far flown the drone into a wall, the ceiling and the TV. I was getting better, but I wasn't there yet.

'Planning, preparation and practice, Ian. The three Ps. There's a reason I have zero convictions and never did anything more than two weeks in jail.'

Ian frowned. 'Is that true, Jimmy?'

'The only time I was ever behind bars for more than a few hours was an early bust. The fucking judge set the bail so high I couldn't get out. But other than that? Zero prosecutions, zero convictions, zero time.'

I could see Ian was impressed. 'All right then, Jimmy, let's go over it again.'

We did. We practiced and we repeated mnemonics, all strangely reminiscent of scenes from *The Dirty Dozen*. And we drank a bit, and it was probably that latter fact, combined with having successfully neutralized Hangwoman that led me to say, 'OK, but just an hour,' when Ian suggested that as a manly man he needed some time in the Red Light District. I would babysit him from whatever bar was conveniently nearby, and I made clear I was allowing for some hurried sex, not granting permission for a bender.

We went out into the night, both desperate for fresh air and movement after breathing epoxy fumes and sitting cross-legged on the floor. Two men of roughly the same height and weight, both white, both more or less the same age. The essential difference for any observer was Ian's longer hair, but we were both wearing knit caps against the chill and the damp, and because I was getting nervous as we rapidly approached D-Day and H-Hour and M-Minute, or however that goes, and didn't want to risk a chance recognition.

But I spotted no one who looked like a tail. No Willy, no Hangwoman, not even any rent-a-tail who might be working for Delia. I did spot a woman on a bike who reminded me of Sergeant DeKuyper, but I doubted the good sergeant would be following me around in the rain with a basket full of groceries.

I walked with Ian for a while as he browsed the offerings, always taking a moment to nod appreciatively or even make a small bow to the ladies who beckoned from their red-lit shop front windows. Irish charm, I suppose.

Eventually Ian found what he was looking for down an alley so narrow a Hemsworth's shoulders would have scraped both sides. And a hundred yards away and just around a corner was a bar where I could sit and sip beer in a slow stand-down from whisky levels of tipsiness.

I had located and co-opted M&M, Madalena and Milan. I had neutralized Hangwoman. I had the golden Hitler still, though I was baffled as to what to do with it. And the most worrying parts of my preparation for the Rijks job – the DIY – had worked out better than I'd feared. Sarip and DeKuyper were still out there, somewhere, and that remained a concern, but not a great concern. The beauty of the law is that it stops cops beating confessions out of you, and short of catching me in the act – a very unlikely possibility – the cops didn't worry me.

The big worry was Willy Pete and the Ontario Crew. They didn't quite know what role I was playing, but they knew enough to be concerned. But I was pretty familiar with Willy now and I didn't spot him.

Half an hour in Ian texted to say he'd done the nasty and was ready to go find a congenial bar. I didn't want that, obviously, so I left my current congenial bar and turned down the alley just as he was emerging from his tryst, bashful grin and all.

He was fifty feet away. I saw him and he saw me and I saw a well-dressed businessman seem to materialize out of the brick wall itself, and move with swift ease behind Ian as Ian opened his mouth to speak and the businessman wrapped one hand over Ian's forehead and pulled back.

Ian yelled, 'What the bloody—'

And a stiletto was at his throat.

I yelled, 'No!'

The hand holding the knife moved, pushing it point first exactly where a well-trained Special Forces soldier would know to stab it, right through the carotid. He pushed it in to the hilt. Then he shoved Ian's head forward, causing the blade tip to sink even deeper. A six-inch blade, I thought, six inches from the carotid to . . .

Ian's mouth opened in a noiseless scream and I saw a flash of the metal blade inside his mouth. The blade that went through Ian's carotid artery, through the soft palette of his mouth, and into his brain.

The killer heard me. Saw me for the first time.

Time froze. I stared at the 'businessman' and he stared at me. I saw the shock and chagrin on his face. He had the wrong guy.

The stiletto was meant for me.

He had not withdrawn the blade, not yet, so the full gusher of blood was delayed, but only delayed. Blood poured from Ian's mouth and drained down his throat.

Ian's jaw worked like a landed trout but no sound emerged. He looked at me, right at me, and I could not look away as I saw the baffled panic grow in his eyes. Ian raised one trembling hand and touched his neck, then held his hands in front of his eyes and saw his own death painted red on his fingers.

Jesus Hippie, aka Turtleneck and now the businessman, but always Willy Pete, had made a mistake. And now he hesitated fractionally, knowing no doubt that once he withdrew the blade Ian's carotid would pump his life away in seconds.

Ian's eyes pleaded with me, but there was nothing I could do. Nothing. Death had come for Ian. He was hemorrhaging in his brain and once Willy Pete pulled the plug it would be over very quickly.

What clever bon mot do you toss off to a man dying for the crime of wearing a similar stocking cap?

With a look of what might be regret, Willy Pete drew the blade out and Ian's carotid gurgled a quarter of a cup of blood per beat of his heart.

Beat . . . beat . . . beat . . . beat. One cup.

The average person has a gallon and a half of blood, that's twenty-four cups. It would take a minute and a half to empty Ian, but of course it wouldn't get to that point. Hearts stop pumping when you're dead.

Ian crumpled to the ground, his body going into spasm, the last dance as neurons fired in panic sending garbled messages to limbs able to do no more than jerk and kick. One foot hit an empty bottle and sent it rattling away.

Willy Pete, bloody knife in hand, measured the distance to me, wondering if he could still . . .

But this was face-to-face, not a sneak attack from the rear and he had no way of knowing just how bad I was at hand-to-hand combat. Then a woman's scream came bouncing off the narrow alley walls from behind me, a scream that would draw witnesses and police, and that was not in Willy's plan.

Willy Pete tried out his tough-guy look on me, like I needed to know he was a bad guy, like I might not understand the threat. Or maybe like I was going to try and play movie-star action hero. But I wasn't being brave standing there, unmoving, I was paralyzed by shock. Paralyzed as well by the sickening knowledge that Ian was dying for my sins.

I should have said something dramatic. *I'll kill you for that*, or its equivalent. But I didn't. For once in my verbose life, I had no words. I just stood there and watched a red puddle grow beneath Ian's slowly quieting body.

Then Willy Pete and I each took a step back. And another step. And another. And then, as if on cue we both turned and fled into the night.

EIGHTEEN

I walked fast, threading my way through the Red Light District crowd, Fugitive Vision turned up to maximum but despite that not really seeing anything but blurs. I was no longer dealing with some ludicrous Frau Goebbels wannabe, Willy Pete was a hardcore criminal with excellent training in the killing of humans.

I texted Delia.

Me: *Meet me.*

Delia: *It's late, see you in the morning.*

Me: *No. Now. And watch your back.*

The Ontario Crew had decided I was a threat. And like a fucking idiot I hadn't even considered that they might attack. I'd been so distracted by Hangwoman and Madalena and my own glorious plans that I had missed the threat. And now Ian was dead. Because of me, because of my lousy tradecraft, because of my failures of operational security. All my cocksure arrogance, my ever-so-superior understanding of all things criminal . . . I'd watched a man die knowing that it was supposed to be me gasping and falling and shitting my pants as my blood formed a shallow lake beneath me.

I was shaking. Trembling, I suppose is the more apt word. I was scared. You can act tough all you like but unless you're a psychopath murder rocks you. More so when you were the intended victim.

'Goddammit, Ian,' I said to the air. Should I apologize? Apologize to the spirit of the dead man? *Hey, ghost of Ian, sorry about that: my bad.*

This was two, two innocent people who had died because of me. The asshole in Cyprus who I'd banged with the lid of a toilet cistern, that was self-defense. It doesn't count if you kill a guy who's trying to kill you. For years I'd tried to convince myself that it also didn't count if some cuckold blew his brains out in a Bugatti. I hadn't pulled the trigger. I hadn't told him to do it. I'd slept with the man's wife and stolen some money that he could easily afford to lose, and he killed himself.

I had really tried not to put that on myself, I had deployed all my writer's imagination to mitigate the guilt, but trembling my way down an Amsterdam street, I was right back there at the moment when I'd heard about the suicide. I had confabulated, I had rationalized, and by God no one's better at bullshit, but lies are for other people, you tell yourself the truth. I had known the truth.

There wasn't even a way to spin this murder. Ian was in Amsterdam because of me. He'd been working for me. And he'd been stabbed to death, while I watched, *because of me*.

But even as all of that boiled within me, a far-off part of my mind, the eternally chilly part of me, my inner psychopath, was calculating the damage done to the Plan, the sacred Plan. *Could I still do it without Ian?*

Delia was just stepping out of the elevator as I plowed may way into the empty lobby of her hotel. I don't think I did a very good job of hiding my feelings because she took one look at me and went from *irritated woman* to *FBI Special Agent* in a heartbeat.

'What happened?'

'Guy just got killed. Willy Pete. I mean, he was the killer.'

There was no one nearby but a bored desk clerk to overhear, but I was being too loud and too careless and Delia at least still had her wits about her. She grabbed my arm and led me like a recalcitrant toddler into the elevator. We didn't speak. I looked at the floor and tried to assemble my scattered wits.

In Delia's room with the door locked I told her about bringing Ian in to help with some (unspecified) preparations. And told her about the killing. She had nothing to drink in her room and no mini-bar, which was not helpful, so I took it upon myself to call down to room service and order a bottle of Glenlivet – the best they had – and charge it to Delia, which was to say, the FBI and the American taxpayer.

'Did anyone see you?'

'Not well enough to make an ID. But there could have been

CCTV.' The whisky came. I poured myself the better part of a tumbler full and drank it down.

'Fuck!'

Delia let that outburst pass. 'The locals will make this their number one priority. Amsterdam isn't Chicago. They'll—'

She was talking, but not looking at me, probably hoping if she kept talking I wouldn't ask my next question, which was: 'Who have you got watching me?' She decided not to answer, but I wasn't having it. 'Goddam it, Delia, someone followed Hangwoman onto the train after Chante saw her boarding. Someone followed her home and told you, and someone managed to track me and . . . my guy. So can we drop the bullshit?' I was yelling. I didn't care. 'My guy just got murdered, Delia. Murdered, working for me as I was working for you, so honest to God, Delia, you fucking tell me the goddam truth, because if you had eyes on me, they had eyes on him, and I want to know where the piece of shit is!'

Delia and I had been standing. She quite still, me jumpy, pacing, using movement to burn off the adrenalin. Now she motioned to the one chair.

'Sit. You're driving me crazy.'

I sat. She sat on the edge of the bed. I refilled my glass. I wanted to cry. I just wanted to hang my stupid head and cry.

'All right, David, I'll go through this again. No one at the Bureau knows who you are. I made it clear that I had to do this alone.' She'd probably have stopped there but she saw a savage look in my eyes, sighed and went on. 'Once here I reached out for some contract help. Guys who'd worked for us in the past, freelancers.'

'Jesus Christ. Contractors, there's a weasel word if I ever heard one. Contractors. And hey, Delia, who else did the contractors work for?'

She swallowed nervously. 'I don't know.'

'The CIA? Delia, do these contractors of yours ever work for the fucking Agency?'

Long pause. 'It's possible. These kinds of people are usually ex-military or ex-intelligence, retired or moved on. You know.'

'Yeah, I know. Thing is, I had a look at Willy Pete's driver's license and credit cards. They track back to a place that sure looks like an Agency safe house or letter drop in McLean, Virginia.'

'How did you . . .' She waved a dismissive hand. 'Never mind.'

'The question is, how *didn't* you? You ran a background on Willy Pete, how come you didn't have him in McLean?'

Now it was Delia's turn to stand up and pace. 'We don't poke our noses into Agency business or the reverse.'

'Great. Great. Fucking brilliant. Contractors work for money not loyalty, and who has more cash to throw around, Delia, the FBI or the fucking CIA?'

I drank some more but when I closed my eyes I still saw a shiny blade going too slowly into bare flesh.

'I am so tired, Delia, just fucking tired.'

She sat beside me and put a hand on mine. 'I know, David.'

Now I really wanted to cry.

'Here's where we are,' I said after a while. 'The Ontario Crew and probably the CIA by extension know why you're here. They have figured out – not too hard to do – that I am your operative. They can't kill you, even the CIA doesn't kill FBI legats, but they can sure as hell kill me. The only question left is whether the Agency has already blown a big hole in my real identity.'

Delia didn't argue. There was nothing to argue about.

'Why would the Agency tolerate let alone support Daniel Isaac stealing art?' I asked, not expecting an answer.

Delia shrugged. I'd never seen her so on the defensive. 'Arms deals and the Agency go hand in hand. Over the years Isaa— US Person One – will have done favors. You know, like, we need to get some shoulder-fired missiles to this group in that country which we can't officially support. The weapons are delivered and the Agency owes US Person One a favor. Multiply that over decades. A lot of favors, a lot of investment in that relationship.'

'Not to mention what Isaac knows and could tell a Congressional committee or the *Washington Post*,' I interjected.

'Yes. That, too.'

'So the Agency did the math differently from you. They

decided it was best to let the crazy old man have his painting if he'd go *quietly* to the grave soon thereafter.'

There followed a period of silence, both of us in our own heads running scenarios. From the length of the silence it was clear neither of us had any brilliant ideas.

After a while Delia said, 'I can go to the embassy and talk to the resident . . . the local CIA chief. Maybe—'

'No,' I said. 'Don't trouble our friendly, neighborhood spooks. That's not going to be helpful with your career.'

'David, this is not about my career.'

'The hell it's not. I'm invested in your career, Delia. You know? As much as I'm not a fan of you showing up at random times to get me in trouble, you're the only Feeb I know. You are the only person on earth who I could call as a character witness if I'm ever popped. Not that I would, it's just . . . I don't know, D. Maybe I just need there to be one person who knows that . . .' I couldn't complete that sentence. It was too needy and vulnerable and all those things big, tough, macho guys like me don't do. Especially when we are already millimeters away from weeping.

Her expression was somewhere between gratified and worried.

Delia's brief physical contact was all that was allowed within the bounds of our relationship, so I didn't grab her and look deep into her eyes, but I did stand up and move close to her because I wanted to tell her something I needed to say that transcended whatever our official roles were within this odd quasi-friendship.

'Listen to me, FBI lady. I know what I am, and what you are, and we both know there's no good reason for you to trust me. But I trust you. And I am telling you, without anything to back it up, that in this, this one thing, you can trust me: I will always protect you. If I go down, if I get caught, I will not take you down with me.'

We had a lovely, unguarded moment, just the law enforcer and the lawbreaker, and I could have sworn there were tears in her eyes, but that must have been a trick of the lighting. I'm pretty sure the Bureau doesn't issue tear ducts to its agents.

And anyway, enough emotion. Enough self-pity. I wasn't

going to be scared off by some piece of shit like Willy Pete. Fuck him, fuck Isaac, fuck the CIA, fuck Sarip and Hangwoman and anyone else who wanted to hurt me. I was going to pull off a heist right under their noses.

But I had less than a full day now.

Tick-tock.

And the guy who was going to help me was dead in an alley.

I left Delia's hotel staying well clear of alleys, pulled out my phone and texted Milan and Madalena.

Hey M&M. Do either of you know how to operate a small boat?

NINETEEN

' I want to be absolutely straight with the two of you.'

Madalena Azevedo, Milan Smit and I were crammed together into the bathroom of their room at the Amrath hotel.

Why the bathroom? Because it was not near a window, and I had made sure that none of us was carrying, holding or wearing any device capable of recording, and because with the shower running the water would confound any listening device.

Paranoid? My guy Ian had eaten a stiletto. The Dutch forensics people were probably still examining his body.

I leaned against one wall, uncomfortable with a towel rack in my back. Madalena sat on the (closed) toilet seat. Milan was against the closed door.

'What is it you wish of us?' Madalena asked. Her English improved when she wasn't furiously cursing me.

I shook my head. 'I'm not going to give you the big picture because then you'd be culpable.' Puzzled looks. 'Then you would know what was going on which would mean you could be charged with being part of something worse than simply following orders I was paying you to follow. Understand?'

Slow nods. Milan's eyes narrowed.

'Paying?' Milan echoed.

I smiled. I drew an envelope from my pocket and handed it to Madalena. 'That is five thousand euros. That's yours. But if you do what I ask you to do, and if I am successful in executing my plan – a plan, I emphasize, that you know nothing about – the payoff won't be five thousand. It won't even be fifty thousand. I am putting you in some jeopardy and I don't use people without offering a substantial incentive.'

I let the suspense build and watched the looks flitting back and forth between M&M.

'If all goes as planned, if I succeed and you've done your

part, I will put a quarter of a million euros in an offshore bank account in your names.'

'A quarter of . . . two hundred and fifty thousand euros?' Milan didn't whistle appreciatively, but the whistle was implied.

'You could live for at least five years on that. Hell, if you decided to get out of Europe that would buy you a nice apartment somewhere with white beaches and water the temperature of a bath.'

'And what is it we must do for you?' Madalena demanded, suspicious girl.

'You, Madalena, must simply carry a mobile phone around to various tourist spots, starting around three p.m. The flower market, the homomonument, the A'Dam lookout. I have a list. You follow that list. At a specified time you will make phone calls to numbers I'll give you, businesses, just stay on the phone for at least a minute. Doesn't matter what you say, ask about their stock or whatever. Then, you'll meet me near the Waterstones bookstore – the specifics are on the list – and you'll give me back the phone. That's it.'

They both shifted uncomfortably, possibly because the humidity in the bathroom with the faucets going full-on was edging into the Mississippi range. But more likely because they could tell from the context that whatever was going on here it was some serious business.

'And the golden *Führer*?' Madalena asked.

'That object will meet with an unfortunate fate, I promise you that,' I said, putting on the smug expression I wear when I want someone to think I've figured everything out, but I haven't. Yet.

'And me?' Milan asked.

'You will get into a boat I've arranged for. You'll be at a spot I name and you'll catch a package I'll give you.'

'Is it drugs?'

'No. It will be a black nylon zippered art bag.'

I badly needed them to agree. I had lost Ian who was to perform Milan's part of the exercise, and I had nowhere else to turn aside from Chante, and I resisted that idea. I might not love Chante but she had never been in the life and these two had been. In the nineteenth century, the Royal Navy had impressed – legal kidnapping – men who had at any time earned a living from the sea and forced them to serve about his majesty's ships. In that analogy Chante had never made a living from crime. She was not in that brotherhood, Milan and Madalena were.

'And then?' Milan pressed.

'Then you will follow a path I'll lay out for you. There will be some switching of boats, some tying off in specific locations, and a bit of work with another phone.'

'And you won't tell us what this is about?'

'No. I'll only tell you that no one will be physically hurt. No one dies. It doesn't involve drugs or human trafficking. That's it.'

Madalena said, 'We must talk. Without you.'

'I'll step out.'

I exited the bathroom and stood staring, waiting and feeling helpless, in their hotel room. I could not hear words, just tones of voice. Those muffled tones told me that the answer was not an automatic 'no.' They weren't yelling. No, they were discussing the possibility of bargaining.

One of them knocked three times on the door and I went back in.

'OK,' Madalena said, speaking for both of them. 'But two hundred and fifty is not enough.'

'Oh? What would be enough?' That they might bargain for more money was not a surprise, it was a victory. I sternly avoided any sign of relief.

Madalena shrugged.

'OK, OK,' I said with a rueful sigh. 'I can go another fifty.'

In the end we settled on three hundred and fifty large. Not the kind of money Isaac was offering the Ontario Crew, but generous enough that I felt a little less bad about dragging them into this.

'But can we trust you?' Madalena demanded.

'Believe it or not, you can. But if you need more reassurance just remember: you're on the bottom of this totem pole, and when it comes to making deals with the police the bottom rolls over on the top, not the other way around. You know my name.' Well, kind of. 'I'm trusting you to do exactly what I ask. *Exactly.* I'm trusting you to take the money and never speak of me or this again. Ever.'

And that was largely true, dammit: they could burn David Mitre. But for a former prostitute and a low-rent conman they seemed sincere. And later when they realized what they'd been part of they would be quite happy to keep their mouths shut and spend the money.

Still. I didn't like it. Not even a little bit. But there it was, and when you have no choice you do what you have to do.

We spent the rest of the morning in that bathroom with the tile walls sweating, going over my lists again and again until they'd both become tired of the repetitions and could do it all by heart.

The lists themselves were a problem, but I gave them explicit instructions as to how to handle that. As each item was performed they were to tear off that part of the list and burn it or swallow it.

I was improvising. And hoping. And not liking it at all. If I were being sensible I'd call off the whole caper. But when has an artist ever been guided by good sense? Also: Willy Pete had killed my guy, I'd be damned if he was going to get his fifty million.

I felt weird, like I was floating untethered, and I couldn't tell whether I was flying or falling.

TWENTY

R-Day. As in 'R' for Rijksmuseum? Or should it be, V-Day, as in Vermeer? I woke up early with frayed nerves from a rapidly fading dream, sat in bed without so much as a cup of coffee and went over my plan. Again. This was the day when it would all work or all fail. I had lost my number two, my guy. Poor bastard Ian. Maybe there really was a heaven in which case I had no doubt that Ian would show up at the Pearly Gates dressed as a priest. Not sure if that would be helpful or not. Maybe St Peter had a sense of humor and a soft spot for losers.

My nerves settled as I went over the beats of the day's planned events. The plan was solid. The moving parts were moving – I opened a confirmation email from the flash mob folks. They had received their props and knew what to do.

I had all the toys I needed, all my purchases and my DIY package and my AirBnBs with their respective Wi-Fi access codes. I had my disguises and my toys and my wheelchair. I had the accounts and the shell companies. The audio I'd recorded with a voice synthesizer was edited and loaded up.

I'm usually calm going into a job – fear doesn't help. Nerves are fine, but only so long as they don't mutate into fear. What was the old Frank Herbert bit from *Dune*?

I must not fear. Fear is the mind-killer. Fear is the little-death that brings total obliteration.

Rather dramatic that, but true enough.

I put it out of my mind. No, that's a lie. I tried to put it out of my mind, but I'm a writer as well as other things, and writers tend to have excellent imaginations. There is nothing quite like a professional-grade imagination to find the worst possible outcomes to play over and over on the movie screen in your head.

Prison. Yes, that was not a good outcome. If I ever went in

I might never come back out. The Dutch would convict me, make me serve my time in the Netherlands, then extradite me to the States. In a very few hours I could be wearing handcuffs and frantically considering means of escape from prison.

Then there was the Ontario Crew. How long would it take them to discover that someone had beaten them to the Vermeer? Presumably they'd find out when everyone else did. And then what? They were salivating over a fifty-million-dollar payday and would not be happy at losing out.

The day was long and I had nothing to do. I tried to write but that was not happening. I tried to think about the Waterstones panel but why bother? Go-time was four thirty and I had nothing to do but fidget.

Until the doorbell rang.

In the catalog of sounds no fugitive is ever going to enjoy, an unexpected knock on the door was right up there with the sound of car doors slamming outside your home at night.

'Can you get that, Chante?' No answer. Of course.

So I walked on rubber legs and peeked through the peep-hole – quickly, because a person on the other side of the door can tell when someone is looking through a peephole and if that person was Willy Pete that peephole could be enlarged by a bullet passing through.

It was not Willy Pete. It was the other face I didn't want to see. I took a deep breath, let it out slowly, plastered on my befuddled half-smile, and opened the door.

'Lieutenant Sarip,' I said, frowning my surprise. 'I hope you've come with good news. Have you arrested the assholes who beat me up?'

'Mr Mitre. You will remember Sergeant DeKuyper.'

'Of course.'

'May we come in?'

'Sure, sure. Chante! Can you put some coffee on? Or would you prefer tea, Lieutenant and Sergeant?'

Chante emerged from her bedroom looking annoyed, took in the tableau and for once didn't argue but went to the kitchen to put the kettle on.

'My personal assistant,' I explained.

I sat. They sat. The coffee table separated us.

'I must confess we have not yet arrested your assailants,' Sarip said.

'Oh. Then . . .'

Sarip nodded at DeKuyper and she drew an iPad from her bag. She fiddled a bit as my blood slowly congealed in my arteries. Then she set the iPad on the table and there in full color, high definition, lay an Irishman soaking in his own blood.

I recoiled. 'Jesus! What is that? Is that . . . is that a dead person?'

Chante interrupted with a plate of cookies. 'Tea and coffee are coming.'

Sarip nodded at Chante and I saw a look of distaste on Chante's face. Good: she didn't like Sarip. Much better than if she'd taken a shine to him.

DeKuyper swiped to a second shot. Then a third, a grisly close-up.

I looked away, not needing to pretend distress. Ian looked so broken, so undignified with his legs splayed and his head sideways as if staring at his own life's blood. 'Why are you showing me this? What the hell, Lieutenant?'

'This man was stabbed – fatally – in De Wallen last night.'

'I'm sorry for his family but what the hell does it have to do with me?' Calculated, calibrated anger, even belligerence. That was the right play now.

'Do you recognize him?' DeKuyper asked and swiped to a close-up of Ian's face in a very different setting. In this shot he was framed against a stainless-steel table. This was a shot taken in the morgue.

'Recognize him? Is he someone famous?'

'Please take a close look, I know it is distressing,' Sarip said smoothly. 'But please, take a second look.'

He wanted to see my expression. He was looking for a reveal. Like I was an amateur. I screwed my face into a wince and with an expression full of disgust and growing anger, looked again at the face I knew.

'OK, again, I don't know that poor man. Why do you think I would? Is he an American? There are a lot of Americans in Amsterdam, are you questioning all of them?'

That brought an answering frown from Sarip and yes, even a hint of doubt. There's nothing quite like a non sequitur to short-circuit the linear cop brain. But he was a clever boy, my pal Martin Sarip, and he recovered quickly. 'It seems he is an Irish citizen. No current address. But fingerprint identification points to a long criminal record.'

'Uh-huh. Whatever. A criminal got stabbed. It was probably a drug deal gone bad.'

'Mmm. Perhaps.'

'I mean if it was one of my books, that's how I'd write it. Now would you mind putting that thing away? It's kind of early in the day to be looking at dead people, don't you think?'

Sarip flicked his cunning eyes sideways and DeKuyper complied, closing the iPad and slipping it back into her bag. *And round one goes to Mitre.*

Coffee came and we all added sugar or milk or in my case, nothing. No one ate a cookie. Chante hanged back in the kitchen ostentatiously wiping down the counter and the stovetop.

'In your books,' Sarip began again, 'Does your hero ever have hunches?'

I shrugged. 'Sure.'

'Well, I have a hunch.'

He wanted me to ask, but all I gave him was an expectantly raised brow.

'You see, like any city, Amsterdam has a certain pattern to crime. There's an ebb and a flow, but it's always the same things. Drugs, sex trafficking, drunk tourists getting into fights . . . But now in, what, eight, nine days, we have three very unusual crimes. Or, if you prefer, incidents. Incident one being your tumble into the canal.'

'OK . . .'

'Incident two, your regrettable assault.'

'Wait, you think the guys who beat me up did this?'

'Why would they?'

'How would I know?' I could play this game all day.

Sarip smiled and said nothing for an uncomfortably long time. So I ate a cookie. Finally he said, 'Ah, well, it is just a hunch.'

'Dude, I mean, Lieutenant, sorry, I don't understand any of this. I don't know what you're talking about. I don't mean to be rude – I'm a guest in your country – but I'm finding this awfully intrusive.'

Time for Sarip's last gambit. He drew out his phone, opened it, turned it to me and aimed a long shot of Delia at me. 'Do you know this woman?'

'Sure,' I said with impressive rapidity. If he was asking it was because he already knew we were connected. 'You could say we're dating.'

'And what do you know about her?'

'Whoa,' I said and held up a hand. 'Now you want to ask me about my friends? This is just not cool. I mean, really.'

'Would it surprise you to learn that she is an agent of the US Federal Bureau—'

'FBI. Yeah, FBI, of course I know. I met her when I was researching a book. But, not meaning to be unhelpful, Lieutenant and Sergeant, I am not going to answer any more questions unless you think I need a lawyer. Do I need a lawyer? I can call my embassy . . .'

And that was check. Not check*mate*, but definitely check. Two minutes later they were gone leaving behind the thick musk of suspicion. So, yeah, sadly, however this came out, I was definitely burned in Amsterdam.

'You are a very good liar,' Chante said when they'd left.

'Chante, I am the living, breathing god of bullshit.'

I checked the time. *Tick-tock*. Hours still to go and nothing for me to do. So I waited an hour then went out ostensibly to shop for food at the Albert Heijn. As I cruised the aisles and loaded my basket I looked for Willy Pete. And for any of Delia's contractors who might still be eyeballing me. I spotted neither. I did however spot none other than the sullen sergeant, filling a shopping cart. I pretended not to see her and not to know that she was following me. Fine, I could always lose a tail I'd spotted. Though, there was a tingling in the back of my head, one of those vague, unsettled feelings. A vague, unsettled feeling that involved DeKuyper and groceries.

But my never-well-concealed arrogance returned as I lost

her. Nice try, Sergeant. I had this. Even under Sarip and DeKuyper's nose, I had this.

At three thirty in the afternoon of a gray and drizzly day, I returned to the apartment, unloaded groceries and wine, and began to get ready for the caper that would make me a legend, or a guy in a prison jumpsuit.

It was time. Time to rob the Rijksmuseum.

TWENTY-ONE

I suited up and went out into the street beneath a very visible umbrella with a Van Gogh *Sunflowers* print. Impossible to miss.

I walked north, wandering this way and that before diving into a coffee shop just off the Nieuwendijk. I had scouted the place and knew the back door led to one of Amsterdam's hundreds of a tiny courtyards, and from there to an alley and by the time I emerged back into the light the umbrella and the hat I'd been wearing were gone, as was my down jacket.

That was a relief: I was wearing layers. Lots of layers. The day was chilly but I was dressed for Arctic conditions.

From there it was a thirty-second walk to an AirBnB with a coded lock. I let myself in and to my relief found the clothing I'd had Ian place there. I changed clothing yet again and exited by a back stair into a rather lovely pocket garden and from there through the back of a sandwich shop and out to the street again. Six blocks south, near the Rijks, a second AirBnB, this one in a building with a rickety elevator. In this AirBnB – very nice artwork, by the way, not worth stealing, but well-chosen – there was my motorized wheelchair and the rest of my necessaries.

Ian had been surprisingly efficient. He'd done well for me. *When a man's partner is killed, he's supposed to do something about it.* That's what Sam Spade said. Ian hadn't quite been my partner, but he had worked for me, and maybe I had an obligation. I wondered if he had a wife somewhere, maybe kids.

I loaded up my small backpack, slid various objects into various recesses of the wheelchair, double-checked batteries, then drove the wheelchair onto the elevator and motored my way out onto the Lijnbaansgracht, not a thousand feet from the Rijksmuseum. Down the street at a blistering three miles an hour, reminding myself not to move my legs, over the canal bridge, then over the Amstel, plowing heedlessly through crowds, head cranked to one side, drooling a little, playing the part, a stroked-out old fart in a chair with a plaid blanket over his paralyzed legs, impatient, probably in pain.

If there were eyes on me now I was screwed. Simple as that. I'd decided in light of his visit that my opponent in this game was Sarip. I had more enemies than Sarip, so many I had a hard time keeping track of them all, but if Delia had managed to call off her contractors then the essential foes were the Ontario Crew and Sarip. It can be useful to personify the enemy. The Ontario Crew wanted to kill me, but if it came down to who had more resources to devote to tracking me it had to be the cop. Was Sarip sufficiently convinced that I was a bad guy playing some nefarious game that he could justify a street surveillance team? I thought not. If he had a full team in action he'd not have used DeKuyper to watch me at the Albert Heijn.

I motored on toward the great Gothic-Renaissance mash-up of red brick and limestone and cloud-dimmed skylights. It was an impressive building from any angle, huge but not intimidating. I was struck by the notion that the architect had had a sense of humor. It was grand and imposing but at the same time gentle, almost self-mocking in the way it tossed styles together to create a sort of *Great British Bake Off* showstopper of a confection.

The ensemble in the Rijks's breezeway was reduced this day, just two violins and the balalaika, playing something melancholy that was probably Russian.

The guard at the entrance did a sort of slight bow, a recognition of my status as an old guy in a wheelchair, someone owed deference and an assumption of harmlessness.

I entered the atrium of the Rijks. In my head there was a score playing, music signifying heightened tension. But in truth I was less tense than I'd been in days. I was at work. On the job. It was too late to worry now, it was all about the plan.

Seen from above the Rijksmuseum is a squared-off figure eight. The holes in the '8' are two courtyards, the first serving as the main atrium and containing the café and gift shop; the other being a sculpture garden.

The exhibits are on four floors, including the bottom level which has some special collections, as well as the two courtyards. On the second floor (or first, if you're European) are artworks from the period 1700 to 1800. On the fourth floor is 1950 to 2000. The floor in-between was the one that mattered most to me – that's where the collection of pretties from 1600 to 1700 lived. I don't know what happened to 1800 to 1950.

Lying along the crossbar on the third floor (my floor) is the vast, ornate gorgeousness of the Gallery of Honor. This gallery stretches from Rembrandt's huge *Night Watch* at one end, to the Great Hall at the other, which actually is pretty great, with an amazing mosaic arched ceiling, and soaring stained-glass windows supposedly depicting various art being done by various men, with some women tossed in beneath as avatars of different schools of art. I didn't figure that out on my own, I'd had to read about it. Suffice to say that the Great Hall was a museum all by itself. The Gallery of Honor acts as the crossbar of our square '8', the other galleries extending in either direction, through a series of smaller interconnected rooms. So if you keep going you circle around to the other end of the Gallery of Honor. Right at the intersection of the Gallery of Honor and the Great Hall are big, wide stairs that lead between floors, as well as doors for toilets and identical smaller stairs, presumably for evacuations.

The Gallery of Honor was subdivided into eight open alcoves defined by partition walls, four on a side. *Jewess at the Loom* had been placed in the alcove second from the Great Hall, on the right if you were gazing toward the stained glass.

My path would go from that open side room in the Gallery of Honor, through the swinging glass doors into the Great Hall, right, into a line of narrower cubbies. At the end of the corridor I'd pull a U-turn into the excitingly named room 2.8.

Room 2.8 had a problem in that the only way out was back the way you came, but it had compensating virtues, among which were that the putty gray security doors were oversized for the wall and protruded a good two feet into the room. This had the effect of creating a small camera blind spot. It could create other possibilities as well.

The atrium is below street grade so that the cloakroom was more or less below me as I entered the museum. I descended via short elevator ride along with a Japanese family and motored my way along in what I'm certain was an offensive parody, and went for the men's room. In the privacy of a handicapped stall I opened my backpack and took out the coffee can that was my bomb. The bomb was a piquant blend of sugar and potassium nitrate, cooked together to form a sort of roux, which was then contained in aluminum foil. I'd worn myself out watching YouTube trying to figure out how to make a simple timed fuse, but Ian had made short work of it. He is . . . was . . . Irish. Ian had joked that bomb-making is in the national patrimony, so to speak.

Of course this bomb was not meant to explode. There would be very little fire and a whole hell of a lot of smoke. Hopefully. We had not had time to test it. If it failed to go off, or for some reason failed to generate enough smoke to look like a serious fire, I might well be trapped in the museum.

I opened my phone and checked the timer again. I was on schedule. *Tick-tock.*

I took the coat check receipt and surreptitiously tore the identifying number out and swallowed it, an inelegant, but effective way of destroying evidence. The remainder of the ticket I tore into little pieces and dropped in a bin.

I motored my way back to the elevator and waited patiently for it to come. An extraordinarily fat family of four – Americans, of course – loaded on with me, all of us crammed in together as the father sent me a greasy, apologetic smile. The door began to close and I saw two women rushing to make it and to my abject horror recognized one of them. It was the rumpy-pumpy woman from Tess's boat.

Jesus H. Christ, what were the odds? But my disguise worked to conceal my undoubted rumpy-pumpiness, so she never so much as glanced at me.

I got off on the third floor, the heart of the Rijksmuseum, all the goodies from 1600 to 1700, the high points of Dutch art, at least the Dutch art the Rijks hosted. The Van Gogh museum might have disagreed as to peak Dutch art.

I motored out of the elevator and into the Gallery of Honor, emerging just to the left of *The Night Watch*. There was as usual a decent crowd gaping at the massive thing – it's the size of a billboard – and gazed down the length of the room. Stairways behind me to my left and right, also restrooms. At the far end of the gallery there were also stairways and restrooms, and in-between about, oh, let's say a billion dollars' worth of art.

Mosaic arched ceiling, pink and green columns arrayed ahead defining the separate alcoves, long gray benches, polished blond wood floors, skylights full of gray and wet. I'd seen this view in the flesh twice, online dozens of times and in my imagination on countless occasions. This was my theater.

I did a discreet time check. The smoke bomb would ignite in 132 seconds.

Text to flash mob organizer: *How's it going?*

Quick response: *Just about to start.*

I pushed on the joystick and slid up next to one of the benches. I reached beneath my plaid lap blanket and pulled out a small Bluetooth speaker. The back of it was covered with the kind of two-sided tape used to hang wall hooks. I looked like I was playing with myself as I switched on the power: all to the good because if no one looks at old dudes in wheelchairs, even more does no one look at old dude in wheelchair possibly adjusting his colostomy bag.

The speaker was small enough to almost be concealed by my hand. I fiddled and stressed over the inexorable *tick-tock* until the be-blazered guard looked away. Then I slipped the speaker under the bench. Press, hold, hold, patience . . . Yes, it was stuck.

The smoke bomb would be going off any second now.

I motored down the length of the hall, past conspiring Batavians on my left and guys dressed like pilgrims on my right, both by Rembrandt. On I cruised, slaloming through the crowd, past landscapes and hunting scenes and paintings of ships by guys who would be household names, maybe, except for the overshadowing existence of Rembrandt.

I approached the third alcove on my right, the target. It was not a huge space, though stratospherically tall. The walls were battleship gray. There was a bench. There were wires stretched

at mid-calf height, not to stop anyone, just to remind you how
far back you should stay. There was some Pieter de Hooch on
the side walls, but it was all Johannes Vermeer on the back
wall, none of which I could see for the crowd gazing thoughtfully at *Jewess at the Loom*, nestled between *The Love Letter*
and *Woman Reading a Letter*.

My heart seemed to be about six inches higher in my
chest than usual, and it was beating heavy, heavy and slow
because I was in it now, it was about to go down; and on
the job my heart doesn't speed up, it slows. Or maybe time
itself slowed, because everything was moving through
molasses now.

A twenty-something couple in near-identical gray coats
shifted from left foot to right, synchronized. A toddler whined
and Mom reached a slow hand to touch the top of the little
girl's knit cap. Three elderly Japanese, two taking pictures,
the other, an old man with the hair-do popularized by Homer
Simpson, nodded to himself as if he'd seen something deep
and meaningful. Maybe he had.

I was at the back of the crowd of perhaps twenty-five people.
I advanced my chair a bit and a woman noticed and moved
aside to let me pass, smiling indulgently.

Down below, down in the cloakroom the timer would have
completed its circuit. The fuse would have been lit. The sugar
and nitrates would sputter and the first tendrils of smoke
would appear in the bag resting on shelves beside purses and
coats and hats. It would take a while, not long, but a while
for anyone to notice.

I forced myself to take long, slow, deep breaths.

This was the last second of time in which I could still bail
out.

I opened my phone.

I twisted around and drew from my pack a smallish
construction of white plastic and black rotors. Was anyone
watching me? I couldn't look, I just had to *do*. I slipped it
beneath my lap blanket.

I'd kept just far enough back from *Jewess at the Loom* that
I still had line of sight to the speaker I'd planted back near
the sacred *Night Watch*. My phone wouldn't reach that far

but it would reach the higher-power Bluetooth emitter I had epoxied to the bottom of my wheelchair.

Ready.

Last chance to back out. This was it.

Well, what the hell. I could survive prison. Right?

Play!

And it worked! A shrill, distorted, frankly crazed-sounding voice began ranting.

The Night Watch *glorifies fascism! It must be destroyed!*

A flicker went through the crowd. I mimed my own concern and said, 'It's terrorists!'

You cannot stop me! I will destroy it!

The guard leaned out of the alcove to see. Further back other guards were moving, slowly at first, then faster toward *The Night Watch.*

Rembrandt was an imperialist apologist!

Guards moved faster now, reinforcing each other in their concern that something was wrong, very wrong. My nearest guard hesitated. I yelled, 'I hope it's not someone slashing the painting!' And that did it: my proximate guard moved out of the alcove. The crowd followed, not all the way, just out of the alcove, curious but not determined, they just wanted to see what was happening.

The hour of reckoning has come! Death to Rembrandt!

Now came the move I had practiced probably two dozen times. The drone was under my blanket, whirring, lifting the blanket in what might have looked like an impressive erection. I switched to the drone's native app and threw back the blanket. The tiny rotors whirred and the drone rose into the air, then veered wildly down the length of the Gallery of Honor, just ten feet in the air, trailing a red ribbon to make it easier to spot. And the Bluetooth speaker shouted, *Drones are the tools of the oppressor made to do the work of Antifa!*

OK, not the most eloquent statement but baby, it worked, because now the Vermeer crowd was all looking away, and all at the same time. As the drone skimmed along the more ambitious or athletic folks tried to leap in the air and bat it down. So much the better: *look away, look away! Follow the drone! Listen to the crazy person's wild threats.*

Did anyone see that I had launched the drone? Three did, a bored teenaged boy and two of the elderly Japanese. And what were they going to do about it? Fuck-all, because they were not guards, just random civilians, and I was a crazy old man in a wheelchair.

I tapped the app and put the drone on hover. It hung in the air maybe twenty feet from *The Night Watch,* right where it could so easily dive right into the massive painting.

And this was the beauty part: the drone wouldn't have so much as knocked away a fleck of paint. It was a plastic toy, it weighed ounces not pounds, it moved at a few miles an hour, it was not a bullet. It was, in short, entirely harmless. And entirely captivating, especially to the eager heroes who leapt from atop benches in wild and awkward efforts to knock it down. Someone was going to break a leg and I wasn't even going to feel guilty. It's not my fault people are stupid.

I stood up. (A miracle! I can walk!) I took six steps, lifted my foot over the stretched wire, and laid my hands on the gilt frame of *Jewess at the Loom.*

I lifted it up off its hooks. It wasn't heavy. I rushed back to the wheelchair, laid the *Jewess* on my lap, and threw the blanket over it. It was not an effective disguise; it was pretty clear that something rectangular was under that plaid wool. But it was enough for my purpose.

'*Was machst du?*'

That was from a frowning, worried woman whose expression was somewhere between thinking I was a senile old fool and a suspicion that the fact that I'd leapt from the wheelchair after clearly launching a drone suggested that just maybe, just *maybe*, I was neither senile nor old. Certainly not crippled.

'It's OK,' I said to her in my best Voice of Authority. I drew a wallet from an inner pocket and flashed a print-off of a police ID I'd found online. It was an ID for Jim Gordon from the Gotham City police, but at a glance it looked official enough. 'Be calm. I'm with the police.'

Only a moron would buy that, but God bless the Germans, they will defer to authority.

I turned the wheelchair, pushed the joystick and sped away, out of the alcove, away from the embattled *Night Watch,* straight toward the swinging glass doors separating the Gallery of Honor and the Great Hall, and plowed right through them. Very Hollywood except for the low speed and total absence of shattering glass or explosions.

Behind me I heard the German woman switch to tentative, plaintive English. 'This man has taken a painting. Is this correct?' Given the state of things in the Gallery of Honor it would take her five minutes just to get anyone's attention.

Then, just ahead, a guard was rushing through the Great Hall toward the Gallery of Honor, which would bring him right by me. So I gave him my best panic face and shouted, 'I think there's a bomb! There's a bomb!'

The guard ran past, through the doors. In a few seconds he might click on the fact that I had something under my blanket but not yet he hadn't, not yet.

At top wheelchair speed – about eight miles an hour for this model – I raced through the Great Hall, past tourists who hadn't yet heard that something was going on. Benches and paintings to my right. Stained glass soaring above me on the left. Old man in a wheelchair, look out, step aside!

'Someone has attacked *The Night Watch*!' I cried, like Paul Revere yelling about the British coming. 'Terrorists!'

That sent the Great Hall crowd scurrying, some heading down the stairs to safety, others milling around and muttering, and still others running toward the Gallery of Honor while pulling their phones out to capture the excitement for their Instagram. This left zero people to chase me.

Three floors down, down at the basement level where the cloakroom was, the sugar and nitrates should be – had damn well *better* be – billowing smoke.

Because the thing was, all the automated security doors could be locked at the first sign of a robbery or vandalism . . . but you can't lock doors when there's a fire. Priority One: safely evacuate the building. There are countries where the security forces might make a decision to save the paintings and to hell with the lives of people breathing smoke, but the Netherlands was not one of those countries.

Nice Dutch people do not lock doors when there's fire.

If there was a fire.

I sped along, heedless, literally shoving people out of the
way and yelling, 'Someone's attacking *The Night Watch*!' and
the always popular, 'Fire! Fire!'

Past Frans Hals's portraits of a husband and a wife, the
man world-weary and not impressed, the woman staring
bleakly.

The next tiny alcove was empty of people and lacked security cameras. Perfect. I threw off the blanket, stood up again
and fumbled at hyper speed with the zippered, black nylon art
bag. I manhandled the *Jewess* into the second bag, the putty-
gray bag within the T-Mobile bag and walked on, leaving the
chair to block the narrow doorway behind me.

By now the Bluetooth speaker would have been discovered
and turned off. The drone, far beyond the reach of my control,
had probably been batted down and everyone in the Gallery
of Honor – with the exception of the German woman – would
be thinking it was all a tasteless prank or political stunt.
They'd be laughing nervously.

And, suddenly, like an answer to a prayer, the alarm blew,
loud ringing, in bursts. Fire!

Excellent!

Then I saw him. He was behind me, just beyond my
strategically parked wheelchair.

Willy Pete!

TWENTY-TWO

'Fuck!' I yelped, with singular lack of originality.

We made eye contact and that was a mistake because I could see mystification turn to sudden, shocked recognition.

'You!' Willy Pete cried.

I ran, clutching the black zipper bag, keeping the pink T-Mobile logo turned outward. Willy clambered over the wheelchair and ran after me. I had maybe fifty feet on him. I ran full-out, as fast as I could while holding a painting into the openness of room 2.9, which was populated by glass display cases holding smashable objects including a very nice replica of a sailing ship.

I had my second Bluetooth speaker in my jacket pocket. I had practiced finding the switch without looking and I turned it on then sent it skidding and bouncing across the polished floor.

Now it was down to how well Willy has cased the Rijks because there are just three ways out of room 2.9. There's the door I'd come in through. There was the door that led to more galleries. And there was the door that led to the cul-de-sac of room 2.8.

If Willy has done his job and properly cased the museum he'd know 2.8 was a dead-end, and he'd guess that I knew it too. In which case the logical move was for Willy to assume I'd run on through the galleries, because that's what a fleeing man would do; a fleeing man did not run into a dead-end, and I was pretty much the picture of a fleeing man.

I ran into room 2.8.

I opened my phone. I hit the second Bluetooth speaker which started yelling, 'There's a bomb! Run, there's a bomb!', the sound of panic filling room 2.9. If Willy wanted to hang around room 2.9 and explain why he was near a speaker yelling threats, that was up to him, but I doubted he'd linger.

Room 2.8 was large, not Gallery of Honor large, but large enough that it was partly divided by a wooden portico set into an abbreviated partition wall. That didn't matter. What did matter was that there was a security camera mounted in the corner to my left as I entered, and it was aimed so as to scan the room.

I heard footsteps go racing past, back in 2.9. Willy was doing the logical thing. Good boy. He was also talking loudly, presumably into a phone. 'Fucker's heading south down the east side, second floor! Repeat. Target is . . .'

I moved well into room 2.8 into camera view. There were two exit doors, the one I'd come in through, and a second one just a dozen or so feet to my left. Both were security doors with large overhangs, almost like shelves about two feet deep and eight feet high.

The camera to my left wouldn't see me and the only other camera was way down at the far end of the room pointed my way. That was the camera I was playing to.

I tore off my duffer's cap and pulled a blue stocking cap from eight my bag. I skinned off my jacket and dropped it on the floor. I did all this while being watched by an older man in the blue blazer of a guard. Was he deaf? Did he not hear the speaker in the next room shouting about bombs? He seemed puzzled. He moved hesitantly, not quite sure how he was to deal with me.

The public address system came on suddenly, making me jump.

Guests of the Museum we are experiencing security issues, please remain in place and remain calm.

'They're attacking *The Night Watch*!' I told the guard, but he didn't move. At first. Then he started toward me and I saw him twist his head sideways a bit to talk into his microphone – not that anyone in the security center had spare time to listen, probably. But I couldn't have it.

I stepped into him and shoved the edge of my zippered painting up under his chin. He staggered back, tripped and fell. He was not unconscious and he was not on his back which was a bad combination for me. I dropped the Vermeer, straddled the elderly gentleman, and pistoned one knee onto his chest. It wouldn't kill him, I hoped, but it knocked the last of the fight out of him. I said, 'Sorry,' and rolled him onto his belly so he was looking away.

I leapt to the second exit door, the one so close to the security camera that it was out of view. There I had some quick moving and shuffling involving the putty-gray bag to do, and some standing on tiptoes, then ran back into room 2.9 clutching a black, zippered art bag with the glaring pink logo.

Room 2.9 still echoed to the cry of, 'Fire! Fire!' No Willy. No guards that I could see. No people at all. The cameras would record that I had run through 2.9 into 2.8 carrying a T-Mobile zipper bag just the right size for concealing a Vermeer, had disabled a guard in full view of the camera, and just fifteen seconds later had reappeared before the cameras in room 2.9 still carrying the black and pink zipper bag.

I went back the way I'd come and found my abandoned wheelchair which Willy Pete in his eagerness to get at me had pushed just far enough to let me slip by without the need to climb or vault.

Into the Great Hall I went, not running now, just walking briskly, turned into the stairwell, taking the steps two at a time, flanked on both sides by confused patrons escaping a bomb or a fire or a crazy person or something, they weren't sure what, they just knew they'd seen about enough art for one day.

A total of two minutes and thirteen seconds had passed since I'd snatched the painting off the wall. People are slow, bless them. And I am not.

I attracted no special attention as I fell in behind a gaggle of Spaniards noisily clattering down the steps. Down and down, but then, pushing against the tide, coming up the stairs came a man, a fit, serious-looking man I'd never seen before who ran right past me, then stopped, did a classic double-take, spun and yelled, 'You there!'

I stopped as well.

'Yes?'

I closed the distance between us. If I have learned anything from reading Jack Reacher books, it is to consider the balance of an opponent. My opponent was half-turned, one foot on a higher step, one foot lower, all the weight on that lower foot.

I stumbled convincingly, fell to my knees right at his feet. My zippered art bag fell and slid down the steps. I wrapped one hand around the weight-bearing ankle of Mr Fitness, and yanked back hard.

He fell, but man, he was quick! He softened his landing like a well-trained martial artist by slamming his hands back to take the impact. He'd be up in a flash but I already had my little spray bottle of hot sauce and grain alcohol out. I pumped frantically as he writhed, getting good coverage on his face.

'Motherfucker!' he yelled. So: American.

He yelled and he got to his feet, just one eye open, streaming tears, and blindly missed a step and tried to catch himself by outrunning his fall. Might even have worked, had I not given him a helpful shove which sent him sprawling face-first down the worn stone.

I snatched up my zipper bag, leapt over him and plowed ahead, down and down, occasionally yelling, 'Fire!' by way of explanation. I shed the blue stocking cap I had on, pulled on a plaid flat cap, slipped off my outer shirt, and debouched back on the lower level which was wonderfully, gloriously smoky.

'Fire!' I cried again in evident panic and raced for the exit already crammed with people having the same thought that this would be an excellent time to GTFO of there.

Concealed by the crowd I collapsed my art bag – this required some brute force resulting in a bag that looked gratifyingly like a woman's purse.

The guards at the door weren't searching, they were hurrying, trying to get bodies through the exit as expeditiously as possible. And all at once I was out in the great arcade, cold, damp wind in my face. The balalaika was not playing. The violinists were gaping at all the excitement, as the crowd in the arcade swelled into the hundreds.

I walked north, toward the street, toward the bridge and the city center beyond. The rain had started again, this time with more vigor, which was all to the good, because rain obscures. Rain makes people hesitate before running out into it.

Rain, fortunately, does not discourage a well-compensated flash mob and there they were, bless their clueless hearts, twenty people, all carrying identical black zippered art bags emblazoned with the T-Mobile logo, and dancing more or less in unison while singing the T-Mobile jingle.

I felt rather than saw pursuit, or maybe I was just imagining it, but I plunged straight into the flash mob, twenty people with identical bags. I pretended to dance along for a few steps, looking for pursuit. There were two Dutch patrol cops watching the flash mob and considering whether they had a duty to break it up. Out here on the sodden plaza no one knew that the Rijks was beset by Dutch masters-hating terrorists who might have set fire to the cloakroom.

If the Rijksmuseum security was really good, really decisive, really quick they would just about now be discovering my smoke bomb, and maybe even starting to realize they'd been duped and robbed. But it would still be too slow, because I was already crossing the wide avenue of the Stadhouderskade, dodging a trolley, plowing heedlessly through the bike lane. The area was an ant colony of commuters and tourists, cars, bikes and the clanging trolley.

I risked life and limb crossing against lights, was sideswiped by a Dutch woman on a bike who yelled at my retreating back – in English because, well, this was Amsterdam: 'Hey watch where you go!'

Onto the bridge, the Museumbrug, with its iron railings lined with pink flowers. I stopped halfway across, breathing hard but still in the dead calm state of mind that often comes to me when I'm engaged in something insane. Praying silently to whatever saints have the job of looking after fools and thieves, I looked over the side.

And there by God was Milan Smit, my faux Hell's Angel, lounging in an open boat drinking beer as if there was no rain.

'Hey!' I yelled.

He heard me and hit the throttle on the boat's outboard and came chugging below me.

I slid the zipper bag over the railing and dropped it into his waiting hands.

TWENTY-THREE

My first thought was, *Oh my God: it worked.*
My second thought was, *Uh-oh: Willy Pete.*
Willy, followed closely by two other guys, one with a splotchy red face sparkling with Tabasco tears, were closing in. I didn't try to run. They were all in better shape than I was. Besides, I didn't need to.

'You!' Willy Pete snarled as he and his boys hemmed me in, doing the chest-push and generally intending to terrify me.

'Problem?' I asked innocently, hoping my panting and my hammering heart wouldn't turn it to soprano.

'Problem?' Thug number two had a lisp. It seemed like not the time to suggest a good speech therapist. 'You stole a fucking painting!'

'Did I?' I theatrically patted my body as if such a thing might be concealed on my person.

I saw a metallic flash. Willy had his stiletto out, but hidden by our tight-packed bodies. 'You have three seconds to live, asshole. Give up the *Jewess.*'

Words that had been spoken in this city before, albeit in German.

'Go ahead. Stab me Willy Pete, aka Carl Willard, who moonlights for the CIA.'

I was not at all sure that would work. Willy Pete's eyes narrowed and his compadres exchanged worried looks.

'You could die choking on that information,' he growled.

'I could die of an embolism,' I said. I was not as scared as I probably should have been. But I just didn't see them murdering me on a busy bridge in broad daylight, especially since they were sure I was the guy with the painting they wanted. But I thought I'd best make that point explicitly, just in case.

'Kill me and the Vermeer is gone,' I said. 'That's a lot to pass up just for the pleasure of stabbing me.'

'Listen, smart guy, if I don't get the Vermeer, you will die. Don't have any doubt about that. Now or later, those are your choices.'

'Well, I'm going to have to pick, later. And as for later, Willy, here's what I've got on you. You lost your wallet, didn't you?'

If looks could kill . . .

'Yeah, I have it,' I said, getting into the whole noirishness of the back-and-forth. 'I have pictures of your driver's license and your credit cards, all safe in the cloud. I know about the safe house in Langley. I know you've been promised a hell of a lot of money to steal the Vermeer, and I know the guy who hired you is Daniel Isaac.' I watched his face. He had the relaxed gaze of a hawk staring down a mouse. I waited for a flicker. And there it was: on the mention of money. I turned to Lisp, the henchman not weeping and wiping his eyes, and said, 'How much of that fifty million bucks do you two clowns get?'

Ah, the information you can get from facial expressions and eye movements. They both – even my weepy friend from the stairwell – shot choreographed suspicious glances at Willy.

Willy hadn't told them what the take would be. I barely resisted laughing.

I said, 'Everything I know is well-dispersed to people and places you have zero chance of silencing. Fuck with me and it all comes out, and I don't think Daniel "the Chipster" Isaac, or the CIA, would be happy about that. Do you?' Time for me to press my advantage. 'You boys want to call the cops? No, you don't. Do you want to stab me on this bridge? Go for it, but you'll never get the Vermeer or the fifty million that way, will you?'

'You don't know who you're fucking with, Mitre,' Willy snarled. But that was weak and we all knew it.

'Nah, see your problem is that I know exactly who I'm fucking with. So you boys toddle off and tell the merchant of death he can have his Vermeer for the low, low price of five million dollars which, gee, is just a tenth of what he was willing to pay you.'

I'd have felt so much better if he had raged and cursed. He

didn't. He went blank. Expressionless. Like he was already gone. It was a cold look. Cold was bad.

But I couldn't show weakness. I had to own the swagger. 'So what's happening now is that I am walking away. If you come after me I will reluctantly have to bring the cops into it. That might cost me the five mil, might even get me arrested, but there is zero chance of conviction. Whereas, if the cops find you being unpleasant to me, it would cost you prison terms. Especially you, Willy, because I was there when you murdered my buddy.'

This part was a combination of chutzpah and information seeking. If he knew who I was – who I *really* was – he'd know I'd never call the cops.

'Now, you three get the fuck out of my way or I'll start yelling for cops right here, right now.'

They didn't move, but neither did they push back as I muscled past them, bringing me way too close to that stiletto, toward which object I affected indifference. I was not at all indifferent but I was pretty sure they'd do nothing.

And nothing is what they did.

Milan would run the boat up the Singelgracht just a thousand feet or so to the Holland Casino which, I may say parenthetically, is a sad piece of work that wouldn't make it in Henderson, Nevada let alone Vegas. Milan would stroll through the casino, looking for tails, then go to a second pre-positioned boat and sail off down the canal and tie-off just a few feet from an AirBnB I'd reserved solely to get their Wi-Fi password. Which, perhaps oddly, was stroopwafels. All lower case.

Milan would then use a burner phone to link to the Wi-Fi and we would begin the live broadcast.

All of this would eat up a half an hour.

I used that time to walk to an actual coffee shop and have actual coffee. What I really wanted was about twelve ounces of Talisker, but I still had a panel to do. I did not concern myself overly much with being tailed by Sarip's cops or even Delia's contractors, in fact I welcomed it. *Look at me! I'm walking along with completely empty hands. Gaze upon my innocence, ye coppers and despair!*

Then it was off to intersect with Madalena's movements in the little square near Waterstones.

I had some moments of anxiety when I couldn't spot her there and I had to kill more minutes than I'd have liked and had to order still more coffee to explain my loitering. But then, there she was. We made eye contact. She walked down a row of parked bikes and dropped her phone into a bike basket. I sauntered by a minute later and picked it up.

And *ping, ping, ping* went the cell phone towers.

TWENTY-FOUR

The blank, nearly emotionless, but hyper-alert condition I'd been in from that first laying on of hands in the Rijks, dissipated to be replaced by a hollow fear. I had experience with moments like this. I knew the dilution of the adrenalin in my system would leave me feeling jumpy and exhausted. You can only maintain that disembodied fugue state for so long before all the suppressed fear comes bubbling up.

My stomach was not enjoying too much coffee on top of too little food and the residue of used adrenalin, all my tangential Nazi bruises were reminding me that they weren't gone just yet, and there was a part of me that really just wanted to sit down, right there on the sidewalk, and weep till it was all over. But again, aspiring criminals, this is where experience is so helpful. This was not my first day of school. I'd been here, I'd done this, I'd felt exactly this way – aside from the bruising – and I had endured.

I walked into Waterstones at 5:51 p.m. A rather disturbing video live stream was about to go public in nine minutes, 6 p.m. local, 9 a.m. Las Vegas time. The dominoes were toppling one by one, and there was now nothing I could do to help things along.

'Hi, I'm David Mitre. I'm on a panel tonight.'

The front desk clerk called his supervisor and there was a blur of handshaking and expressions of delight and I was whisked away to the green room – a musty office with some ragged lounge chairs, bottles of water and packaged snacks of various kinds, all encroached upon by cardboard boxes and steel rolling carts piled with books.

'Am I signing stock? Because I'm early and I'd just as soon start.'

I was indeed signing stock, and they had a decent but not amazing pile of three dozen of my latest, and another dozen of my previous works. So I sat there opening my books to the copyright page and scribbling my deliberately over-dramatic but entirely illegible scrawl with a fine-tip black Sharpie, all the while waiting for . . .

Ting!

I opened my phone, opened my Signal app and there was the single word: *Gouda.*

Because when your crime partners – Milan and Madalena, M&M – want to tell you they've launched something you don't want them saying, 'Hey, we launched something!'

I instantly wiped the message. I double-checked that the cloud was turned off and for extra measure, deleted the app and restarted the phone. I excused myself to the restroom where I smashed the phone against the porcelain until the guts were exposed. I used my pocket Swiss Army knife to pry out the battery and dumped it in the trash. Then I used my cigar torch and burned a good forty-five seconds' worth of butane flambéing the memory. I pried out the heat-blistered flash memory and flushed it down the toilet, muttering, 'There you go, NSA, read *that*.'

I then carefully wiped down the case and the starred screen and tossed the mess in the bin along with the battery.

I went back out to the green room to finish autographing, a task made more difficult because I'd singed my ring finger burning the phone.

So far, so good, as the man who'd jumped off the Empire State Building was heard to say as he passed the fiftieth floor. It was up to the Fates now.

I hate when things are up to the Fates.

By now the Rijksmuseum security, no doubt aided by Dutch police, perhaps even my friends Sarip and DeKuyper, would be going through all the video footage. They would know they'd been robbed. They would know the 'fire' was just a harmless smoke bomb. They'd have the drone and the Bluetooth speakers and the motorized wheelchair. Battalions of *Koninklijke Marechaussee* would be frantically comparing serial numbers to shipping lists and they'd be cursing as they discovered that none of my toys had come from Amsterdam.

So inconvenient.

Beat cops would soon be showing up at shops in Rotterdam

and beyond, looking for credit card details that would lead to stolen numbers and irrelevant addresses.

They'd probably be able to pull up footage of me walking out of the main door with my black zipper bag and down the archway to the street. Right through a flash mob whose presence would only serve to confirm that I had been very damn serious about getting away with the Vermeer.

The one thing I worried about was in the queue to exit when I'd collapsed the art bag, but I was reasonably confident that this move had been blocked from camera view by the crowd. What Rijksmuseum security would see was an old dude in a wheelchair suddenly spry, snatching the Vermeer, hiding it in a zipper bag, carrying it away, appearing before sequential cameras, swapping disguises and in the end walking off through a confusing flash mob and into the sunset.

'Are you David Mitre?'

I jumped. The Sharpie flew from my hand, spiraled through the air and left a small black mark on the spine of a *Harry Potter* book.

'Sorry, I didn't mean to frighten you, I'm Jennifer Choo. We're on the panel together?'

She looked like her author photo: Asian-British, or British-Asian, early forties, graying gracefully, dressed in jeans and a down jacket. I forced a greasy grin onto my face and stuck out a hand. 'Sorry, I didn't mean to fling a Sharpie at you. Too much caffeine.'

We chatted: publishing people we'd dealt with. Agents. Deals. Options. The usual artsy, literary stuff we literary artistes talk about in real life. This was in lieu of either of us having to pretend to be big fans of the other.

A third author showed up, one of those fusty old men with dandruff and nose hair who wrote a single book ten years ago and fuck-all since. His name was George, I think. George something. Didn't know him either, but he'd read my books and managed without saying so to convey that he was not impressed. He wore a vest, a too-colorful vest, like something one might wear at Christmas if you were drunk enough and your maiden aunt had knitted it from her cat's fur and was waiting there all dewy-eyed for you to offer effusive thanks.

I didn't like George. I'm funny that way with people who don't like my books.

More blather and time passed and I didn't pull my phone – the phone Madalena had handed off to me – out to check the time because I had to appear cool and in no hurry.

Did Mr Mitre appear distracted?

No, officer, he was just rambling on about IP lawyers versus agents.

There's nothing worse than waiting, waiting for your future to be decided when you had no ability to influence the outcome. Well, maybe not the worst thing. Ian would argue that his end of this caper was worse.

The event was running late because we were waiting on the arrival of the night's big star. Meanwhile the first video stream had been up online for ten minutes. I kept chatting with no bloody idea what I was saying because in my mind I was with Milan. Everything now relied on a headbanging pickpocket I barely knew. If he wandered off, all was lost. If he decided to chat on the phone with some friend, all might be lost. If he just got tired and fell asleep, all was lost.

At the twenty-minute mark, in just ten minutes, Milan would shut down the transmission. Then he would sail off to the next AirBnB and resume transmission there on the hour.

Suck on that NSA. Good luck GCHQ. As for the Koninklijke Marechaussee? Puh-leeze.

Sure, if somehow a land-speed record for bureaucratic cooperation had been set, the big eyes and ears in the sky would track the broadcast to Amsterdam. But that just added to the authenticity, because of course the signal would originate in Amsterdam. Given the elapsed time it would have to.

And the sigint folks would be able to locate the AirBnBs in time, but that was crucial: *in time.* Not in twenty minutes. Not in a time frame that would give them an ability to react. They could send action teams all over the city and they wouldn't get to any of the Wi-Fi sources in time.

Yes, they would realize – again assuming unprecedented levels of interagency cooperation – that the thief was using AirBnBs, and they'd pop the top on AirBnBs servers like opening a beer can, and they'd get the credit-card data which would show . . . a stolen credit-card number bought online.

Maybe they would share that info with Sarip's people and the law enforcement folks would hastily track down the owners of the apartment who would admit that, nope, they never did meet the tenant. Just gave them the combination to the front door lock and, oh, right, also the Wi-Fi password.

But this would be where the LEOs would get clever. The second broadcast which would also be tracked back to an Amsterdam AirBnB – quicker this time because they knew what they were looking for – and the LEOs would rejoice because they had a pattern.

Round three of the broadcast at nine p.m. local would confirm the pattern. Their excitement would be unbounded. 'Pattern!' Sarip or his equivalent would cry in their simple-minded way. *Quick, everyone start calling AirBnB owners who've rented recently to someone they didn't meet in person. We've got 'im now!*

Do you though? Do you, Lieutenant? Check the fourth broadcast. Oh look! That's not an AirBnB ISP, that's a fucking coffee shop. Hah!

Would it be oversharing to admit that as this scenario played out in my head I felt something bordering on sexual gratification?

I was good. I was better than good. I was a fucking criminal genius.

If it all worked.

'So what are you working on?' George asked, head tilted skeptically to hide his shame at being a mere one-and-done in the presence of Mr Five Books.

I shrugged. 'Same old, same old,' I said. 'Joe Barton's been good to me.'

'You don't ever aspire to anything else?'

Why? Is that what you're doing? At the end of a ten-year-long 'aspire' are you, George? Muse-talking on a regular basis, are we? Of course I didn't say that because it would be unkind. Also my mouth was as dry as a college freshman who'd been up all night smoking weed and snorting Adderall.

Right about now Milan would disengage the first Wi-Fi link. If it was actually working. If, if, if. Aside from that single, *Gouda*, I couldn't be sure any of this was happening.

The Star of the Evening strolled in, accompanied by a publicist. Polly Addison Theriault, the arriviste, the social media force, the kid who already had a Nero Award and was in hot contention for an Edgar.

This new arrival, not so far from being half my age, had her phone open and without preamble or introduction said, 'Hey, are you guys watching this?'

'Watching what?' were the words strangled out of my throat.

'It's kind of amazing,' says she, talking too loud because she had Airpods in. 'Some, like, famous painting's been stolen from the big museum they have here. And someone's threatening to destroy it unless he gets five million euros.'

Don't be the first, don't be the first, don't be the first . . .

'What the hell?' George demanded, taking it so personally that he stood up.

'What's that you're looking at?' I asked with mild concern, coming in second. 'I'm David Mitre by the way, big fan.'

'And I've read, I think, one of yours, David. I'm not sure.'

I've always insisted that I don't kill people, well, not deliberately, but if someday a tram happened to be coming by and I happened to be standing behind Polly Addison Theriault . . .

'Oh. The live feed cut off,' she said. 'No . . . wait there's a message. Heh. Intriguing.'

'Are you going to share with the class?' Jennifer Choo asked impatiently.

'Let me see if I can rewind . . .' She took out the earbuds.

We all waited, open-mouthed as Polly Addison Theriault, author of two gimmicky books in what was to be the *It All Started With* series, swiped and frowned and then turned the phone around and played it for us.

I had of course seen the video and heard the audio – many times – but not in an active context, so to speak.

The picture on Polly's phone showed *Jewess at the Loom*. It appeared to be tacked to a piece of plywood. It was dimly lit, but you could still see the diligent *Jewess* looming away. Beside it a digital timer ticked down from twelve hours.

Eleven hours, thirty-seven minutes left.

The tinny audio, obviously a mechanical voice, said:

> Hallo, guten tag, bonjour, hola, boa dia, hi and g'day, mates. We are the Children of Abraham. We are not terrorists. We are not politically motivated. We are simply businessmen looking for profit.
>
> As you see, we have the Vermeer stolen from the Rijksmuseum. In twelve hours a small but effective bomb will go off, destroying this priceless Vermeer.
>
> There is only one way to stop this from happening.
>
> The price is five million dollars.
>
> At the bottom of this video is a link. Those who wish to contribute to save this beautiful and irreplaceable artwork, please click on the link and donate what you can afford in any common cryptocurrency.
>
> This video will stream for twenty minutes. Then it will fall silent. And then reappear in another stream.
>
> We don't wish to harm the painting. It is a magnificent piece of priceless art. But our need is dire and we will carry out our threat.
>
> Twelve hours.
>
> Five million dollars.

'Children of Abraham. Jews,' sniffed Jennifer Choo.

'Not necessarily,' George rebutted. 'Abraham had two children, Isaac and Ishmael. Ishmael was the father of the Arabs.'

So the whole Children of Abraham thing was working as anticipated. Some would blame Jews, some would blame Arabs, both would be wonderfully embarrassed when it became clear that it was neither. But in the meantime various intelligence agencies would be squeezing their sources amongst Jewish and Palestinian extremists and wasting time chasing down blind alleys.

'But I haven't even heard that a painting was stolen,' I said with appropriately befuddled expression. 'A Vermeer did he say?'

'The message kept just replaying until, like, a minute ago. It must be a prank,' opined Polly Addison Theriault.

George blew out a snort. 'Won't work. No one's going to fall for this, that's probably not even a real painting.'

'You're right,' I agreed. 'Unless it turns out some painting really was stolen.'

At which point Polly Addison Theriault, the clever girl, checked Twitter. 'OMG! There's a bunch of people talking about . . . like a drone? And a fire at the Rijksmuseum?'

She pronounced it Ridge-ex-museum, which made me obscurely happy.

Now my mood brightened, not because I had achieved success, I wasn't going to know that for twelve hours. But the second phase had well and truly begun and there was absolutely nothing for me to do.

The bookstore manager popped in to tell us that it was time, and that we had a surprisingly large crowd waiting for us.

And, oh, did we ever.

TWENTY-FIVE

There's not a lot of showbiz in book panels and signings. The very best you're going to get is an introduction. That's it. No triumphal music playing us on or off.

The stage was a towering six inches high with five stools crammed into too little space. There was a moderator and I'm sure she had a name but I hadn't managed to remember it, being somewhat distracted by the fact that I was either pulling off the heist of the decade (if not century) or embarrassing myself spectacularly en route to many years in tiny rooms without windows and an en suite right next to the cot. Also a roommate.

The moderator sat at the far end. Then came the star of the evening, Polly Addison Theriault, then me, then George with Jennifer Choo bringing up the rear. We all had individual bottles of water but we were sharing a mike.

Facing us, or being faced by us, depending, were about fifty folding chairs containing approximately fifty rear ends. And there were standees. This was good, it's depressing when the crowd is three old ladies and a homeless guy talking to the voices in his head. More than fifty people? That was pretty good, even if only eight of them were there for me.

But it's not just about numbers. It's also about the quality of attendees and I absolutely did not love the fact that there was not one, but two faces in that audience that I did not want to see.

Willy Pete was now dressed in the kind of mid-range dad clothes military guys think of as civvies. He was standing at the back, fixing me with a white-hot glare. There was another guy, too, one of the muscular fellows who'd been with Willy when he'd confronted me on the bridge, the Lisp. They stood apart but were clearly together.

'Helloooooo, book lovers,' the moderator crooned into the over-amplified mike. 'Waterstones Amsterdam is pleased and honored to be able to bring four brilliant mystery writers together. I'm going to start off with a few questions and then we'll throw it open to all of you to ask your own questions. Then we'll have a signing right there at that table.'

The table was your standard folding leg object with four chairs and four name tags. Willy Pete was leaning against said table. He reached over and took the folded paper reading *David Mitre* and crumpled it in his fist.

I almost laughed, because as tough-guy moves went it was pitiful. Which is not to say I wasn't scared. I was. I was facing two guys who could jointly or severally kill me.

We started with the inevitable 'tell us briefly about your work' question which Jennifer and George filibustered. Polly was brief, which made me hate her slightly less. And I did my usual sardonic, faux-modest routine and about halfway through that Willy and his sidekick left. I wondered why. Had they just showed up to glare balefully for three minutes? Had they spotted someone else in the crowd, say, law enforcement unfamiliar to me?

Whatever the reason, I welcomed it. My sphincter was already tight enough, thank you very much, without a pair of thugs giving me the death stare.

'Tell us about what inspires you, David.'

'I don't really think in terms of inspiration,' I said. 'For me it's my job, a job I love, but there's nothing mystical involved.'

Then we did the literary role models question. I hate this, it forces me to kiss Lee Child's ring, which in turn forces me to throw subtle shade on Lee by mentioning Raymond Chandler. Because Child may be mystery writing's current Thor but Chandler is Odin, the all-father, the occupant of the throne to which we all must bend a knee. Some people memorize poetry, I memorize Chandler.

There was a desert wind blowing that night. It was one of those hot dry Santa Anas that come down through the mountain passes and curl your hair and make your nerves jump and your skin itch. On nights like that every booze party ends in a fight. Meek little wives feel the edge of the carving knife and study their husbands' necks.

Meek little wives feel the edge . . . How the hell do you

write better than that? You don't, that's how, and all of us in
the business of trying to do so know it.

'My question is for Mr Mitre. Mr Mitre, are you married?'

Sometimes my female fans flirt a bit. It comes with the
territory, though not for poor George.

'I am not married,' I said with a greasy smile, tossing off
a quick joke. 'Who would have me?'

There followed the usual back and forth, mostly involving
Polly Addison Theriault, with occasional nods to Jennifer Choo
and me. George was growing restless and resentful.

At this point in the evening I either had bank accounts filling
up with bitcoin, or the whole charade had collapsed. I couldn't
check, I only had one phone on me at the moment and it had
a specific, limited purpose.

We reached the end at last and were to head to the signing
table. I settled in with my Sharpie, ready to mumble my humble
thanks to all who had spent the eighteen euros to buy my
book. I wasn't even looking up when I was handed a book
and a horribly familiar voice said, 'Autograph it for Martin
Sarip, please.'

Ah.

Fuck.

OK, it was time for this.

'Happy to,' I said.

'I need some of your time.'

'I won't be more than another twenty minutes.'

'Now,' said the lieutenant who was without his usual shadow.

'But the people in line . . .' I waved a hand at them.

'Now.'

He put steel into that, so I pushed back and in a loud voice,
said, 'Folks, I'm sorry but it seems the Koninklijke Marechaussee
needs to consult with me.' I offered the next person in line an
apologetic shrug along with an expression that suggested I
was a sort of Hercule Poirot and Sarip was the hapless Inspector
Japp. Duty called, and all that.

We went back to the green room and shooed away two store
employees who were opening boxes and stacking fresh books.

'Your phone,' Sarip snapped, holding out his hand.

'What?'

'Your mobile. Give it to me.'

I'm not sure I've said this explicitly, but I have a problem with being told what to do. I suppose that's obvious, really. So I didn't answer. I also didn't give him my phone. I just met his gaze and without intending it – well, OK, intending it, but I shouldn't have – I smirked. After I'd left his insistent hand hanging in mid-air for a good ten seconds, I said, 'Is that the law in the Netherlands? Any cop can just walk up to an innocent person and demand his phone?'

Sarip was not happy about that. He looked very much like a guy who might just try to snatch my phone away from me but for the fact that I was bigger than he was. He literally ground his teeth. 'If you have committed no crime then you should have nothing to fear.'

'Aside from trusting you not to violate my privacy?' I sighed. I could resist further, I could probably demand a lawyer from the embassy. I could do those things, but since I *wanted* Sarip to have my phone, had in fact counted on him asking for my phone, I did the generous, innocent thing. 'I will voluntarily hand you my phone – I'll even unlock it for you – if you first explain why you want it.'

Sarip was coldly furious. And maybe if we'd been in a nice, quiet cinderblock-walled interview room he might have smacked me around a bit. Maybe. He was mad enough to, and I knew why he was mad; his cop gut was telling him that the Hangwoman incident, the skinhead beating and the murder of poor Ian were all connected to the theft of the Vermeer. And since he knew for a fact that two of those incidents involved me . . . He was worried that he'd had the perpetrator in his sights for days and had nevertheless failed to stop me. That wouldn't look good on his quarterly performance review. He answered me but in a tone full of gravel and malice.

'There's been a painting stolen from the Rijksmuseum.'

'Oh yeah,' I said. 'Polly Whatsername was showing us a bizarre video just before we went out. Huh. OK, but what's that have to do with me?'

'That is the question,' Sarip answered. 'If I could access your mobile we could quickly eliminate you by checking your GPS data.'

'Really? Hmmm,' I said. 'OK.'

In that moment Sarip realized what my phone would give him. He would find no messages, no emails, no texts and if he checked my browser history he would conclude that I seldom used the internet. The phone, an Android, was just a few days old and sure, that in itself would be suspicious, but what it would not be is evidence against me.

When Sarip got the phone back to his in-house geeks, those geeks would turn up very few indications that the phone had moved – I'd only had so much time to set this up – except for today. And today's GPS record would show me nowhere near the Rijksmuseum at the time of the heist.

It took every bit of my maturity, not something I have in surplus, not to laugh in Sarip's face, the poor bastard. He'd just insisted on, and I had reluctantly turned over, exculpatory evidence. The Netherlands tries criminal cases before a three-judge panel, harder to bamboozle than a jury, but nevertheless, my phone, the phone taken from me by Sarip, the phone he'd insisted on, would show me in one place and the Rijksmuseum in another.

'Where were you from four to six p.m.?' Sarip snapped.

I shrugged. 'Dude, seriously? You seriously think I stole a painting? Me?' I shook my head and laughed at the transparent folly of it all. 'Look, I wandered around town, I wasn't taking notes. I mean, check the phone, it will be more specific.'

At that point, having signed so few books that it had only darkened his mood, George came in, stopped, stared at the two police, picked up the bag he'd left in the green room, and stalked off.

'Where's your better half this evening, Lieutenant? The lovely sergeant?'

'Under the weather,' he said.

Polly and Jennifer entered, laughing like old school friends. They eyeballed Sarip and me, but didn't ask questions. What they did instead was watch the second broadcast. Same recorded message, same threat, same demand.

'It's on again, the thing about the painting,' Polly said. Sarip watched me for my reaction.

'See? There you go, Lieutenant. Unless you think I can be in two places at once.'

Sarip, who looked set to spontaneously combust, stabbed an angry finger at me and said, 'Do not leave Amsterdam,' and stormed off, accidentally knocking a pile of books over.

I called after him, 'What, ever?'

Because while it's never smart to tweak a cop, it is fun.

TWENTY-SIX

don't think I've ever been more frustrated than I was as I left Waterstones at about nine p.m. I had built and let loose upon the world a brilliant plan which, at that very moment, was either working or not. And I could not find out. There was an excellent chance that Sarip had eyes on me – possibly the eyes of his missing partner – and if I was seen whipping out a phone that would drastically diminish the exculpatory power of the phone I'd had Madalena take on a tour around Amsterdam and handed to Sarip.

I could go back to my apartment and there I could check, but there were two problems with that. One was that there might be all manner of active electronic snooping aimed at my place. And two, Delia might be there and I wasn't ready to deal with her. It was entirely possible that she might yell at me.

So I walked over to the Singel and followed it north, hung a left on Blauwburgwal and crossed to the Arendsnest, a sardine tin of a brown bar, and after some jostling found a few bare inches free. I usually avoid the brown bars because they represent a sort of sacred space for locals in a city devoted to tourists. But I was pretty sure I'd be leaving Amsterdam soon and not at all sure I'd ever be able to return. I was feeling pre-nostalgic.

The Arendsnest was about as narrow as a bike lane, wonderfully shiny with bottles and mirrors and stacked glasses and knick-knacks. Behind the bar loomed a chalkboard beer menu listing nothing but Dutch artisanal beers. I craved whiskey, but the job was not yet done and I might yet have another encounter with Lieutenant Sarip. I ordered a Seabeggar rye pale ale on the grounds that I'd never had a rye beer and started to run through the plan again, obsessively searching for holes.

I tried a couple other beers as well in the course of killing a couple of hours. I watched the fourth broadcast on a stranger's phone, looking over his shoulder. The theft of the Vermeer was definitely a topic of conversation, though in this bar, at this moment, people were speaking Dutch so I gleaned no new data.

Just before midnight I left, swaying a little perhaps, but sober enough. Six hours in. The halfway point. A light rain fell through a clinging mist leaving the brick sidewalk slick. The mist turned lights dim and starry and deepened the darkness of the Herrengracht canal, which was on my left, as I walked south toward what passed for home. Between me and the canal was the narrow one-way street and a long line of parked cars, all angled in and facing the canal. Wherever there wasn't a parked car there was a cluster of chained bikes. Elm trees dripped and rustled fitfully in a downright cold breeze that somehow penetrated to the bone without clearing the mist away.

Half a block down the street I saw a woman leaning against a parked orange VW Polo and talking on her phone. She was turned in my direction and I had the impression that she reacted to seeing me. Nothing dramatic, just a sort of subtle pushing away from leaning on the car.

It was nothing, I told myself, just a woman getting home late, or maybe about to take the drive of shame after a tryst. But I hadn't survived as a fugitive by ignoring the little warning bells tinkling in the back of my brain.

I mimed forgetting something, patted my pockets, and turned around, instinct telling me to walk away. Then, behind me, I heard the door of the Polo open, then slam shut. And a second or two later, the engine came alive with a diesel rattle.

I turned my head, still affecting a casual lack of concern and the Polo was creeping down the street in my direction, headlights blinding. Wrong way on a one-way street. But slow. Not looking to run me down, more like the driver was following me.

Then, ahead of me, an unmarked white-paneled van turned off Blauwburgwal and came toward me, creeping as cautiously as the Polo. I was between a van and a VW, a Mitre sandwich. Too late to turn back now, I kept walking, very casual, seemingly unaware, toward the panel van. The van continued closing the distance as did the Polo, the two vehicles no more than ten car lengths apart now.

I heard the sound of the van's transmission shifting gears and the engine revved. It lurched forward, came right at me and would run me over in about two seconds . . . except for the fact that Amsterdam canal houses are all slightly elevated with front doors reached by anywhere from three to eight or nine steps. I danced nimbly aside and took seven steps in two leaps. I tripped at the top and stumbled into the black iron railing. The van screeched to a halt just beside me, the Polo screeched to its own halt just twenty feet away to the south.

I saw the van's sliding door open. At that moment what I expected was half a dozen guys in black tactical gear to pile out, grab me and force me into the van. I mean, that's the way it works in the movies. And what the Ontario Crew, the CIA and the Dutch cops all had in common was that none of them wanted me dead. Yet.

No one wanted me dead . . . except the man who had tumbled from the driver's seat into the back, snatched up a shotgun and leveled the thing at me. It was a double-barrel shotgun, side-by-side, old school. A hunting weapon presumably.

At six feet you have to really try to miss a target with a shotgun and I'd have taken a whole bunch of buckshot onboard had Hangbrother, the Naked Nazi, not been in such a hurry to grab his gun that he neglected to take the van out of gear. The van rolled, Hangbrother pulled the trigger, there was a catastrophically loud explosion that echoed and reverberated, lengthening a half-second explosion into a three-second-long blast, which annihilated the window and shredded the curtains of whichever unlucky person lived at number 98.

The van rolled on and crashed into the Polo, not enough to do much damage, but enough that the van's engine shuddered and died. Hangbrother scrabbled to get himself back into firing position. I let loose a terrified whinny and vaulted the railing and only when I was airborne did I see that I would fall into a well leading to a basement door, a fall that was guaranteed to break an ankle at very least. I executed a graceless half-pirouette and managed to land one foot on a low planter and the other foot on a concrete post which was some pretty impressive acrobatics, except that I was now turned away from the shotgun and I knew I had to jump again and right the fuck then, so I tried to reverse my pirouette, caught my foot on the planter and fell hard onto the brick sidewalk as a second shotgun blast blew out the windows of number 96.

At this point no one within a square block could possibly still be asleep unless they were passed out, but no one was quick enough or perhaps foolish enough to open their windows and yell for quiet.

I twisted a bit, fell face down, rolled, then slithered up out of the well and scooted like an alligator under the van.

Hangwoman yelled something furious in a foreign language that probably translated to, 'He's under the van! Drive over him!'

There was not a lot of clearance under the van, and by not a lot I mean that my behind was pressed against a hot muffler. I heard the transmission being shoved into gear and I heard the engine respond and the vehicle jumped forward just as I slithered through to the other side. The rear tire caught just the very tip of my left foot which caused me to leave a shoe behind. The second time I'd lost a shoe in Amsterdam, thanks to these crazy bastards.

I jumped to my feet and found myself making eye contact via the wing mirror with Hangbrother.

'What the holy fuck!' I roared, outraged.

His window was down and I was well past common sense, so I tried for a grab, got my hand briefly on the steering wheel, but he was in reverse, so he pulled back, bashed into a bike stand and in panic threw the van into first and hit the gas. The van shot forward, Hangbrother hit the brakes too late, and the van smashed into the front of the Polo, this time for real.

Anyone who'd slept through the shotgun blasts would be awake now. It wasn't a totaling crash, just some bent sheet metal, but car crashes have a very distinct noise and there's no one alive who won't take a moment to look at a crash.

The smart way to run seemed to me to be south, away from the van, past the Polo. Hangwoman had come running around the back of the van, maybe assuming I'd go that direction, or maybe just to berate her brother, but it was too good an opportunity for me to pass up: there was the open door of the Polo and steam rising from its exhaust pipe and I did not fancy testing whether I could – with just one shoe – outrun a shotgun blast. I thrust my rear end into the car, pulled my legs in after me, stood on the clutch pedal, ground the gear shift in what I hoped was the right direction – left and forward? God, I hoped so.

The engine revved, the gears ground and there was a sphincter-tightening moment of hesitation as the Polo's bumper, entwined now with the van, did not want to yield and Hangbrother piled out of the van, fumbling bright red shells into the chambers of the shotgun. He was ten feet away, snapping the double-barrel gun closed, all the while being goaded by his furious sister, and I was in the car, stuck in the car, not nearly time enough to run.

Then the Polo's bumper broke free and I reversed, fish-tailing wildly. Ahead of me, back up the street, the Hangsiblings had climbed back aboard the van, brother behind the wheel, and my female nemesis now leaning out of the passenger side window with the big gun.

They were coming after me, the lunatics. Every cop in Amsterdam would be heading our way and these assholes didn't know when to walk away. I was in reverse, they were in a forward gear, and that was not a race I'd be winning. My only hope was reaching the cross street and turning around. Turned the right way the Polo would easily outrun the van. But the cross street was still a hundred yards off and suddenly I saw just about the last damn thing I wanted to see at that moment: bikes, four of them, turning onto Herrengracht, going the wrong way right down the middle of the street. Tourists. Drunk tourists on bikes!

I could of course plow right through them. But even in my panicky state I had the feeling that maybe killing or maiming four people would be what Delia calls, 'wrong.' I braked hard and saw an opening: an actual empty parking space. I'd go in rear-first, throw it into gear, and at least be ready to race away once the two-wheeling idiots passed.

Which would have worked had Hangbrother not panicked

on seeing the approaching bikes and swerved.

Right into the Polo. Right into the Polo which was backed right up against the canal.

I felt a sickening thump when my back wheels rolled right over the ridiculous six-inch-high iron barrier. I dropped the clutch and gunned it. The powered front wheels squealed and – oh, that was a mistake: I was still in reverse.

The Polo didn't so much slide off the quay into the canal as execute a perfect backward dive. It was a five-foot drop, not enough to break my neck as the Polo's hatch back hit the water, but enough for the back of my head to bang the head-rest. There was a shriek of metal on concrete, and a second hard bump and the front wheels spun madly in the air.

And then, the Polo was a boat.

TWENTY-SEVEN

S ome emotionless corner of my brain was keeping track
of time. 12:30-ish, after midnight, and Milan would no
longer be in a boat. He would – assuming always that he
was still free and on-schedule – have carried the package half
a block from the last boat to a rented hatchback and driven it
across town to a rental from an AirBnB competitor. He
wouldn't use that Wi-Fi, but would leach off the Wi-Fi from
a different apartment across the street. I'd allowed for him to
spend two broadcasts at this new location, after all, the man
had to eat and take a pee at some point.

At three a.m., with just three hours left till my cut-off,
Milan would carry the package up onto the roof of yet
another canal house, which would give him line of sight to
our final rental and its Wi-Fi. There was some risk in this,
running the final three broadcasts through a single Wi-Fi – it
would mean leaving the package untended for three hours.
But it was more important that Milan get well away: better
to lose it all than have Milan picked up. It wouldn't take Sarip
five minutes to get Milan to name me. This way he could
walk from that final location, reunite with Madalena at the
Amrath, then trot over to Centraal and catch the 6:15 to
Brussels. Their train would be pulling away just as the final
broadcast ended.

All of which would hopefully work as planned. But I had
more immediate problems: VW Polos float better than one
might expect, and I was now drifting along the canal at a
speed only a snail would envy. Drifting right toward a bridge,
indeed racing the white panel van to the bridge. The van won
easily. Out they piled, Hangwoman and Hangbrother and the
big shotgun in her hands. I flashed on our first encounter when
she'd tried to lynch me from the bridge. Now she was aiming
to blow my head off from a similar bridge.

The Polo was skewing sideways, spinning slowly, which

complicated Hangwoman's aim. She leaned over the railing
of the bridge and fired from not twenty feet away.

In movies bullets don't always penetrate sheet metal,
but this was real life and the first blast blew buckshot right
through the windshield, shredded the dashboard, broke the
steering wheel. Nothing hit me. Then I was under the bridge,
but not for long because when I drifted out the far side I'd
be a sitting duck.

So with water rising in the foot well and the canal water
within sloshing distance of my windows I tried to push open
the door and get out, but the water pressure kept the door
tightly shut. So I started climbing out through the window but
already I was coming into view on the opposite side of the
bridge. Hanging halfway out was going to be bad.

Out the other side and *blam* went the shotgun again, a
hurried shot that left an uneven field of holes in the hood.
Then I got lucky. The car rolled onto its side, a solid wall of
water rushed in, and the Polo sank.

Down went the Polo. The front, the engine, where all the
weight was, plunged straight down, the rear end went straight
up, and the Polo dived down and down as freezing water
filled the cabin. Down and down through black water, falling
a good, oh, six feet or so until the front bumper hit canal
debris and stopped. I was completely submerged. The Polo
was not. What I needed to do was get out through the window
and swim as far as I could underwater. Which would have
been a good plan had the suddenness of the plunge not caught
me unawares and with empty lungs.

Fortunately the back window of the hatchback was intact
and back (up?) there was an air bubble. So I crawled and
kicked my way over the seats, rose up into the air bubble
and sucked air. Through wet, starred glass I saw Hangwoman
reloading.

She saw me looking at her, so I gave her the finger and
before she could cock and aim, I submerged. I got tangled in
a floating shoulder belt but freed myself and shot through
the window. There was no light, no detail, no way even to be
sure what direction I was pointed in. I had to risk a quick
glance if I wasn't to swim right into a wall of concrete or

bricks. The water stung my eyes but I pried one open enough to differentiate the slightly brighter direction that should be 'up'. I pivoted and kicked and my foot went through something that scraped and when I tried to kick free, I just managed to entangle my leg further.

The Dutch pull something like 12,000 bikes out of the canal each year and I had just stuck my foot through the spokes of one. It did not want to let me go. My trousers were well and truly snagged.

So, with lungs burning, I did what I had to do. Then I swam as far as I could underwater, surfaced just long enough for a gulp of air, submerged and swam on, and when I surfaced next I looked back and saw the bridge had become a sort of art installation of flashing blue lights.

Had the cops arrested the Hangsiblings? I couldn't tell. But cold, scared, shivering from both cold and fear, trouserless and shoeless, I was hoping for a shootout in which the Dutch cops would kill both the crazy Nazi bastards.

TWENTY-EIGHT

Amsterdam is a famously tolerant city, but even so a grown man walking around trouserless was going to attract attention, so I swam and drifted as far as I could without contracting hypothermia, and finally hauled myself onto a moored houseboat. There was a light on inside or I'd have kicked a door or window in to look for clothing, but the last thing I could risk was another incident. So I disembarked and walked shoeless, bare-legged and with an utter absence of dignity, to my apartment.

The astonishing thing turned out to be the fact that I walked right past a beat cop resting on his bike, and he said nothing. Amsterdam cops were on high alert for an art thief, not an escaped lunatic in his underwear.

I slogged up the stairs to my apartment, acutely aware of the fact that I had, just nine days earlier, arrived similarly wet but minus only a shoe. One more round of this and the next time around I'd be stark naked.

I had left my key in my trousers and thus in the canal, so I knocked, loudly. Chante would be asleep by now, it had to be after one a.m. The caper had almost five more hours to run and I had no idea whether it was working. As soon as I'd had a warm shower and a room-temperature whisky I would be able to at least check mainstream media and Twitter, even if I dared not survey the accounts. But first: hot water, whisky and dry clothing.

I knocked again, thinking Chante was asleep and in mid-knock the door opened. It was opened by Tabasco, the guy I'd sprayed with my hot sauce mixture in the Rijksmuseum.

I saw past him and my heart stopped. Across the living room, Delia was sitting in a chair, ankles tied to the chair legs, hands behind her back, mouth stuffed with a napkin and secured by duct tape wrapped around her head.

Willy Pete stood behind her.

I could do one of two things: go in, or run away.

The decent, heroic thing would be to walk in, face the situation squarely, and hope for a deal to be struck, or at least stall until rescue arrived. Only there was no rescue coming. Also, decent and heroic were not the point, winning was the point and Rule Number One is never let the enemy write the narrative. Never follow the enemy's plan.

So I didn't do the decent, heroic thing, I did the smart thing: I ran.

I ran almost three feet before plowing straight into Lisp, the third member of the Ontario Crew. I ran into him and bounced back. He shoved me hard and I stumbled backward into Tabasco, who wrapped big arms around me, pinned as his fellow minion zip-tied my hands in front of me. Then Tabasco shoved me backward and swung a hard fist into the side of my head. My knees buckled and it was several seconds before I could see properly.

When the spinning geometric patterns subsided I saw that in addition to Willy, Tabasco and Lisp, there was a fourth person. A woman. Wachmeester Olivia DeKuyper, pride of the Koninklijke Marechaussee.

'Oh,' I said, being too weary, cold and defeated to think of something clever.

'Are you drunk?' DeKuyper demanded, turning her nose up at my wet, canal-smelling trouserlessness.

'No. I just went for a swim. And frankly I could use a drink.'

'Could you?' Willy sneered. 'Well, fuck you.'

'Mind if I stand up?' I asked this of the policewoman, who shrugged.

I struggled without the use of my hands, but got to my bare feet and without asking further permission headed for the sideboard where the whiskey beckoned to me. Hands secured in front I poured myself a glass of Talisker and drank half of it.

'Anyone else?' I asked, nodding at the bottle.

'This is not a social call,' DeKuyper said.

'No?'

That earned me a punch in the kidneys from Lisp, which sent

electric eels shooting up my spine and down my arms. It was a struggle not to collapse again, and I was proud that I held onto my glass.

'We're not really in the mood for bullshit,' Willy Pete said by way of explanation.

'Pity,' I grated. 'I'm so good at bullshit.'

'We want the painting. Just the painting,' DeKuyper said. 'Give us the Vermeer and we will leave you alone, unharmed.'

'I assume there's an "or else" coming?'

'Or else,' Willy Pete said ominously. He grinned at me and produced a glass vial, a bit larger than the sort of thing used to package crack. He shook it and I saw that it contained water. Water and a few little, irregular pebbles, yellowish in color. 'See these harmless-looking little pebbles? They're nothing so long as they are submerged and not exposed to the air. But these are special pebbles, these. White phosphorus. And white phosphorus, when it is exposed to oxygen, will begin to grow warm and to smoke. It's what they use for smoke grenades, you know. White phosphorus. Willy Pete.'

'Yeah, I get the connection, Willy. But thanks for the exposition dump.'

'Leave white phosphorus in the air and it will burn all by itself. Spontaneous combustion.' The man had knowledge and was determined to share it. 'It will burn and there's not a single thing that will stop it burning. Put it on flesh and . . .' He pulled his turtleneck aside, exposing flesh like melted wax. 'Painful, too.'

'Ah, so we're doing torture,' I said.

He shrugged. DeKuyper looked uncomfortable, but not uncomfortable enough to do anything.

And Delia? Not happy. She was gagged and bound, but it all felt like one of those movies where the baddie has Bruce Banner all tied up. Agent D was itching to do violence.

'There will be no need for torture if you simply hand over the Vermeer,' Willy said.

'No can do, I'm afraid.'

Willy made a sarcastic *tsk-tsk* sound. 'Yeah, I thought you might say that. And if I threaten to kill you?'

'I'll point out that if I'm dead I can't tell you much.'

'Exactly. So here's what I'm going to do. See, I am going to place one of these little pebbles of white phosphorus on Agent Delacorte's head. And then we wait for a while till it combusts. Or, if you're impatient, I can speed things along a bit by lighting it. After which it will begin to burn down through her hair. And then through the thin flesh of her scalp. And then it will begin to melt and crack the bone of her skull. Then, Mr Mitre, the real damage starts, because it will just keep burning and burning and it will melt its way through the gray matter, burning away Agent Delacorte's brain, destroying memories and abilities and perhaps depriving her of speech. The pain would be hideous and—'

'Not really,' I interrupted.

'What?'

'It won't be that painful. I mean, the human brain has no pain receptors. You can stick pins in a brain, or drop bits of white phosphorus on it all day long and the brain won't feel a thing. I mean, the rest, sure, it would definitely make a mess of her brain, but it wouldn't be a bunch of screaming, it'd be more like, you know, Daisy.'

It had been no empty boast to claim skill at the spinning of bullshit. There's an old saying among lawyers: *If you have the facts on your side, pound the facts. If you have the law on your side, pound the law. If you have neither on your side, pound the table.* My own rather less elegant version goes, *If you don't like the story, write a different one.*

'More . . . Daisy?' DeKuyper frowned confusion at Willy who wasn't so sure he understood, either.

'Oh, come on, you guys haven't seen *2001: A Space Odyssey*? You know, the part where Dave is pulling processors out of the HAL 9000? And HAL sings "Daisy"? But slower as each processor is removed? '"Daisy, Daisy, give me your answer, do. I'm half crazy, all for the love—"'

'Shut the fuck up!' Willy yelled and I imagine he'd have liked one or more of his henchpeople to punch me, but they'd become caught up in the story.

'He's right,' Tabasco said, nodding vigorously. 'That's in the movie.'

I turned to him. 'It's a masterpiece. One of the greatest movies of all time. Don't you agree?'

'Stop wasting time,' Willy snarled. 'Give me the Vermeer!'

All through this my thoughts were at least partly on Chante. Where the hell was she? Had they hurt her? Would I find her lying dead in her bedroom? Delia's laser eyes were intense but not conveying anything helpful.

'So a pebble of white phosphorus, how long will it keep burning? I mean, after it melts down through her brain, what happens next? Does it drop into her sinuses? Does it burn down through her soft palette and into her mouth? Because then . . . I mean, if I were writing the scene . . . then she'd spit the thing at you.' Now Delia's eyes seemed to be telling me something, but I was pretty sure it was something like, *what the fuck are you babbling about?* I didn't know what the fuck I was babbling about, I was stalling. Stalling and signaling indifference because that's the thing with a hostage, you have to devalue them. What Willy expected me to do was plead for Delia. Well . . . no.

'Or maybe,' I said excitedly. 'Oh oh, this is even better. There's something flammable or even explosive. Right? Like dynamite or Molotov cocktails. The white phosphorus burns down, into her mouth, she spits it into the dynamite and boom. It's a sacrifice play.'

'What the fuck are you . . . Shut the fuck up and—' Willy began.

'Oh wait, I have another idea! OK, now follow me on this.' They were. All four of them were listening like children waiting on the next development in a bedtime story. 'First of all, it would require a fairly detailed notion of brain physiology, but once the white phosphorus has burned through the skull, she could tilt her head this way or that and sort of guide the path of the burning white phosphorus.'

'Why are we listening to this—' the dirty cop interrupted, but then she saw the puzzled look on Willy's face and fell silent. I had caught Willy's interest.

'The thing is,' I babbled on. 'The victim – agent Delacorte here – could, if she knew enough about brain physiology, sort of aim the burning pebble to annihilate one kind of memory, or shut down some portion of her brain, which would, might, have the effect of enhancing the activity in other parts of her brain. I'm not saying superpowers would be involved, but you can't be sure.'

Through all this Delia was not happy. She had blood running down the side of her neck from where someone had smashed her with enough force to render her incapable of resisting as she was zip-tied to a chair. I avoided making eye contact, any expression of concern, even non-verbal, would weaken my position. And my position was plenty weak as it was. Weak to the point of being gossamer.

'Very interesting,' DeKuyper said, thinking she was clever and calling my bluff. 'So shall we put it to the test?'

'Well,' I said, 'You're going to want to move her.' I pointed. 'She's awfully close to that smoke alarm. And you all know what burning hair is like.'

Four sets of eyes went to the smoke alarm. No, they had not thought of that. They were not an imaginative bunch, they were more the direct-action kind of folks, to whit, the placing of a gun barrel against the side of my head. This was Tabasco. But I wasn't worried, he wasn't going to shoot me.

'Go ahead, genius, pull the trigger and then toddle off and explain to Daniel Isaac that you failed to get him his Vermeer. Failed despite what I'm guessing was a healthy up-front payment and a whole lot of expenses.'

'How about I just shoot the bitch, then?'

'I don't think Sergeant DeKuyper would . . . oh, you mean the FBI agent. Go ahead, shoot her. You still won't get your painting, will you? Because as soon as you kill her you're right back to threatening me. And see, here's the thing: the four of you can't walk away from this and leave either the Feeb or me alive, so let's cut the bullshit and talk business.'

I waited to see if any of them would argue that point but, sadly, no. We were all in agreement that the Ontario Crew, plus their corrupt cop, would need both Delia and me dead.

'So, here's where we are,' I said. 'You have empty threats, I have the Vermeer, we all know Isaac's behind this, we all know that at least some of you have worked for the CIA, and the CIA may be fine with lots of shit, probably including the

murder of an Irishman in a dark alley, but I don't think they're
fine with either torturing or murdering an FBI agent. No, you
are way off the reservation on this, which means you have to
cover your tracks and Agent Delacorte and I are tracks.'

'There are lots of ways to die,' Willy said. 'There's quick
and painless, and there's slow and agonizing.'

'Kind of a lousy choice there, Willy. May I call you Willy?
See, here's my guess. You've been on the phone or on a secure
app, whatever, talking to the Chipster. That's what I call Isaac,
do you think he'd mind? No? Anyway, the Chipster would
have been furious. What the fuck is this shit, he'd have said in
his reedy, gasping old man with COPD voice, "How did you
let someone else steal my Vermeer?" Right?'

No answer necessary. That was exactly what had happened.

'And you said, "Just hold on, moneybags, we'll get you the
painting. Don't pay the ransom." But Chip was like, "Hey, I
was going to pay you fifty million. I can pay this thief off
with just a tenth of that, and I won't risk the Vermeer." Right?
Did I miss anything?'

Willy's silence was confirmation.

'And now, the clock is ticking down. What is it now, two
a.m.?'

DeKuyper glanced at her watch and scowled.

'Four hours left. Tick-tock. Four hours for you to convince
me to hand over a painting which, should I actually hand it
over, would mean getting a bullet to the back of the head a
minute later. You see the problem. Right? Right. The cool
thing is, I actually have a solution.'

None of them wanted to ask. To ask was to concede that
I was now running the meeting. DeKuyper stared daggers at
Willy. The other two carefully avoided making eye contact
at all, but it was clear that they wanted to hear the solution.
We were in what used to be called a Mexican stand-off,
though I imagine someone's come up with a less ethnically
offensive term. A stand-off which, if nothing changed radic-
ally, would leave old man Isaac Vermeerless and the Ontario
Crew scrambling to repay whatever earnest money Isaac had
fronted them.

'Just for our amusement,' Willy huffed, 'tell us.'

I shrugged. 'It's simple. Look, you don't give a damn about the Vermeer and neither do I. In what, a little less than four hours? Yeah, in just less than four hours a timed incendiary device goes off and the Vermeer is destroyed. Live, on YouTube. Well, none of us care about the art, but we do all care about money. Money is rather the point, isn't it? You had your eyes on a massive haul, fifty very large. I mean, fucking hell. Fifty! But that fifty million is gone now. Poof! Not happening. So now we are down to what *could* happen.'

I would like to point out that all through this I was standing in my underpants (black, three-inch boxers) and bare feet and stinking of canal water. I heard about an actor once who played all the way through *Macbeth* with a broken ankle. This was kind of like that.

'Here's what *could* happen,' I said, and gave DeKuyper a saucy wink. 'What *could* happen is that Isaac ponies up the five million. And I tell you where to find the Vermeer which you move – I assume you planned that part carefully – to Isaac's secret museum for him to drool over as he gasps his corrupt last breath.'

'You think that old bastard will pay us out if he's already paid you five million? He'll tell us to fuck off with whatever spare change he happens to have in his wall safe.'

'Maybe,' I admitted. 'But that'll be better than what you've got now. I mean, you'll have the five million.'

'We'll have the . . . what?'

'The five million. See, as soon as I have it in my account, I'll move it to yours. Well, all but half a million. Because that half a mill is what we're putting in the account of Agent Delia Delacorte.'

That stunned 'em. Stunned Delia, too, judging by the furious glare.

'See, the thing is, we need mutual assured destruction. Like the cold war. Mutual assured destruction. If Delacorte opens her mouth, we leak details of the half million. Now, maybe the Bureau buys her explanation, but probably not, they're suspicious people those Feebs. In any case they won't buy her explanation, certainly not after this catastrophic failure on her part. They'll investigate and find, surprise! that Delacorte asked for this assignment. Asked. And then a half mill shows up in her name.'

Four sets of eyes turned to Delia who strained angrily against her bonds, putting on quite a show. I wondered if it was genuine or whether she was acting the part I needed her to play. Either way, it was effective.

'And what about you, Mitre? What do you get out of all this?'

'Me? Oh, I keep whatever cash comes in that's not from Isaac. I'm a man of simple needs. You get four and a half mill, Agent D gets half, Isaac gets his painting, and I get whatever money all the other good, art-loving citizens of the world have donated.'

DeKuyper shook her head. 'It will not work. The FBI will know that money sent to Delacorte's account is an attempt at discrediting her.'

'Maybe,' I allowed. 'But not if the money went to a private offshore account she's never disclosed.'

Blank astonishment in Delia's eyes, which I hoped no one else noticed.

'In fact,' I said, 'just to prove my bona fides, how about I make a small contribution of my own. Say ten thousand euros?' I mutely held up my zip-tied hands. At a nod from the bemused Mr Pete, Lisp used a wickedly unpleasant-looking knife to cut the tie.

Then, DeKuyper watched over my shoulder as I opened a bank app, tapped in passwords, and transferred ten thousand euros from an account I controlled, to another account I controlled.

No, of course the second account wasn't in Delia's name, why would I give her my money?

'You boys – and lady – actually believe I'd be dealing with an FBI agent and not have a way to compromise her?' I laughed and shook my head ruefully. It may be the oldest con in the modern world. I mean, back in caveman days I'm sure the cons involved bones and grubs and whatnot, but in the modern era it's all about money. Money, money, money. This was a variation on what's sometimes called the *in-and-in*: the conman appears to put his own money into the scheme.

I prayed to the Great God of Grifters that these three did not know anything of the game. The ex-soldiers were not the big concern. There are exceptions, but as a rule there are few suckers quite like a man in uniform who is not in uniform. If you can't con a soldier or sailor on leave you're just not trying.

DeKuyper was the more likely problem. As a cop she'd have seen grifts before. Maybe. Then again, maybe not, she wasn't a street cop, she was part of an elite. I wondered how they'd gotten to her. You can't just go around fronting random cops and offering them bribes. Sure, you could do that in New Orleans, but this was Amsterdam.

But as DeKuyper watched the little animated GIF showing money flying from one account to another she seemed fascinated. The page also showed something else I wanted her to see: my balance in the first account, which was just shy of a million. People respect people with money. You'd think after decades of banks and politicians and billionaires exposed as cheats, regular folks would stop assuming that people with money don't steal. But no, folks will still insist on confusing money, IQ and virtue – three very different things.

'There you go,' I announced and closed the app. 'Ten grand in our trussed-up Feeb's secret account. Agent Delacorte now has a choice.' I walked up to Delia, swaggered a bit actually, playing my part. 'Now you have a choice, Delacorte. Keep the ten. Keep the five hundred that will be along shortly. Your account isn't compromised, not as far as I know, anyway. I only know it because I creeped your phone while you went to the bathroom last week.'

She glared, but Delia is not a stupid woman, rather far from it, and she had figured out my game. Anger, defiance and then, just a bit of softening, a downward look as she considered.

'Your choice is simple, Delacorte. Really very simple. On the one hand, you run to your bosses and claim you were used, which, when you consider the context of this whole fiasco, probably means your career is already a bit fucked. Or you keep a nice little nest egg and no one is the wiser. The Vermeer ends up with Isaac, I make money, the Crew here makes some money, and you make some money. You report that your effort to block the theft failed. Just that.'

I resolutely maintained eye contact with Delia. I was hoping Willy and DeKuyper were looking at her as well, it would mean they were buying it.

'So, are you in and wealthy, Delacorte, or are you going to fuck yourself?'

Delia tried to speak, but there was the small matter of the gag.

'Let her speak,' I told Willy. And he began to unwind the tape around her head.

When I was a kid I used to watch the old *Charlie Brown* specials. There was always a time when Snoopy would have a little interlude of happy dancing. That's what I felt like doing, because as long as nothing else went wrong, I had won.

Delia, may the blessings of a just God rain down on her, did the exactly right thing. Once the tape was loose she spit out the gag and said, 'Half a million my ass. If I'm selling my soul it will be for the full seven figures. I want a million.'

'Fuck you,' Willy shot back.

And we were off to the races: the bargaining had begun. The consensus seemed to be that if anyone was making up the rest of Delia's piece, it should be me. Willy's logic was impeccable. 'You've already cost me enough, Mitre. Keep pushing and I may decide to hell with it and put both of you down.'

So DeKuyper watched again as the animated GIF flew $490,000 – five hundred minus the ten I'd already transferred – from account A to account B.

I transcribed the number of Delia's supposed account and gave it to Willy.

'And now,' I intoned, 'We're all in this together. No one says a word, now or ever. As Benjamin Franklin said, we must, indeed, all hang together or, most assuredly we shall all hang separately.'

TWENTY-NINE

Throughout my masterful – if I say so myself – improvisation one question had remained pressing: where the hell was Chante? It was coming on to three a.m., and unless she was off on a one-night stand, unlikely, she should be in the apartment, somewhere.

I had the uneasy feeling that Willy and his people might have hurt her. Perhaps fatally. It was Tabasco who escorted me into my bedroom to get trousers and I half expected to find her there. But no. So I dressed under Tabasco's watchful eye.

Then I told him I had something valuable to retrieve from the other bedroom. Chante's room.

Look, I don't like the girl, in fact I can't stand her most of the time. But she can cook, and well, she was in some attenuated sense my responsibility.

Chante was on her bed, face down. The duvet under her head was red with blood. Her ankles were zip-tied as were her hands. Though at a glance it struck me that her wrists were not cinched enough to make her hands swell, so Willy must have been kind. After he or one of his people had turned her lights out with a punch to the face or a cosh against the back of her head.

'She dead?' I asked.

'Not as far as I know,' Tabasco muttered. 'Not yet, anyway.'

'Mmm, well, leave her to me. I hate the bitch, I'll do her myself.' I walked past into the bathroom.

'What are you after?' Tabasco demanded.

'Something of value.' I gave him a leer. 'I hid it in the cistern of her toilet.' I removed the toilet lid, a nice, heavy piece of porcelain very much like the object I'd used to kill a man in self-defense. That had worked because I'd had the advantage of surprise. Wouldn't work now.

I looked into the cistern, expecting to see *der Führer* glaring up at me. But Hitler was gone.

'Well, fuck me,' I snapped. 'Someone fucking ripped me off! Well, that's some bullshit, that was not part of the deal, give it back!'

I stood with my back to the toilet. Tabasco stood facing me, filling the doorway. I resolutely avoided looking past him and kept my accusatory gaze fixed on him.

'We didn't take nothing out of your toilet!'

'Yeah, well it's gone, isn't it?'

'What the fuck are you even talking about?'

'Hitler,' I said. 'You know, funny mustache, crazy eyes? Liked to kill people? Usually in a sneak attack, coming up from behind like a sneak and—'

And Chante swung the golden Hitler hard, old school, from above, a chopping motion. Gold is soft for a metal, but quite a bit harder than skull. I heard bone crack. Tabasco's eyes rolled up, his knees bent, and I rushed to catch him before he could complete a noisy fall. He was no lightweight and it was all I could do to slow his collapse and let him rest his face on the toilet seat.

And there went all my brilliant improvisational grift right down the drain.

I motioned Chante to remain silent.

Tabasco was down, but Lisp, Willy and the crooked cop were still muttering in the other room. I searched Tabasco quickly and found his pistol. Which would be great if I were Clint Eastwood entering through saloon doors. But I had little to no confidence in my ability to shoot Lisp, Willy and DeKuyper before they could get me. Or before a random bullet hit Delia.

The really frustrating thing was that if I succeeded and somehow took down three trained soldiers, I'd have failed: it's mighty hard to disappear four bodies. Even one is an unholy challenge. Besides, my remit from Delia had not been to cause a shoot-out certain to draw police and press attention and create an international incident exposing Isaac.

Also: I really didn't want to kill anyone. I suppose that seems almost quaint in a world where we're used to action heroes massacring endless streams of minions and henchmen. But I'd killed one guy, entirely in self-defense, totally justified, but it had never become OK to me, it had never quite settled down in my brain.

In seconds Willy would come see what happened to Tabasco. No time. My negotiations, clever as they were, had been blown up by Chante's unexpected bravery and resourcefulness.

Amateurs. They always think they're doing the right thing.

'Now what?' Chante whispered.

Now what? Now that all my beautiful bullshit was useless?

An answer came. It always does. The answer came but it was utterly mad. Mad and stupidly risky. I would be relying on one thing to save me: the fact that Willy Pete, and the Ontario Crew were, as I had once been, professionals.

'Now,' I said, heart in my throat, 'we change the narrative. Again,' I said.

I walked back out into the living room, knees locked stiff, trembling, a voice in my head screaming, *It won't work, it won't work.*

The pistol hung at my side. Delia was still tied up but no longer gagged. Willy was turned away, pouring himself a drink. Lisp was at the window, eyeing the street, on the look-out for trouble, unaware that I was the trouble.

I raised the pistol, saw DeKuyper's eyes go wide, aimed and squeezed the trigger. The noise in the apartment was stunning. A wine glass on the sideboard shattered. And Sergeant DeKuyper screamed, because I had just blown a bloody hole in her calf.

DeKuyper roared and thrashed and fell hard on her rear end, an almost comical collapse. She screamed what I have to assume is the Dutch equivalent of, 'Fuck! Fuck!'

Lisp spun, so did Willy, and they both had pistols coming into view.

I dropped my gun to the floor, raised my hands high and yelled, 'Vermeer!'

Willy Pete froze. He had his gun out and could shoot me. Would shoot me unless he did the math quickly and correctly.

Here was the math: if he shot me, no Vermeer and no money. He had not yet run the equation far enough ahead to realize there never was going to be a Vermeer or the money. He'd only calculated far enough ahead to hesitate.

DeKuyper had both hands clamped around the wound but blood was oozing between her fingers. Not an artery, she wouldn't bleed to death, but she wouldn't be walking out of there, either.

The rug would be ruined. I'd never get my deposit back.

I had to shout to make myself heard over the police woman's furious cursing. 'Go ahead, Willy: shoot me.'

'You motherfucker!'

'You used to be a soldier, Willy, can you still think like one? You've got two men down, including a police woman no less, and my guess is you recruited her less for the heist and more for the surveillance and the getaway. She's the one who put the button on me and ended up getting my buddy killed. A woman with groceries, that's good tradecraft, who suspects a woman with groceries, right? But I imagine her larger purpose was to guarantee your safe evacuation, right? Get you past the roadblocks? Now she's gone from asset to liability. Also, I just fired a gun in central Amsterdam, which is not Chicago where folks might ignore such things. So tick-tock. Grab your two boys and get the fuck out of here. Then you get the fuck out of Amsterdam.'

My life hung by a thread. If Willy Pete was just a thug he'd blow a hole where my stunted heart beats. I was hoping, in fact betting my life, on Willy still being enough of a soldier to adapt quickly to this sudden reversal of fortune, and enough of a professional criminal to know when to stop digging.

'I'm not going anywhere without the Vermeer!'

'Yeah, you are, Willy. Because, here's the thing, dude: I don't have the Vermeer.'

'Don't fucking bullshit me, I was there. I saw you!'

'Yep. You saw me. You chased me. But you missed me, didn't you? Then, a bit later, you saw me walk out of the Rijks carrying a black nylon art bag and hand it off to my compatriot in a boat. Thing is, though, Willy, I never took the painting. The Vermeer is still in the museum.'

I stood there with two guns aimed at me. A few pounds of pressure on a trigger and all my cleverness would be reduced to a red mist sprayed on the walls. I had nothing else to say, and the artillery barrage laid down by my pounding heart and my lungs, which had forgotten to breathe, would have made it hard anyway.

I was dancing right along the tightrope of life, one wrong move, a wrong gesture, a random emotion in Willy's brain, a sudden noise, anything could push me right off and the story of David Mitre (and Martin DeKuyper) would be all over. Type the three hashtags marking the end of the manuscript, that's all folks.

Well, I thought, I can't say it's been a good life, but it was interesting.

'You motherfucker,' Willy said, but no longer as furious. And that was when Willy Pete, professional thief, ex-special forces, surrendered. To me.

'The thing is, Willy, I actually want you – you of all people – to appreciate what I've done. I mean, I'm not a professional thief like you, I'm just a fiction writer. But I have re-imagined art theft. I solved the problem of monetizing art theft by re-imagining it,' dramatic pause, 'as art extortion.'

'*National Lampoon*,' Willy said, sounding deflated. 'The famous dog cover.'

I could see that the reference baffled Delia, but I got it and I laughed because Willy, aka Jesus Hippie, had it right.

'Exactly. Buy this magazine or we'll shoot this dog. You and I both know that any mook can steal the *Mona Lisa* or *Starry Night*, but you can't fence it. You can, however, steal *Starry Night* and threaten to destroy it.'

'Motherfucker,' he said for a third time. 'The video? How did you . . .'

'I made a copy of the Vermeer. The copy of the painting and a video camera are in a box. A box being moved between various internet nodes. Broadcast for twenty minutes, kill the signal, move the box.'

'Good Opsec,' he allowed grudgingly.

'It was probably a bit much, but you know how it is, you don't prepare for the best scenario, you prepare for the worst.'

We were now having a professional chat. Like a pair of orthodontists discussing the best way to wire up a crooked molar.

'How did you set the flash mob up without leaving a trail?'

'All online, man. Bogus credit card, burner phone.'

There came the sound of police sirens. Our eyes met. He sighed.

'Well, we best get the fuck out of here.' With a rueful shake of his head he repeated, 'Art extortion.'

'It's my gift to you, Willy, you and the whole Ontario Crew. I've just shown you your future. I've shown you how to make back that fifty million.'

Tabasco came staggering back into the room, face red with blood.

'Delacorte is compromised now, she'll keep her mouth shut. Won't you, oh so very Special Agent?'

Delia knew enough to spit contemptuously, but say nothing. I winked at Willy.

'Now, dude, you do need to get the fuck out of here. Walk away. Walk away and tell Isaac to go fuck himself. And as for the Agency and its involvement, leave them to me. They won't bother you, either. Guaranteed.'

'What about her?' He jerked his chin at the writhing police woman.

'Who, Sergeant DeKuyper?' I shrugged. 'You're going to take the gun I lifted off Tabasco – sorry, that's my name for him – and drag his sorry ass outta here and leave DeKuyper, who is going to claim that in the course of fighting a burglar her service weapon accidentally discharged, blowing that nasty hole in her leg. With a bit of luck she'll get a medal.'

Chante was at the window. 'Police.'

I saw the reflected blue lights on the window glass.

'There's a back way. Down the stairs till you see a side door. It leads to the gift shop. Kick it in or pick the lock if you're quick, and leave through the shop.'

And that was what they did.

There's no honor among thieves, but there can be admiration. Willy was a thief, and already the wheels were turning in his brain. He was already imagining stealing the *Mona Lisa* and threatening to destroy it. He was a pro, and so was I, and neither of us saw much profit in digging this hole any deeper.

'Help Alfonse,' Willy said to Lisp.

'Alfonse?' I echoed.

'Yeah, but I think from now on we may have to call him Tabasco.'

'You can't leave me behind!' DeKuyper cried, still trying to stem the flow of blood, like the famous little Dutch boy who stuck his finger in a dike.

'Stick to the story,' Willy snapped at her. Then, under his breath, 'Dirty cops. They're useful, but they're still garbage.'

That, he addressed to me. Then he actually stuck out a hand. 'Sorry about the guy in the alley. It was supposed to be you.'

'SNAFU,' I said and shook his hand. It's military slang I learned while researching a book. *Situation Normal: All Fucked Up*.

Willy sighed and shook his head. 'Charlie Foxtrot,' he answered, which in mil-speak was CF: clusterfuck.

And with that he and Tabasco and Lisp were gone, leaving me with a bleeding LEO, a tied-up LEO, and Chante who had put the blood-smeared *Führer* on the kitchen counter and was hastening to untie Delia. I threw a towel over Mr Master Race – none of the bullshit I was frantically spinning in my head accounted for a random Hitler. Yet. But then my always helpful, well, usually helpful, imagination came up with the answer.

It took the cops a few minutes to get their act together and come storming up, bristling with guns, their heads encased in helmets, their bodies burdened by Kevlar.

'Hey, asshole,' I said to DeKuyper. 'You were surveilling me in the course of your duties. You saw me attacked by a crazy woman in a VW Polo. You followed me and as we approached we both heard Chante cry out. We ran up, found Chante beaten and Delia tied up, and there was a struggle. Bang! And the bad guy panicked and took off.'

The cops banged hard, just like in the movies, and yelled even as they were pulling back the steel door-rammer. I opened the door and was all but buried in fast-moving cops. They were good, very well-trained, so that by the time Lieutenant Martin Sarip arrived the three of us – Chante, Delia and I – were all face down on the floor and an ambulance had been called for poor Sergeant DeKuyper, injured in the line of duty.

Sarip knew Delia was FBI and that chilled his jets just a bit. He took us all in, he couldn't *not* take us in for questioning, but we were not handcuffed. And at the station they gave us coffee and a plate of *stroopwafels*, all very friendly. Nevertheless I knew a forensic team would be going over the apartment with a fine-tooth comb. They'd find blood. Eventually they'd discover that some of the blood matched Chante and some matched me and a lot matched Sergeant DeKuyper, and some matched a person unknown.

But DeKuyper was going to tell my little story and there would be plenty of evidence that was true, the Polo was presumably still in the canal and both Chante and Delia had been struck hard by the guy attempting to rob me.

Rob me of what? Why, of the golden Hitler, of course.

There'd been a melee during which time Chante had smashed the burglar with Hitler and DeKuyper had accidentally discharged her weapon while fighting bravely with the thief.

Like I said: conman, fiction writer, it's pretty much the same gig.

THIRTY

D id Sarip buy the story that Chante, Delia, DeKuyper and I all told? Nah. It rested on too many unlikely elements. But law enforcement officers can only enforce the law – it's right there in the job title – and the law needs evidence. Four witnesses, including a Dutch police woman and an American FBI agent all told the same tale, and four witnesses beat the hell out of mere gut instinct.

They questioned us separately. After a few minutes of me recounting the same story, a policeman came in and whispered dramatically in Sarip's ear. The lieutenant grinned wolfishly and with admirable dramatic flair left the room, only to return two minutes later with the news that Chante had flipped and told them the whole story. If I was hoping for any leniency, now was the time for me to confess.

It was all credibly performed but I had not just ridden into town on the back of a tulip truck. I didn't laugh at him; the poor guy had had enough trouble lately. I just repeated my story, the same story Chante and DeKuyper would tell. I worried a bit that Delia might be overcome by some sense of duty, but the thing was that she was under orders not to tell the Dutch anything.

Sarip let me stew for a while and presumably eyeballed me via the CCTV in the corner of the room. When he returned he had a little surprise for me. He opened an iPad and cued up some video.

'This is from the security cameras at the Rijksmuseum,' he announced. What he played was an edited supercut of the robbery.

'Some old fart stole the painting?' I asked in wonderfully convincing surprise.

I don't know what he expected. But he nodded to himself, heaved up a sigh and sat back in his chair. It was over and we both knew it. He'd keep investigating, but he'd never get it all. He didn't even have enough to hold me: I was the victim of a series of shocking crimes, after all: lynched, beaten, roofied and stabbed, shot at and nearly drowned before barely surviving a confrontation with a Nazi burglar. Thank goodness Sergeant DeKuyper had been there to save me!

'You've had a very interesting time in Amsterdam,' Sarip said with a nasty sneer. 'It's good that your last visit to this city will be memorable.'

I did not miss hearing that 'last'. Interesting, I thought, that in the end I'd found Willy Pete more gracious in defeat than this cop.

I glanced at the clock on the wall and smiled. Six forty-one a.m. The final broadcast had ended. All that was left now was to find a peaceful, secret moment to check the accounts.

Well, that and send the final message to the Rijksmuseum.

'I imagine I'll be leaving Amsterdam soon,' I said with genuine regret.

'Yes,' he said. 'You will.'

And I did. Chante and I packed up our things and I called a taxi to Schiphol. There, in the anonymity of the first-class lounge, I opened my latest phone, downloaded the necessary apps and signed in.

'Jesus!' I nearly spilled the free lounge Scotch.

Chante, seated across from me, looked up from her magazine.

'Nothing. I was just checking the stock market.'

That was related to the truth, in that money was involved. Credit cards, PayPal and sweet, sweet cryptocurrency had swelled my accounts. The largest deposit had come just minutes before the deadline. Five million. But there was more because people are suckers. Or, if you wanted a more charitable take, they were good, decent people who didn't want to see a priceless work of art destroyed. Those good, decent people together had ponied up just under two million. A bunch of that would be clawed back by the credit-card agencies, but not all. I'd be left with something on the order of six million dollars.

We flew from Schiphol to Nice, and grabbed a limo to the Hotel de Paris in Monte Carlo. Monte Carlo, a very expensive place for rich people to spend their money. A tiny country with a royal family and no pesky intelligence service. Don't get me wrong, if you steal something in Monte Carlo, the bastards will get you and they won't waste time doing it. But law enforcement from other countries? Not really made welcome in a country where probably half the money spent came from an offshore account.

I was poolside enjoying something tall and cool which, frustratingly, was not as good as the cocktail Chante had mixed up, when Delia Delacorte came striding purposefully on her long legs. She took the chaise longue next to mine. We were both dressed, it wasn't as warm as all that.

'You couldn't find anyplace nicer for a rendezvous?' she asked without preliminary. 'What's a room go for in this place?'

'Your monthly salary,' I said. 'Unless you want a suite.'

She looked at me. I looked at her. I flagged down a waiter and said, 'Would you bring us a bottle of the Pol Roger? The Churchill, if you would.'

'OK,' Delia said. 'I'm here as instructed.'

'Far from prying eyes and listening microphones,' I said.

'Uh-huh.'

'So, any news from Amsterdam?'

She nodded. 'Why yes, David, there is. It seems that sometime this morning someone using a voice synthesizer called up the Koninklijke Marechaussee and told them the Vermeer was still in the museum. In room 2.8 as it happens. Sitting all by itself in a gray zipper bag, lying flat on the top ledge of a security door.'

'Really? Huh. Interesting.'

'Yes,' she said dryly. 'Interesting. It seems *Jewess at the Loom* never left the building.'

'Just like I told Willy. Well, I'll be.'

'Yeah, you'll be something,' she said, trying for threatening but not getting there because, well, much as she'd have denied it, the woman liked me. Women do. God help the poor creatures, but deep in the heart of even the most upright of women there is a kernel of affection for bad boys.

'So the Vermeer is safe?' I asked. 'I don't mean to sound off-brand, but I'd hate to see it harmed. It's a good painting.'

'Yes,' she said, 'many people are of the opinion that Vermeer can produce a good painting. And yes, it is safe. Or as safe as it can be in a world full of people like . . .'

She stopped there. I think she intended to say 'people like Willy', but since I am (or was) people like Willy she went elliptical. But I wasn't insulted. I know what I was, what I am, and occasionally I even think about what I might become. Work in progress, as the saying goes.

'Tell you what it looks like to me, Delia. It looks to me like things worked out the way you wanted them to. Isaac wasn't exposed and the painting stayed where it was. So, well done Agent D.'

That earned a long sigh.

The Champagne arrived. The waiter poured. I raised my glass. 'To Amsterdam. I will miss it.'

'Amsterdam.'

We sat quietly for a while in companionable silence, casting sidelong glances at a woman on the other side of the pool who might have been Jennifer Lawrence, but probably wasn't.

'The Bureau's forensic accountants are tracking the money,' Delia said.

'That should be interesting,' I opined. 'Who knows what they might find?'

'They think, based on very early estimates, that they're looking for about nine million dollars.'

'Nine? Nah. I'll bet it's less than that. In fact, I'll bet most of the money will have been shuffled along from one account to another.'

'You'll bet that, huh?'

'I will. Speaking purely from imagination, you understand, as a fiction writer I mean, I'd guess careful investigation will find that a lot of that money ended up in the political action committees of Congressweasels who have also, over the years, benefited from US Person One's own campaign contributions.'

She had not expected that. Her shock was so profound that an entire eyebrow moved a millimeter. 'That would be . . . interesting.'

'Indeed! I mean, what if two million dollars – to grab a number out of the air – had made its way over the internet from offshore accounts to most of the defense-friendly and law-enforcement-loving folks in the government? Wouldn't that just present a dilemma.'

'Two million. Out of . . . I mean, if you were to speculate.'

I shrugged. 'Hmm, this calls for some mighty speculation. But let's say around seven mill. A lot of people will have ignored the whole "bitcoin-only" instruction and given money on their credit cards. The card companies will claw back most of that. Figure five, five and a half tops. Some of that would have been expenses.'

'Receipts forthcoming no doubt,' she muttered.

'So I'll have to do this in my head, but if you started with five and a half, spent a quarter mil on this and that . . .' This and that being Madalena and Milan. 'Then take away two million for political contributions and you're down to three. Of that I'd speculate that a million might have been spent to compensate a family in Ireland.'

Sorry, Sam Spade, I know when you made that remark about partners and the requirement to do something you meant, revenge. But revenge is for amateurs, and I am not an amateur. A million to whatever family Ian had was fair trade for a scoundrel.

I told myself that and almost believed it.

'A family in Ireland.' She frowned. 'The man stabbed in the alley?'

I didn't answer directly. 'That would leave just two million by my rough math,' I said. 'Isaac's a bit poorer, some pols can buy a few more TV ads, neither the FBI nor the CIA have been publicly embarrassed . . .'

'The Agency will figure out who you are,' Delia said, and the thought worried her. Which was sweet. It made a little lump in my throat.

'Oh, them,' I said. I leaned down and fished my bag out from under the chaise. 'I have something for you to give them, a *quid pro quo.*'

'I don't think they'll want your money.'

'Nah, they have all the cash they need. But do they have a hard drive full of names of tangential Nazis eager to commit assassinations?' I handed her the hard drive. 'If I was you I'd download a copy for the Bureau, then give it to the Agency.'

'Hangwoman?'

'It was supposed to be Uber for murder.'

'And I assume that gold statuette came from the same source?'

'Mmm, more or less.' Madalena and Milan were still out there somewhere, opening their account to find they were quarter millionaires. I hadn't given them more, just my first offer, but I suspected they'd not complain. I might well have use for them at some point in the future, and it wouldn't do for them to have too much money to spend.

Chante appeared, shadowed as always by the dark cloud that follows her everywhere. Delia and I watched her weave her way through the lounges and tables.

'Waiter? Another glass please.' I don't know why I was proposing to give her a glass of bubbly that'd probably cost fifty bucks all by itself. Just politeness. That plus, goddammit, she was a writer, part of my tribe now.

'What do you think Sarip will do with *der Führer*?'

'Evidence locker. There to gather dust.'

Chante arrived as did the glass, which the waiter – excellent service, by the way – filled.

I raised my glass. 'I propose a toast. Death to Nazis, tangential or otherwise.'

'*Sic semper tyrannis*,' said my FBI pal, and we three clinked glasses.

'This is wonderful,' Chante said. 'I shall order a bottle from room service.'

I spit out a good twenty dollars' worth of Champagne and said, 'You'll what? Do you know what this stuff costs?'

'I see,' Chante said, crestfallen. 'I don't deserve to enjoy, to savor, to appreciate art. I am, after all, a servant. I can only thank you for this small taste of that to which I have no right.'

I am not weak, and I am not easily intimidated, so to her departing back, I defiantly yelled, 'Wait . . . No, that's not what I . . . I . . .'

'You know she's ordering herself a case, right?' Delia said.

'It'll go well with the caviar,' I said.

'Well, David,' Delia said, tapping her glass against mine, 'you can afford it.'